The French Escape

Suzie Tullett

www.bombshellbooks.com

Print ISBN 978-1-912604-80-7

Also By Suzie Tullett

The Trouble With Words

Little White Lies and Butterflies

For Elijah

You make my heart sing

CHAPTER ONE

In two hundred metres, cross the roundabout, third exit.

Flick let out a heavy sigh, wanting to just throw the satnav out of the car window. After hours of driving she was sick of listening to it, its voice having long gone from politely monotone to distinctly patronising. Forced to ignore the temptation though, she resisted tossing it out onto the roadside. With only a vague address to go off and no idea how to get there, she needed all the help she could get, even if that did mean being spoken down to by a bit of technology. Easing her foot onto the brake, she slowed the car, ready to do as she was told.

Cross the roundabout, third exit.

Turning the wheel, she glanced at her mum, Brenda, snoozing in the passenger seat. "A fine travel companion you turned out to be," she said. Not that she begrudged her mother sleeping, of course. Well, maybe a little. A rhythmic guttural sound emanated from the woman's gaping mouth and unable to help herself, Flick stifled a laugh. Her mum might not be providing much by way of conversation, but she still managed to entertain, and Flick shook her head, intent on teasing her about it later. She chuckled, knowing her mother would never admit to snoring. Purring maybe; this, definitely not.

Flick returned her attention to the road ahead, wishing her dad were here too. Flick felt sure he wouldn't have abandoned her for the land of nod; his excitement at having crossed the Channel wouldn't have let him. A definite Francophile, he loved everything that France had to offer – its history and culture, the food, and most certainly the wine; *J'ai le hangover* being an often-used phrase of his. She smiled, recalling his linguistic efforts. Try as he might, the language was one of the things he never could quite master. The man spoke more Franglais than Français.

It might have been a year since his passing, but Flick still had to swallow hard, attempting to quell the lump in her throat that always accompanied thoughts of her dad. Tears sprang in her eyes and blinking them away, she silently scolded herself, insisting she was merely being daft. Thanks to recent events, her emotions were all over the place and if truth be known, she didn't really know what she was crying about these days. Her father? Matthew? The Andrex puppy on the TV ad?

She wished she could be more like her dad. He had had such an enthusiasm for life no matter what it chucked his way. Like now; Flick knew if he were here he wouldn't just be sharing the driving, he'd be sharing all the information he'd gathered about where they were headed. "Unlike you," Flick said, back to looking at her mum, a woman who'd been determined to share nothing.

She thought back to when her mum first suggested their holiday. Flick hadn't been sure, it felt like too much of an upheaval. She'd gotten so used to hiding herself away, summoning up the motivation to go anywhere with anyone proved hard. Not that she'd really had a choice in the matter. Her mum had an uncanny knack of persuading people around to her way of thinking. And when all else failed, she wasn't averse to just putting her foot down, a tactic she'd resorted to in this instance.

"It'll be an adventure," Brenda had said, ignoring Flick's pleas to the contrary. "The beginnings of a new start, which is just what you need after everything you've been through."

Flick had scoffed, insisting what she needed was to remain in the safe confines of home. The last few months had provided her with all the excitement she could take, thank you very much. Besides, could a mother/daughter trip to this part of France really be described as adventurous?

Flick took in their surroundings. Weaving through the sleepy Breton village with its shuttered stone cottages and quiet cobbled streets, a part of her could still argue not. Yes, she appreciated the place's natural charm, who wouldn't? And passing through the village square, she easily envisaged herself sitting outside the little coffee shop enjoying a *pain au chocolat* and a *grande café crème*. Looking at the currently empty tables, however, the words *fun* and *frivolity* didn't exactly spring to mind. The village couldn't have been further from *Gay Paris* if it tried. "Still, it is beautiful here," she supposed, trying to remain positive as they meandered out of town, leaving it behind in favour of cornfields and autumnal sunshine as far as the eye could see.

In two hundred metres, keep right.

As she once again did as instructed, the car groaned. Flick sympathised. No doubt it felt as eager to reach their journey's end as she, due to all the weight it was carrying. Also courtesy of her mum, Flick noted, who'd insisted they pack everything from a pair of sleeping bags, to their Sunday best, along with everything in between. Unable to see through the car's rear window, Flick yet again had to wonder what this French escape of theirs entailed. Even her dad's casket of ashes had been squeezed in, for goodness sake, her mum describing his presence as some sort of *swan song*, whatever that meant.

Naturally, Flick had enquired about where they were headed. Numerous times, in fact. But while, much to Flick's relief, her mum had readily confirmed they would not, indeed, be camping, no other clues had been forthcoming. She glanced her mother's way once more, recalling how according to this particular Sleeping Beauty, the element of surprise only added to the adventure.

Continuing to drive, Flick knew her mum meant well. Both her parents had never had anything but her best interests at heart. And now they'd gotten to France, she had to admit she was glad of the opportunity to get away from it all. In France no one knew, no one could judge.

She tried to dismiss the unwanted thoughts invading her head. The shock and confusion at Matthews' disappearance, the downright humiliation as events had unfolded. She didn't think she'd ever forget the gossip she'd had to contend with, she could still hear the whispering behind hands as if she'd somehow brought everything on herself. Thanks to everyone's eagerness for the next juicy instalment, it was as if her life had turned into a soap opera. She cringed. No wonder her embarrassment over the whole thing was as strong as it had always been. No wonder she had a mother hell bent on getting her away from it all.

As usual when Flick thought about Matthew, the same question arose over and over – *Why?* The hours she'd spent wracking her brains trying to come up with some sort of answer. She'd even questioned herself. *Should she have seen it coming? Were there any clues that she'd somehow missed? Did he try to tell her that he'd changed his mind and she just hadn't heard?* To this day she came up with nothing and with Matthew in the wind, it wasn't as if she was going to get an explanation any time soon.

Brenda's snoring suddenly got louder and Flick grimaced, as it went from slightly hoarse to downright throaty. She struggled to decide which was worse, thinking about Matthew or listening to this? Thankfully, she spotted a tractor up ahead and, forced to slow down and drop a gear, she breathed a sigh of relief. Never had the sound of a rumbling vehicle engine been so welcoming. She wound down her window, happy to amble along behind. Not that she expected her respite to last, if her instincts were right the tractor would be turning off into an adjacent field soon, its driver intent on harvesting his crops in preparation for the coming winter.

Passing a line of trees, she took in the fallen leaves and spikey chestnut husks that littered the ground. She'd always loved this time of year and not just for the windfall of food supplies it provided; thanks to the rich riot of colour, in Flick's view, autumn seemed to show nature at its very best.

Sure enough, the tractor's right indicator blinked, signalling it was about to turn before going on its way. Back to focusing on their journey, Flick checked the timer on the satnav. According to its display, it wouldn't be long before they reached their final destination and she'd, at last, find out what she was letting herself in for. Her stomach churned. She didn't like surprises, not any more.

She caught her reflection in the rear-view mirror and giving herself a long hard stare, the face looking back wasn't pretty. Even to her own eyes she looked tired and miserable, she'd lost her spark. Her once bouncy, dark hair appeared dull and lifeless and her skin on the wrong side of pale. Not that her choice of wardrobe helped. Looking down at her all-black ensemble of jeans, T-shirt and cardigan, she looked like a vampire on hunger strike.

Fed up of looking at herself, she flipped the mirror away from her eye line, one voice in her head blaming *him* for the sorry state looking back at her, another insisting that she had to take some responsibility. After all, it wasn't as if anyone had forced her to live on a diet of self-pity and ice cream for the last six months. Not exactly the best combination when it came to looking after one's personal health.

Her mother stirred. *Thank goodness*, Flick thought, as the snoring stopped.

"What time is it?" Brenda asked. She straightened herself into a more upright position. "Sorry about that. I must've dozed off."

Flick cocked her head in her mother's direction. "Mum, you've been asleep for hours."

"Give over."

"For at least the last couple." Flick paused for effect. "And you were snoring."

Brenda scowled, just as Flick had anticipated, refusing to believe her. "Rubbish. Now I know you're exaggerating."

Flick laughed, as her mum glanced left and then right through the windows as if trying to get her bearings.

"Are we nearly there yet?" Brenda asked.

Flick shook her head at the question, considering all the secrecy how would she know? Looking to the satnav for the answer, the chequered flag suddenly appeared on the screen, leaving Flick wondering how on earth her mother did it. Either her mum's awakening was pure coincidence, or she'd developed yet another uncanny ability. And knowing her mother, Flick was inclined to believe the latter. "It would seem so."

In two hundred metres, turn left.

Flick slowed down and indicated, before turning onto what appeared to be a little-used lane. Bumping along thanks to the potholes, goodness knew where it led. "This doesn't seem right," she said, hoping it wasn't one of those occasions when satnavs got it wrong. Not only were they in danger of losing a tyre, one she wouldn't have a clue how to change, being stranded in the middle of nowhere would be just her luck.

"I'm so excited," Brenda said, failing to share Flick's concern. "Are you?"

Trees towered above them, a ceiling of yellow and orange leaves blocking out the sunlight as they approached an open set of large iron gates. Covered in what looked like years of rust, they definitely hadn't been cared for in a while. Flick scanned her surroundings. The atmosphere felt almost eerie, as if they'd driven into a Hans Christian Andersen fairy tale. "What is this place?" Flick turned to her mother, eager for an explanation.

"You'll see," Brenda replied, all smiles and anticipation.

CHAPTER TWO

Nate stood, his eyes closed, motionless under the shower. Steam bellowed as hot water washed over him, taking all traces of shampoo and soap with it as it streamed down his body. Thanks to the soothing flow, he felt his muscles relax. He just wished he could say the same for his brain, but no matter how long he stood there his mind still raced. Finally opening his eyes, he ran his hands through his hair before switching off the shower and grabbing a towel, wrapping it around his waist as he headed for the bedroom to get dressed.

Making his way downstairs, he felt a chill in the air and he could hear the wind getting up outside. "The winds of change?" he asked himself. Nate laughed and, having never been one for superstition or flights of fancy, insisted he was just being foolish. "The end of summer, more like."

Turning on the stove, he set the kettle to boil, the shrillness of its whistle soon piercing the quiet of the room. He poured himself a coffee and sat at the table. Leaning back in his rickety old chair, hands wrapped around his coffee mug, he'd forgotten about the cardboard box that lay in front of him. "What do you think it is, Rufus?"

The little Jack Russell sat obediently at Nate's feet, his head tilting first one way and then the other at the sound of his master's voice.

"An antique lamp? Some fancy vase?" A gift from his Aunt Julia, Nate knew it had to be something like that; his aunt never did do minimalist. He leaned forward, tempted to open it. But leaning back again he changed his mind, telling himself that with a bit of luck, she'd still have the receipt. After all, considering the circumstances, she'd be better investing her cash elsewhere.

Of course his aunt meant well. He could just hear her now, telling him the place needed softening up. Or in one of her blunter moments that it needed a woman's touch, her way of suggesting he should find himself a lady friend. *A lady friend, someone special, a partner in crime*, however she phrased it, a woman was something he most certainly didn't need. As for the house, like he'd said when he'd first arrived, there was no point doing anything with it, he wasn't staying. He was just hiding out until the dust settled.

He let out a short sharp laugh as he recalled his unwavering certainty. That was almost two years ago.

Scanning the room, he supposed it no wonder she'd taken matters into her own hands; as with the rest of the house, the room was basic. White walls, a couch, and a wobbly coffee table that he'd fully intended on fixing one day, he had to agree his so-called home was more function than form. But it suited him, he liked it that way. It meant he could pack up and leave at a moment's notice.

He put down his cup, rose to his feet and headed for the window. Gazing out at the lake before him, he wondered if that moment had finally arrived. He sighed, he normally loved autumn. The tourists had all but gone and he could, at last, breathe a little easier. The season brought with it a sense of calm.

Not this year though.

He tried to tell himself he was overreacting, but his heart still felt heavy at the thought of having to leave. He'd grown to love the place. He didn't just think it beautiful, he fully appreciated the solitude it offered him. He let his eyes slowly span the vista, determined to commit every ripple, lily pad and swaying tree branch to memory, just in case. He sighed. This had been his perfect sanctuary from a less than perfect world.

Turning to look at the cardboard box again, he couldn't help but contemplate his time in Brittany, remembering how when he'd first arrived he hadn't just wanted to escape his woes, but to retreat from civilization altogether. Back then, he'd quite fancied himself as Brittany's first *Mountain Man*. Ludicrous, of course. He could see that now. Although in his own defence, he hadn't exactly been thinking straight. Even more laughable, he realised, was the fact that he hadn't banked on his Aunt Julia. There was no way she was ever going to let him withdraw from the world completely. He smiled as he recalled the number of times she'd dragged him out of his comfort zone, even managing to build up a network of trust amongst the locals. He felt his smile fade. Locals he now considered friends. People he'd miss.

He let out a long hard sigh as he pictured each and every one of them. What would he do without the protective blanket they'd wrapped around him these last years?

Again, he tried to tell himself he was just being a drama queen, over the top. But as desperate as he was to believe that, he knew the odds were against him. Thinking back to his old life, if there was one thing experience had taught him it was that people couldn't help themselves and they most certainly couldn't be trusted. He shuddered, his insides filling with dread. When it came to strangers, one whiff of him in the vicinity and any peace he'd managed to find would be gone.

His mobile rang, but Nate didn't have to check the number, he knew exactly who was calling – another unwanted reminder that there were still those out there who never forgot, someone would always be eager to drudge up the past. He shook his head at the continuing ringtone. "Some people just don't know when to give up, eh, Rufus?" Nate said and with no intentions of answering, he let it go to voice message.

Rufus suddenly whined and smiling at his faithful friend, Nate's mood began to soften. At times, he could've sworn the dog could read his mind. "Don't worry, boy. I'm not going anywhere just yet." He reached down and patted his lower leg, a signal for the little dog to join him. Rufus dutifully raced over, his tail still wagging as he threw himself down on his back. Nate crouched, equally enthusiastic as he rubbed the dog's tummy. "Besides, where I go, you go."

Standing up straight, Nate watched Rufus spin back onto his feet and head for the door, the dog bouncing up and down in a never-ending effort to reach the door handle.

"All right, all right." Nate grabbed his jacket from the hook and put it on, before reaching for Rufus's lead. Stuffing it into his pocket, Nate took a deep breath, knowing full well a walk would do them both good.

CHAPTER THREE

Finally, the canopy of rustling branches started to clear and sunlight once again shone down. The road widened out into the longest driveway Flick had ever seen, with untidy expansive lawns laid to either side. Looking ahead, she spotted what could only be an abandoned chateau dominating the landscape and although not on the scale of *Versailles* or Buckingham Palace, to her it was still grand and imposing. "Wow." With its grey craggy stonework and numerous large chimney stacks, the building certainly commanded attention.

"Wow, indeed," Brenda replied.

Flick turned to see another wide grin spread across her mother's face.

"Isn't it incredible?" Brenda asked.

Flick had to agree, she'd never seen anything like it. Surrounded by a perimeter of thick woodland, it was certainly a sight to behold. Although even from that distance, she had to admit it looked more haunted than habitable.

Brenda let out a wistful sigh. "*Chateau D'Enchantement.* That's what it's called, you know."

Halfway up the drive, Flick brought the car to a standstill. She whistled in appreciation. The place certainly lived up to its name. Staring over at its tired and weather beaten exterior, she couldn't help but think about the rich history the building must have and the stories it could tell as a result. She shivered, goosebumps pricking at her skin. It was hard not to imagine a couple of lovelorn ghosts wandering through the long echoing halls, no doubt, within.

"You can see why your father loved it so much, can't you?" Brenda said, a revelation that snapped Flick back into the present.

"What? You've been here before?" Convinced she'd remember the two of them mentioning a place like this, it was news to her. Flick faced her mother. "When?"

"It was a while ago. A bit before he… you know."

Flick reached over to give her mother's arm a comforting rub, sorrow had made a habit of creeping up on the both of them when least expected. She thought it heartbreaking how her mum still couldn't bring herself to say the words out loud, that her husband was dead. They'd *both* lost so much when her dad had passed away, but her parents had shared a love, it turned out, she could only dream of.

Realising time was getting on, Flick pulled herself together. "Maybe we can have a proper look around tomorrow," she suggested, getting back to the task at hand. "We should probably think about finding where it is we're sleeping tonight." Manoeuvring the car forward again, she looked around, expecting to spot a cosy little cottage tucked away somewhere.

Brenda let out a short sharp laugh.

"What?" Flick asked.

She caught another glimpse in the rear-view mirror at all the boxes and bags forced into the space behind them. As realisation dawned, she suddenly felt uneasy and hit the brakes, jolting the vehicle to a second halt. "Please tell me we're not staying in that." She looked at the chateau once more. Granted, it didn't seem to be falling down, but there was no getting away from the fact that it needed a lot of care and attention.

Brenda leaned forward and switched off the satnav, an action that said it all.

"You are joking, right?" Flick said.

Brenda remained silent.

"But look at the state of it." Flick couldn't imagine a place less welcoming.

"It's not that bad."

Flick's eyes widened. "Compared to what?"

With her mum's gaze stuck firmly on the chateau, Flick didn't know whether to laugh or cry. Yes, the whole point of their holiday was to take her mind off her problems back home, and holidaying in the building before her would definitely score ten out of ten on that front, it was so run-down. But trying to look on the bright side was easier said than done when she couldn't see one. No wonder her mother had kept their destination a secret.

Flick found herself torn. On the one hand she didn't relish the prospect of roughing it, and if they stayed here they'd certainly be doing that. On the other, she felt ungrateful. Her mother had obviously put a lot of thought and effort into their trip and the last thing Flick wanted to do was spoil it. Especially when holidays even in the most dilapidated of chateaux probably didn't come cheap.

Staring at the building, Flick thought about her dad again, questioning what he'd do in her shoes. Not that she needed to ask. Unlike her, he'd have seen everything about this trip as exciting and would have delighted in the opportunity to stay in what could very well be a haunted castle. Flick despaired over both her parents, she was obviously adopted.

She tried to reassure herself in the knowledge that images could be deceiving. For all she knew, the chateau's austere, yet tired, exterior could belie a world of luxury within. After all, it had to have some appeal; it wouldn't be let out to holidaymakers if it didn't. She crossed her fingers in sheer desperation, but it was no good, reality prevailed. If they'd had to bring sleeping bags, she could forget all about opulence. They'd be lucky if this place even had the basics. "Please tell me you're kidding."

Flick's question was met with a raised eyebrow and a knowing silence. Her shoulders slumped, she knew when she was beaten and shoving the car into gear, she lifted the clutch, slowly moving the vehicle forward. "Don't tell me. It's all part of the adventure."

As they reached the chateau's main entrance, Flick brought the car to a final stop and she and her mother disembarked.

"What do you think now?" Brenda asked.

Flick gave the building another inspection. Its humongous wooden front door appeared knotted and sun bleached, and white paint peeled from the three sets of large windows that flanked either side. Equally neglected, seven more windows spanned across the whole of the second floor, giving the façade its symmetry and a line of dormers extended across the roof. Against her right mind, she couldn't help but smile. It might not have been her first choice when it came to their accommodation but seeing it up close she actually quite liked it in an eldritch kind of way. She turned to her mother. "Let's just say I'm reserving judgement. Shall we see what it's like inside?"

Brenda strode over to the front door and after scouting the ground for a moment, spotted what she was looking for. She reached down and retrieved a large metal key from underneath a flat piece of stone. "*Voila*!" she said, excitedly holding it up for Flick to see. Unlocking the door, she stood aside allowing her daughter to do the honours. "After you," she said.

Flick turned the knob, forced to give the door a good old shove before it would open. Finally able to enter, her breath caught and she immediately understood why her parents had been so enamoured with the place. The entrance hall's white washed walls, stone floor and ornately carved staircase gave the chateau a grand, yet welcoming, rustic feel. There was a distinct lack of decoration adorning the room, but as far as Flick was concerned it was definitely a case of less is more. "How did you and Dad come across this place?"

Without waiting for an answer, she approached a door to the right and popping her head through, she felt a tinge of excitement. Light flooded in from the huge windows, although it too was void of furniture and accessories. "This would make a great study or library," she said, already imagining wall-to-wall and floor-to-ceiling book shelves. Spinning around, she headed for the door on the left. "A reception room," she informed her mum.

The two women stepped inside and again high ceilings and exceptionally large windows made it bright and airy. Flick ignored the brown floral wallpaper that had seen better days, focusing instead on the wood panelling adorning the walls below. Clearly original, she easily saw how beautiful the room could be with a bit of hard work and a serious wad of cash.

"The fireplace is lovely." Brenda ran her fingers across its giant stone mantel. "And look at the parquet flooring. It's in such good condition considering its age."

Flick continued to take in the room. "Shame about the furniture though, eh?" She indicated to the scruffy sofa. Covered in dust, she had to question what the chateau owners were thinking. The room and its guests deserved better. "They could have at least put a throw on it. No one in their right mind would want to sit on that."

Brenda laughed in response. "I suppose we should unpack the car," she said, ever the organiser. "It'll be getting dark soon. We can check the other rooms out properly once we're sorted."

Tempted to let their belongings wait, Flick reluctantly conceded that her mum was right, exploring the chateau would have to come later. But as Flick dragged her feet towards the door, the sound of a dog yapping caught her attention. A little Jack Russell suddenly scurried into the room. "Where did you come from?" Flick asked, before turning to her mum who simply shrugged. Crouching down to the dog's level, Flick gave it the fuss it seemed to be after. "Maybe the owners have come to settle us in?"

Scooping him up, the dog wriggled as she headed outside to find out. "Stop that," she said, giggling as the Jack Russell eagerly nibbled at her ear. With no one in sight, she at last heard footsteps crunching on the gravel, before some chap rounded the corner from the rear of the building.

"*Alors, te voilà!*" he said.

As he continued his approach, Flick felt a slight panic and her mind scrambled as she tried and failed to remember her schoolgirl French. If ever there was a time she wished she'd paid more attention in class, it was now. "*Bonjour,*" she said, refusing to let her accompanying smile falter at the sound of her own voice. Even to *her* untrained ear, she couldn't have sounded more foreign if she'd tried. Not that it mattered, Flick quickly realised. As the man silently took the Jack Russell from her arms and set it down on the ground, it was clear he hadn't been talking to her anyway, he'd been talking to the dog.

She watched the man gently stroke its back, as he produced a lead from his pocket and clipped it onto the dog's collar before straightening himself up again.

"Sorry about that," he finally said, his switch to perfect English coming as a surprise and a relief. "He must have heard you coming up the drive."

Flick expected him to carry on chatting, but without warning let alone another word, he began to leave, something she found a bit odd. As far as she was concerned, the least he could do was introduce himself and she suddenly stopped him. "I'm Flick," she said, before he could get off altogether. She felt a tad awkward standing there with an outstretched arm. Clearly reluctant to accept the gesture, the man seemed more interested in getting back to wherever it was he'd come from. "It's a sort of nickname," she added, refusing to give up. "Short for Felicity."

Their eyes locked, her tummy doing a little somersault as he finally shook her hand. The man might border on rude, she considered, but with his unruly blond hair and gorgeous green eyes she couldn't deny his good looks, he was drop dead gorgeous. Not that she was bothered one way or the other, she decided, pulling herself together. After Matthew, this man could have had two heads for all she cared.

She continued to wait for him to tell her his name in return, but he persisted in revealing nothing. Instead he just stood there.

"Ahem," he finally said, nodding towards his hand.

Realising she was still holding it, Flick felt herself blush and immediately let go again. She could see her embarrassment amused him but chose to ignore the little smile that appeared on his lips and the twinkle glistening in his eye. "And this is my…" She looked over her shoulder for a much-needed diversion. However, while expecting to see her mother, Brenda wasn't actually there. "Oh," Flick said. "Never mind."

Turning her attention back to the man, she couldn't help but carry on staring. The more she looked, the more something about him seemed vaguely familiar; curious considering she'd never visited that part of France before. She hastily wracked her brain in an attempt to figure out where else she might know him from, except try as she might she couldn't place him.

"Right, I'll be off then," he said.

"This is going to sound strange," Flick said, stopping him for a second time. "But have we met before?"

Flick saw the smile in his eyes immediately vanish, the one on his lips go from natural to fixed. Her question had clearly made him uncomfortable, guarded even. Not that Flick could think why.

"No. Not as far as I know."

"Really? Because…"

"I think I'd remember."

As he cut her short, Flick didn't know how to respond. Going off his tone, his statement clearly wasn't a compliment. Then again, she supposed it didn't matter anyway; he obviously didn't own the chateau. The man might not want to give his name, but common sense told her there was no reason he should omit to being their host. "Sorry," she said, telling herself she must be wrong. "You're probably right. Things have been a bit fraught lately. It'll be my mind playing tricks."

The man's caution remained. "Or I just have one of those faces. In any case, I'll leave you to it."

Flick watched him turn and hastily head back the way he'd come, the little Jack Russell dutifully tottering alongside. *That was weird*, Flick thought.

CHAPTER FOUR

Flick opened her eyes. Still half asleep, her strange surroundings confused her and she wondered where she was for a moment. Realisation dawned as she hunched up onto her elbows and looked around. "How could I forget?"

She took in the sparsely furnished room with its outdated wallpaper and threadbare rug, wondering what her mother had been thinking when she'd booked them into this place. Whichever travel agency or accommodation site she'd used there had to have been pictures. "Of course there were." Flick looked down at the sleeping bag she was wrapped in. "How else would she know to come so prepared?"

There was no denying their accommodation had potential, its original features continued to wow even then her they were so impressive. There couldn't be many bedrooms that housed a fireplace as big as this one. Still, in reality the building's potential meant nothing. When it came to her and her mum's holiday, what mattered was having the odd home comfort, like bed linen and a duvet. Flick slumped back down onto the pillow insisting she was just being ungrateful again. The chateau might not be perfect, but her mum had gone to a lot of effort. "And it's not as if it's all bad," Flick had to admit. Despite spending the night on what had to be the oldest bed in France, she had just enjoyed a very long restful sleep, something she hadn't experienced in quite a while.

She stretched herself out, before reluctantly unzipping her warm cocoon. Getting out of bed, she hastily grabbed her dressing gown. Regardless of the sunlight streaming in, there was a definite autumnal chill in the air and stuffing her feet into her slippers she moved towards one of the old cast-iron radiators. Flick had never seen a radiator as ornate as this before and reaching out to touch it, she traced the swirling leaves and flowers that were moulded into the shiny silver metalwork. "At least you look the part." She let out a wry chuckle. Feeling the cold metal against her fingers, the heating system was clearly like the rest of the chateau, knackered.

Deciding to go in search of her mother, Flick made her way out onto the landing and down the wide sweeping staircase. As her hand glided along the well-worn bannister, she wondered about the building's history, envisaging a host of giant portrait paintings of owners past displayed on the walls. She felt a frisson of excitement. To think she could be walking in the very steps once taken by French nobility really was quite something.

Nearing the bottom, the smell of freshly brewed coffee wafted her way. A welcome aroma, she had to admire her mother's organisation skills, the woman had thought of everything. She headed towards the kitchen at the back of the house and from what she'd seen of the chateau so far this was definitely her favourite room. From the huge soot-stained fireplace with its massive stone mantel, to the chunky original beams that spanned the ceiling, she loved everything about it. She didn't even mind the dark wood cupboards, although they did need a bit of a tidying up. A long oak table sat in the centre, old mismatched wooden chairs lining either side. Despite the neglect, it was as if the room was still the heart of the home having somehow managed to maintain its soul. Flick found it easy to imagine the family gatherings that had taken place here, everyone chatting as they tucked into a *Cassoulet* or *Poulet* à *la Bretonne* cooked on the range that was, without doubt, big enough to feed the masses.

Wondering where her mum had got to, Flick picked up one of the cups that had been set aside and poured herself a coffee. Taking a sip, she almost jumped when her mum suddenly appeared at the patio doors. Her arms full of logs she struggled to tap on the glass, let alone grab the handle to let herself back in, and Flick rushed over to help. "Please don't tell me we brought an axe over from England as well," she said, something that wouldn't have surprised her.

"I was just having a scout around and I found this fabulous wood store," Brenda explained. "It's stocked from floor to ceiling." With nowhere else to put it, she dumped her find straight onto the stone floor by the fire. "Have you been out there yet?" She brushed off the splinters that had caught in her dressing gown. "The courtyard is stunning. It's got views straight onto the lake."

Flick's eyes widened. "The chateau has its own lake?" she asked, wondering how on earth they'd missed that when exploring the building. Then again, by the time they'd gotten around to it she supposed it had been pretty dark.

"It most certainly does. Go and have a look."

Flick stepped outside onto the gravelled courtyard. Glancing around, outbuildings sat to the left and a path led off into the woods on the right. But it was what lay straight ahead that really caught her attention. With nothing but a low-level wall separating her from the water, the lake was breathtaking and she'd never seen so many lily pads. "Amazing," she said, soaking up the scene. "It's like we're in a different world."

"Isn't it," Brenda said, appearing, coffee in hand, at Flick's side.

Flick continued to take in the view. As locations went, this place certainly had it all. She suddenly spotted a stone structure in the distance. "Do you think that's a boat house?"

"Could be," her mum replied. "It's close enough to the water. We should go and investigate once we're washed and dressed."

"I'd like that."

The two women stood side by side in companionable silence.

"Here, hold this," Brenda said suddenly.

Flick took her mother's cup, watching her disappear back inside before returning with two of the oak table's chairs.

"That's better," Brenda said. Plonking them down, she retrieved her drink and took a seat.

Flick followed suit and sat on the other chair, happy to enjoy the peace. *Who needs a sheet and a pillowcase when they've got this?*

she asked herself, her need for home comforts almost a thing of the past.

"How are you feeling this morning?" Brenda asked. "Did you sleep okay?"

"Like a baby."

"I'm not surprised after the drive we had getting here. It seemed to take forever."

Flick laughed and despite recalling how her mother had slept for most of it, she resisted giving her a jibe. "Worth it just to see this though, eh?"

Brenda smiled in response.

"You know, today was the first day in a long time that I didn't wake up with a knot in my stomach."

Brenda reached over and patted Flick's knee. "I told you a break would do you good."

Flick breathed in the still morning air. "It's just so magical. And calming." She knew she shouldn't but feeling a million miles from the turmoil she'd left behind, she allowed herself to consider her situation for a moment. "I really thought what Matthew and I had was special. I thought we were like you and Dad, in it for the long haul." She laughed. "Long haul. I certainly got that wrong, didn't I?" She took a sip of her coffee. "Why do you think he did it, Mum? I mean, who does a runner from their own wedding reception? It would have been better if he just hadn't turned up, left me circling the block. I'd have got the message he wasn't coming, sooner or later."

Brenda scoffed. "Because the man's a fool, that's why."

Flick didn't agree. Thinking back to her wedding day, as far as she was concerned, she'd been the foolish one. She recalled Matthew's momentary pause before saying *I do* and how she'd naively put his hesitation down to wedding day jitters. "I just wish I could be angry with him."

"Don't worry, love. I've got enough anger for the both of us. And if I ever get my hands on him, he'll know that too."

"One minute I feel numb and confused, in the next it's like I'm about to have a panic attack."

Brenda softened. "You need to stop torturing yourself. You've wasted enough energy on that man already. It's time to move on with your life, forget about him."

Continuing to stare out at the water, Flick knew her mother was right. But that didn't make following such advice any easier.

"Anyway, you weren't the only one stupid enough to fall for Matthew's charm."

Flick sighed, remembering how her parents had welcomed him into their family with open arms. "I'm sorry, Mum."

"What for?" Brenda asked. "None of it was your fault. Anyway, I thought we weren't going to talk about him? I thought we had a pact."

Flick reflected on the agreement they'd made at the start of their journey. "We do."

"Well then." Brenda raised her cup. "More coffee?" she said, letting Flick know that was the end of the subject.

Flick nodded. Besides, it wasn't as if going on about Matthew changed anything.

Following her mother back into the kitchen, she leant against the worktop watching her pour them another drink. "Thanks for doing all this."

Brenda dismissed the appreciation with a wave of one hand, as she passed her daughter a refill with the other, but Flick wanted her to know just how grateful she felt. "I might not have realised it before but getting away is exactly what I needed." She considered the misery and heartache she was trying to escape. "In fact, a part of me wishes I didn't have to go back, that I could stay here forever."

Brenda closed her eyes for a moment, her relief at hearing this obvious. Opening them again, she smiled as she threw her arms around Flick, giving her an unexpected hug.

"Careful," Flick said, her coffee almost spilling.

"You don't know how happy that makes me feel," Brenda said, regardless. "I mean it might not be the most modern of buildings, but…"

"Yoo-hoo!" a female voice suddenly called out. "Is anyone home?"

CHAPTER FIVE

Surprised by the interruption, Flick let her mother's words of relief hang in the air as she looked towards the courtyard, wondering who their unexpected visitor could be. She turned to her mum who didn't seem to have a clue either, both of them placing their cups on the side as the woman in question appeared at the patio doors.

Putting her in her fifties, Flick would've thought she'd be more at home in Paris than in the wilds of Brittany. The woman was stunning. Tall and lean, her mid-length dark hair hung loosely around her shoulders and her black skinny jeans, draping, silk Tee and charcoal, lapelled jacket exuded style. As for her boots, Flick couldn't help but admire both them and the woman. In her view, anything with heels that high were definitely not for walking in, especially when that included negotiating gravel.

Having not even brushed her hair yet, Flick looked down at her own attire. Thanks to her dressing gown and slippers, she felt positively dowdy in comparison and she could tell from her mother's sudden awkwardness that she felt the same. Not that the woman seemed to notice any of this. Rather, as she confidently let herself in, she enthusiastically threw herself into France's *faire la bise* and feeling the woman's face brush against Flick's own, the woman was clearly an expert cheek kisser.

"I come bearing gifts," she said.

Flick cautiously accepted the paper bag being handed to her and despite still wondering about the woman's identity, she couldn't resist peeking inside. "Thank you," she said, looking down at the most buttery and sweetest smelling of croissants.

She returned her attention back to the newcomer. "That's very kind, but…"

The woman put a hand up to silence her. "Now I know what you're thinking. That it's very remiss of me to turn up unannounced like this. But as soon as I heard you'd *finally* arrived, I simply couldn't wait, I had to come and say hello. Now, how are you settling in?"

"Okay," said Brenda, hastily stepping forward. "We're settling in fine."

Flick wondered if it was her imagination, especially when her mother usually relished the opportunity to meet new people. But on this occasion, she appeared nervous, tense even. In fact, watching her mum position herself, it was as if she was steering the woman back towards the door.

"And is there anything you need? Anything I can do?"

"No, I think we've got everything covered," Brenda said, once again subliminally guiding their guest towards the exit.

As far as Flick was concerned, however, a woman as glamorous as this had to be the chateau owner, who had, at last, come to introduce herself, and considering their dismal facilities, Flick wasn't about to let her just disappear. Unlike her mum, she could think of a couple of things they needed. Like a heating system that worked, for one. Deciding to start simple, she thought she'd begin with their lack of bedding. "Actually, we're a b–"

"Absolutely fine," Brenda jumped in, before Flick could get her words out. "Aren't we, Felicity?"

Felicity? Flick stared at her mother, really wondering what had gotten into her. She hadn't called her that in years, and even then, only when Flick was in trouble.

"Because if there is, you only need ask."

Again, Flick went to bring up the bedding, but again her mother got in there first.

"Honestly," she said, this time remembering to smile. "We're all good."

Training her eyes on her daughter, Flick immediately recognised Brenda's determined glare. It was one of those looks that willed her to play along at all cost and, despite failing to understand her mum's reasoning, she knew better than to challenge it.

"As long as you're sure?" the woman replied. "Now before I forget, let me give you this." She rummaged in what was obviously a designer handbag and pulled out an envelope. "Your invite."

With her confusion growing, Flick accepted her second gift of the day.

"It's just a little soirée I'm putting together to welcome you to our village, nothing fancy."

Flick looked down at the envelope. Rather than wining and dining her guests, she considered, surely the money would be better spent on upgrading their amenities? Not that Flick was allowed to point this out, not if her mother's continued expression was anything to go by.

"I know it's short notice," the woman continued, "but everyone is so excited to meet you."

"Thank you, I think." Flick struggled to get her head around why anyone would be interested in her and her mother. "It's not like we have anything else on, is it, Mum?" she said, not sure what else she could say.

Brenda nodded, her smile still strained.

"Fabulous. Now I shall leave you both to enjoy the rest of your day." Heading for the exit, the woman paused, returning her attention to Flick. "I'm Julia, by the way."

"Julia," Flick replied. "Pleased to meet you."

Watching their unexpected visitor leave once and for all, Flick waited until she was out of earshot before speaking. "That was a bit weird," she said finally, her eyes still on the door. She recalled the previous day's chap with the Jack Russell, remembering he was a bit odd too. "I wonder if there's something in the water."

She turned to her mother. "And what's got into you? You looked like you couldn't get rid of the poor woman quick enough."

"Rubbish," Brenda said, getting back to her coffee.

"Oh, come on. It was obvious you didn't want her here. What's going on?"

"Nothing."

Irrespective of any denial, Flick wasn't buying it. She knew when her mum was being less than truthful. "Mother?" When it came to Sunday names what was good for the goose and all that.

Brenda's shoulders suddenly dropped as she let out a relenting sigh. Picking up both their cups, she indicated they should sit down.

Doing as she was told, Flick took a seat at the table and waited for her mother to speak.

"I wish your father were here," she said finally.

Seeing the desperation in her mother's eyes, Flick felt her heart break all over again. "Me too."

Brenda took another deep breath, as she glanced around the room. "It wasn't meant to be like this."

Flick had to agree. Life could be so cruel sometimes. "I'm sorry, Mum."

"Why do you keep saying that? What have you got to be sorry for?"

"For not being there for you like I should have been. For being so wrapped up in my own problems that I didn't properly see you were still hurting."

"Don't be daft. These last twelve months have been tough for the both of us." Brenda reached out with a comforting hand. "The last thing I want is you feeling guilty when you've nothing to feel guilty for."

Flick sat there silent, her mum's kind words doing nothing to ease her regret.

"Remember how he used to say you were his little princess?"

Flick smiled. Of course she did. From when he read her fairy tales when tucking her into bed at night, to the Disney movies she'd always loved so much, her dad had called her that for as far back as she could remember. Even when she grew into a stroppy teenager and then a young woman, she'd been his little princess.

"He always did know how to make me feel special," she said. She wished he was still around to make her feel special again. "Thanks to Matthew, I've forgotten what that feels like."

"Yes, well, as much as we said we wouldn't talk about him, it's because of your relationship with Matthew that we're here."

"I know," Flick replied, not that she was ready to thank him for it.

"No. You don't."

Flick's expression turned quizzical. "What do you mean?"

"I mean that's why I needed to get rid of that woman. I couldn't have some random stranger letting things slip, could I?"

Flick narrowed her eyes even further. "What're you talking about? Let what slip?"

She watched her mother take a second to gather her thoughts. She finally looked Flick directly in the eye.

"What else was it your dad used to say?"

Wondering where this was all going, Flick tried to think. Her dad used to say lots of things. "That I'm beautiful. That if I work hard and stay focused I can achieve anything I want in life." She smiled. "That one day I'd be a famous artist... I'm sorry, Mum, but you've lost me. What does any of this have to do with Matthew? With that woman?"

"And you wonder why I wish your father were here. He was always better at this stuff than me." Brenda took another moment. "Look, when you and Matthew got serious, your dad wanted you to know that, no matter what, you'd always be his little princess. He knew you'd eventually get married and it was supposed to be a wedding present, extravagant I know, but that was your dad all over when it came to you. Then he had to go and have a stroke, and then what happened happened and there was no way you could give it back like you did all your other gifts. So, I ended up not giving it to you at all."

Flick struggled to keep up with her mum's rambling.

"And the longer I left it, the harder it became... Don't you see, that's why we had to come here, why I had to stop that woman from opening her mouth, and why everyone in the village can't wait to meet you."

"Mum," Flick finally interrupted. "Take a breath, you're not making any sense."

Brenda fell silent.

Flick could see she still felt frustrated, but at least she did as she was told and inhaled. "You're right, we need to start from the beginning," Brenda said. "So, you remember your dad calling you his little princess?"

Flick despaired, wishing her mother would just cut to the chase. However, the expectation on her mum's face told her she had no choice but to, yet again, play along. "Yes, I do."

"And what does every little princess have?"

"A tiara?"

"And?"

This was getting stupid.

"A throne?"

"And?"

Now it was getting hard. Searching her mum's face for some sort of clue, Flick didn't have any proper idea as to what real princesses did or didn't have. Forced to think for a minute, she wracked her brain until the penny finally dropped.

"You're not suggesting…"

Brenda slowly nodded. "I'm afraid I am."

Flick's heart skipped a beat. This had to be some sort of joke, her mother couldn't really be saying what Flick thought she was saying. She looked around the room, the enormity of her mother's revelation slapping Flick in the face. "Oh, Lordy."

"Exactly," Brenda replied. "Welcome to your new home."

CHAPTER SIX

Nate popped his head through the kitchen doorway. "Anything I can do to help?"

"Nope," Julia replied. She wiped her hands on a tea towel, grabbed a bottle of white wine from the fridge and took a glass from the cupboard. Handing him her wares, she took him by the shoulders, turned him around and gently pushed him back towards the lounge. "You go and relax. I've got everything covered."

Reluctantly doing as he was told, Nate realised he should have known better than to try to make himself useful in the kitchen. Letting her get back to putting the finishing touches on the dainty bite-sized canapés she was making, *everyone* knew that room was Aunt Julia's territory. It was a domain she guarded fiercely, shooing anyone and everyone offering assistance out of the way.

Feeling at a loose end, he sauntered into the living room. He wondered what he was even doing there. He didn't share everyone else's excitement for the newcomers, especially when the new chatelaine had already recognised him, albeit in a vague kind of way. And how long before it dawned on her where from? Then what? He dreaded to think. Oh yes, he'd have much preferred to stay away that night, but as usual when it came to her gatherings Aunt Julia was having none of it.

"It won't be the same without you," she'd insisted. "Besides, everyone will be expecting you."

With nothing else to do, he found himself glancing around. He felt strangely comforted. From the *toile de Jouy* armchair and the lush cream sofas, to the antique display cabinet and the opulent chandelier, the whole ensemble reminded him of his mum.

She and Aunt Julia might not look alike, but they certainly had the same sense of style – expensive.

He pictured one of his favourite moments with his mother. It wasn't anything spectacular, but just the thought of it and Nate felt his mood begin to lift. He must have been about fourteen at the time and he was struggling with some algebra homework. He smiled as he recalled his mum's frustration at not being able to get her head around it either. So much so, that in the end they both just gave up, opting to watch a film instead and as usual, his mother talked all the way through it. She might not have been any good at maths but she certainly knew how to ruin a good movie, correctly anticipating what was going to happen next, and why, at every twist and turn. Nate didn't mind though. He enjoyed listening to her. To the outside world such an evening might be deemed typical when it came to family life. For the two of them, it was such a rare occasion.

Dragging his mind back into the present, Nate continued to take in his surroundings, his eyes resting on the silver-framed photos adorning the console table. Approaching them, he poured himself a glass of wine and setting the bottle down, took in the images before him. Mostly pictures of himself as a boy, Aunt Julia had always been a second mum to him, providing a home from home when things got too chaotic back in the UK. Having never had children of her own, she seemed to relish having him to stay; his holidays here were always packed full of fun and adventure from the second he stepped off the plane.

He picked up the one and only photo of his mother, a relaxed head and shoulder shot taken before he was born. As usual, he found looking at her image unnerving, the likeness between mother and son was striking even to him. He stroked the corner of the frame with his thumb. She might not have been the most conventional of mothers, but he supposed under the circumstances she did her best. What he'd never understand though were the choices she made. Or the pandemonium that surrounded her – even to this day. "Sorry, Mum," he said, as he opened the table drawer and carefully slipped the photo inside.

"Everything okay?" Julia asked.

Hastily closing the drawer, Nate spun round as she made her entrance, making sure to smile as he looked her way. "Fine." Scrutinising her expression, if she'd seen him hide the picture she certainly wasn't letting on. Instead, she raised her empty glass and taking the hint, Nate picked up the wine bottle to fill it.

"I'm ready for this," she said. "And with a bit of luck, we'll have five minutes to ourselves before everyone gets here."

They sat down on opposing sofas and Nate watched his aunt make herself comfortable. She seemed to come over all tense, as if readying herself to say something.

"Bruce phoned," she finally said.

Nate scoffed. He knew it.

"He thinks you're ignoring him."

"That's because I am."

"Why?" Despite knowing that he and Bruce had never seen eye to eye, Nate's response seemed to have caused some confusion. "Don't you agree with what he's doing?"

Nate shrugged. "I don't care one way or the other."

"You don't think you should be involved?"

Determined to keep his irritation in check, Nate took a sip of his wine. "I think we should change the subject."

"But this is about your mum. You can't stay mad at her forever."

He begged to differ. "Watch me."

His aunt shook her head, her expression showing a mix of disappointment and frustration. But as far as Nate was concerned that was the end of the subject. The last person he ever wanted to talk about was his mother, a fact Julia knew all too well and as he drank another mouthful of wine, an awkward silence descended, but Nate didn't care.

"I wonder what they'll do with the place," Julia suddenly asked, clearly wanting to lift the atmosphere. "It's such a beautiful building, I can't wait to see it come back to life."

Nate wished he could share her enthusiasm, but the chateau was another topic he had no interest in. In fact, imagining the night ahead he didn't know who he felt sorry for the most. Himself, for being forced to be here or the newcomers for the grilling they were, no doubt, about to experience? His aunt and her circle might not be malicious when it came to their chit-chat, but they did like to keep up with the goings-on in and around the village. Poor Flick and her mother didn't know what they were in for.

He watched his aunt circle the rim of her glass with her index finger, failing miserably in her attempts to appear casual.

"She's very pretty," she said. "The daughter."

"Is she?" Nate refused to get drawn in, it didn't take a genius to see where this was leading. When she wasn't sticking up for his mum, the woman before him was forever trying to remedy his non-existent love life. "I didn't notice."

He was lying, of course. Recalling their brief meeting, he'd surprised himself at how alluring he'd found her. There was something about the way she looked at him. Most people either avoided eye contact, even when talking to him, or they did their utmost not to stare too hard. Flick, however, did neither of those things. Although she did hold on to his hand longer than necessary, an action that amused him even now. Plus, she was stunning, she had an unassuming beauty, her looks were natural. Not that he was interested, of course. Having been burned in the relationship department too many times already, no way was he going to risk that happening again. As far as he was concerned, Flick might look all sweet and innocent, but she still had the power to hurt him.

Julia froze. "What? You've met her?"

He took another sip of wine, half of him wishing he'd kept his mouth shut. Julia would want a blow-by-blow account of their exchange despite there not being much to tell. The other half felt determined to play it cool and enjoy the moment. Catching his aunt off guard didn't happen very often, so he had to make the most of it. "For all of sixty seconds."

Julia leaned forward in her seat, maintaining a calm composure clearly no longer an issue. "When? You didn't mention anything."

Nate laughed. "I didn't realise I had to."

"So where did this meeting take place? What did you talk about? More to the point, why didn't you tell me you'd spoken to her?"

Wondering which question he was supposed to answer first, a car horn suddenly beeped, putting an end to their conversation. A welcome reprieve, at least on his part, from the interrogation about to ensue. High pitched, yet hollow, he recognised the sound as belonging to a particular Citroën 2CV. *Thank you, Gigi*, he thought, amused by her perfect timing. *I owe you one.*

Unable to quite hide her annoyance, his aunt rose to her feet. "We'll talk about this later," she said, something Nate didn't doubt for one minute.

CHAPTER SEVEN

Nate watched his aunt fix a smile on her face, ready to welcome the first of her guests, still laughing to himself as he followed her outside.

"*Bonsoir*, Gigi," Julia said, ever the consummate hostess with the mostess. "*Ça va?*"

"*Bonsoir*, Julia. *Bonsoir*, Nate."

Following the customary exchange of kisses, Gigi reached into her vehicle. She had to be as old as the car, and that was ancient, yet despite her years and rather slight frame, she easily pulled out a huge basket of just-baked bread. The smell alone made Nate realise how hungry he felt and taking in the array of *baguettes, bâtards, flutes* and *ficelles*, his stomach rumbled. "Talk about a feast." He reached forward, attempting to snaffle a piece of bread, but catching him in the act, Gigi playfully tapped his hand away.

"*Pour toi*," she said, handing the whole lot over to his aunt instead. She lowered her voice. "Are they here yet?"

Nate smiled. Her warm personality belied a shrewd head for business. An artisan *boulanger*, Gigi's award-winning family-run patisserie was renowned across the whole of Brittany for a reason. And with the business acumen to match her extensive bakery skills, she never missed an opportunity to expand their reputation.

"I'm afraid not," Julia replied.

Seeing Gigi's disappointment, Nate couldn't resist teasing her. "Looking to add the new chatelaine to your list of esteemed clients?"

Gigi gave him a cheeky grin. "Of course, *mon ami*."

Nate laughed in response. At least she was honest. Then again, he'd always admired her ability to say it like it was. He thought back to when he'd first arrived. Whereas some of Aunt Julia's friends initially pussyfooted around him, Gigi told him straight, that he needed to stop being such a spoilt brat and *se faire pousser des couilles*, grow some balls. In France this might be a phrase to make even the most hardened of navvies blush, but not her.

As Julia and Gigi headed indoors, Nate hung back, wondering if he should seize the opportunity to sneak off home. Naturally, Julia would be disappointed by his absence, but he knew she'd get over it eventually. At any rate, if their excited chatter was anything to go by he wouldn't exactly be missed. Listening to them, the two women were far too preoccupied discussing the chateau and its new owner to even notice he'd gone, at least for a while.

Feeling like a naughty schoolboy, he giggled to himself as he turned, ready to slip around the back of the house and head off home.

"Hi, Nate," a voice suddenly called out to him.

Nate stopped. *Bugger! Jess!*

"Where are you sloping off to?" she asked.

Nowhere by the looks of things, he wanted to say but didn't.

He sighed, supposing a disappearing act would only be delaying the inevitable. Being his nearest neighbour, his and Flick's paths had already crossed once and were bound to cross again. As much as he wanted to, he knew there wasn't really any point in hiding, he had to just put himself out there and hope for the best.

Putting a smile on his face he turned back around ready to greet Jess as she tottered towards him. He almost didn't recognise her. Usually sporting a pair of jeans and flats, it was the first time he'd ever seen her in a dress, let alone stilettoes and whereas her hair was usually tied up in a knot, her blonde locks hung loose. Momentarily forgetting his plight, he whistled to show his appreciation, she'd certainly gone all out.

Jess blushed in response. "I couldn't meet a real chateau owner in my scruffs now, could I?"

Nate shook his head. What was wrong with everyone lately? "I don't see why not," he replied.

She looked down at her attire. "Too much?" she asked, screwing her face up.

"Not at all," Nate said. The poor woman looked self-conscious enough, he decided, she didn't need the usual teasing from him. "You look lovely."

"Really?"

"Really."

"Although there does seem to be one thing missing," he added, unable to completely refrain from their customary banter.

"What?" Mortified, Jess again looked from him, to her attire, and back again.

"Pete," Nate said.

Jess immediately slapped him on the arm. "You had me worried there!"

"Ouch!" Nate laughed. "So, go on then, where is he?"

She rolled her eyes. "Let's just say he's planning his own grand entrance."

Nate had seen that long-suffering expression before. "Another new venture?"

"You know Pete."

"Come on," Nate said, putting all thoughts of sneaking off home behind him. "You look like you need a drink."

She pulled a bottle of wine out of her oversized handbag. "One step ahead of you."

"I hope you've got enough for me!" another voice loudly interrupted.

Nate looked over Jess's shoulder at the next new arrival. "Dee. Great to see you."

Catching up to them, she greeted first Jess and then Nate with a kiss. "I've had the day from hell," Dee said. "Four viewings this morning, followed by three hours at the *notaire's* office, which I really could have done without. You know what the French system's like for dotting the Is and crossing the Ts. Still, at least the clients were happy when they finally got the keys to their new home." She took in Jess's outfit. "Unlike some, I didn't have chance to go home and change."

"The life of an estate agent, eh?" Nate said.

"You got that right."

"Think yourself lucky," Jess said. "At least you're busy. Now summer has been and gone, the bar's been dead. At this rate, we'll be lucky if we have enough cash to see us through the winter."

"If I've said it once, I'll say it again. You need to turn that place into a restaurant," Dee said. "It's in a prime location and with your cookery skills, everybody knows you'd make a killing. Anyway, that's enough work talk for today, thank you very much. Now where's that corkscrew?"

As she marched on ahead, Nate followed behind with Jess. He leaned in to speak, careful to keep his voice down. "It's because of her bloody work that we're all here," he said. "I mean, did she really have to sell that chateau?"

"I heard that." Dee stepped inside the house.

Nate winked at Jess as they too entered. Happy to leave everyone else to catch up, he poured himself another glass of wine and headed for a corner of the room. Observing them, he couldn't help but think the group a funny bunch. The only obvious thing they had in common was their shared love of France and, being honest, he couldn't imagine any of them becoming friends back in the UK. They were so different from one another.

Like him though, it was obvious they were each running away from something.

Nate laughed to himself. *Take Dee*, he thought. She often said she came here to escape the rat race back in England. Although listening to the complaints about her work load this side of the Channel, she hadn't escaped anything of the sort.

As for poor Jess, thanks to Pete they were probably running away from one debt or dodgy deal too many. Despite his best efforts, the man was most certainly no entrepreneur. In fact, Nate sometimes questioned why Jess bothered putting up with her husband and his mad ideas.

Turning his attention to Julia, Nate didn't have a clue why she was here. By all accounts she simply got up one morning, threw herself and an overnight bag into her car, and once on the road, just kept driving; refusing to turn the vehicle around even when she hit Dover. Nate had often wondered what had informed that decision all those years earlier. Julia, however, still refused to divulge.

Continuing to watch everyone, Nate was surprised Philippe hadn't landed yet. Although as mayor, Nate supposed Philippe could easily have gotten waylaid with his official duties. Nate smiled; he liked Philippe. He was good for his aunt. He didn't just adore her, he gave her the emotional security that had been lacking in her previous relationships. Philippe saw behind the confident façade. He was Aunt Julia's rock. Of course it wasn't all one-sided. It was clear to Nate that she was good for him too. Julia brought out Philippe's softer, more fun, side. She was the antidote to the stresses and strains caused by his political and professional life. Forced to wear many hats, being *Monsieur le Maire* wasn't exactly easy. At least not the way Philippe described it.

This was something else Nate hadn't really discussed with his aunt. He observed her discreetly check her watch, no doubt, because she also wondered where Philippe had got to. Nate smiled. Despite being the worst kept secret in the village, as far as the two star-struck lovers were concerned, no one actually knew they were an item. *Bless them*, thought Nate. They were so happy in their misguided belief. So much so, not even he had the heart to tell them their secret was well and truly out.

Nate's thoughts were suddenly interrupted when Gigi squealed.

"There's a car pulling up in the lane. I think they might be here," she said. Hopping up and down, she stared out of the window.

He watched everyone follow her gaze, hoping to spot the newcomers for themselves. And while Julia straightened herself up ready to receive the guests of honour, Nate found himself automatically looking out for them too.

"What the…?" he said, his eyes widening as a big black vehicle pulled up in front of the gates. He again looked around the rest of the group, each as surprised as him by what they saw. All except Jess, he noted. She appeared mortified and checking out the driver, Nate couldn't blame her. He crept over and whispered in her ear. "You could have warned us."

"What was I supposed to say?" Jess asked.

Struggling to stifle his laughter, Nate watched Pete, clearly proud of his latest acquisition, beaming as he climbed out of the car. "But it's a hearse."

"You think I don't know that."

CHAPTER EIGHT

Flick brought her car to a standstill and staring at the vehicle in front, she turned off the engine. She hesitated, wondering what to do for the best. Unlike her mother, who already gripped the door handle ready to disembark, Flick wasn't sure if announcing their arrival was such a good idea.

"You ready?" Brenda asked.

Feeling uncomfortable, Flick frowned, as she looked from the big black hearse to her mother. "You do see what I see, don't you?"

Brenda scoffed. "I think if someone's dead they'd have sent word telling us not to come, don't you?"

Flick didn't agree. Thinking back to the immediate aftermath of her father's passing, she easily recalled how dazed and disoriented she felt. Neither she nor her mother had the wherewithal to start informing anyone of anything. "I think if someone were dead, we'd be the last people on anyone's mind."

Brenda automatically released her door hold and like Flick, stared straight ahead. "So, what now?" she eventually asked.

"We can't just sit here."

"And we can't go knocking in case."

Flick took a deep intake of breath, filling her cheeks with air before blowing it all out again. "Then we go home, I suppose."

She could see her mother's disappointment. Having gotten the big reveal about the chateau out of the way, her mum had made no secret of how much she'd been looking forward to that night. In fact, she'd gone all out, insisting they both get dolled up for the occasion, which for some reason included the need for Flick to wear a dress. Apparently, the midi-length floral number that her mother had picked out was more befitting than the clean black denims she had chosen. But Flick had remained steadfast, only conceding in the shoe and make-up departments.

Self-conscious enough already, Flick felt relieved that they weren't staying. As much as she hoped the hearse's presence was purely coincidental, she had to admit she was glad of the excuse it had given her. She'd been the centre of attention for long enough back home and the last thing she needed was yet more scrutiny.

Putting one hand on the wheel, Flick reached for the ignition. But just as she was about to turn the key her mother put a hand out to stop her.

"Looks like that's here for someone else," Brenda said, suddenly smiling again as she indicated first to the big black car and then towards the house.

Following her mum's gaze, Flick looked out of her side window to see Julia tootling towards them, a glass of something in one hand while waving with the other. Flick's heart sank, the soirée was back on. As if life hadn't already been cruel enough.

"You found us all right then?" their hostess called out.

Flick let her hands drop back down onto her knee. "At least we know everyone's still alive and kicking," she said, trying to look on the bright side.

"Smile," Brenda said, more than happy to wave back. "It's not every day you get a party in your honour."

Realising her mum was as bad as the rest of them, Flick did as she was told and widened her lips. "Traitor," she said, through gritted teeth.

She could just imagine what lay ahead. The locals were obviously keen to know what plans she had for the chateau, that night's event in itself was enough to prove that. She tried to tell herself it was understandable, that they were bound to be curious. In their shoes, she'd probably be curious too. The trouble was, she didn't have any plans. "How could you and Dad do this to me?"

"You'll be fine," Brenda said, clearly of the opinion that Flick was worrying over nothing.

Flick unclipped her seatbelt. "Easy for you to say," she said, before climbing out of the car.

"It's so lovely to see you again." Julia threw her arms around each of them.

Flick noted how she expertly steered both her and her mother passed the hearse and towards the house, as if pretending it wasn't even there. And although Flick's naughty side was tempted, she thought better of making her face it with an enquiry, instead, choosing to focus on the rest of her surroundings. Stepping through the gates, she felt her breath catch. They weren't so much met by a walled garden, but the most romantic of courtyards she'd ever seen. It might've been the beginning of autumn, but the sweet, calming fragrance of lavender still permeated the air. Blue salvia, phlox and grasses came together perfectly and pendant, bean-like seed pods formed on the branches of the wisteria that twined its way across the front of the shuttered stone house. "This is beautiful," she said. A far cry from the neglected chateau, with its flaky paint and crumbly pointing, that she owned.

Julia downplayed the compliment. "It wasn't always like this. You should have seen the state of the building when I first bought it. More of an old ruin really. Transforming it has been a labour of love, something you'll no doubt experience with your place."

It was an assumption with which Flick struggled to agree. When it came to her place, she'd so far experienced nothing but sheer panic. She'd spent the last few days pacing its corridors and wandering from room to room, all the while wondering what on earth her parents had been thinking. As far as she was concerned, the whole situation was nothing short of surreal.

She and her mum followed Julia through a set of patio doors that led straight into the lounge. As expected, with its posh décor and expensive furnishings, the room was as beautiful as the garden. Continuing to feel uncomfortable, Flick silently took in the welcome party that had gathered, all eyes full of anticipation as the group looked back. She felt the same fight or flight sensation that had enveloped her during her wedding reception. Everyone had stared at her then. *How disappointed all these people must feel*, she considered, to be met by little old her instead of an individual more becoming of a chateau.

Julia immediately began a round of introductions. It felt odd kissing strangers, but if anyone picked up on her unease they certainly didn't show it. In what Flick could only describe as a polite production line of embraces, one by one they more than happily stepped forward, greeting first her and then Brenda. Her mum wholeheartedly throwing herself into the experience, she noted.

It began with Dee, a tall haughty woman, probably in her forties. Flick almost winced as she grabbed her shoulders, holding them in a vice-like grip as she planted her lips on Flick's cheeks.

"Pleased to meet you at last," Dee said, finally releasing her hold. She tilted her head, her face suddenly serious. "I was sorry to hear about your father. I might have only met him professionally, but in my game you meet all sorts, and believe me, your dad was definitely one of the good ones."

"You sold him the chateau?" Although after that embrace, Flick thought it more plausible her dad had been strong-armed into the deal.

Dee stood proud. "I certainly did."

Knowing the woman had only done her job, Flick smiled, trying not to hold it against her.

Next, a tiny elderly woman stepped forward. Dressed entirely in black, she wore minimal make-up, just a bit of powder and a pale pink lipstick. Her white hair was pulled back into a neat yet stylish bun. "*Enchanté.*"

From her appearance, Flick wasn't at all surprised to hear she was French.

"*Je m'appelle* Gigi." The woman's smile shone as much as the welcome in her eyes and as she leaned forward, Flick had to stoop in order to accept the delicate kisses Gigi placed on her cheeks.

"*Je m'appelle* Flick." Once again, her attempt at the lingo sounded embarrassing to her own ears, but thankfully it seemed to please the old lady.

"*Très bon.*" Gigi clapped her hands in delight. She then stood back, allowing the next of the guests to introduce themselves.

Flick felt an immediate affinity. Out of everyone she'd met so far, this woman appeared as awkward about the situation as Flick felt. A fact made even clearer when the poor woman tripped, almost toppling into Flick, but managing to quickly recover her stance before any real damage was done.

"Sorry," she said, trying to control her blushes. "I knew I shouldn't have worn these shoes."

Also forced to shift from one foot to the other, this was something else Flick could empathise with. Her own footwear might not have been quite so high, but thanks to her mother's insistence that she make more of an effort, they were certainly higher than she was used to.

"Anyway, I'm Jess," the woman continued. "And this is my husband Pete." She turned, indicating to the man at her side. "We own the local bar. In the village, on the main street. You might have seen it? I know, I'm rambling. Shut up, Jess."

Yep, Flick definitely liked this woman.

"Nice to meet you," Pete said, coming to his wife's rescue.

"Likewise."

"I hope we'll see you down there sometime," he carried on.

Flick looked forward to it. "I'm sure you will."

As Julia moved in to make the final introduction, Flick immediately recognised the man before her.

"I believe you've already met my nephew," her host said.

"Indeed," Flick replied, silently noting that he looked just as gorgeous as he had the first time round. As she waited for him to speak, however, he once again seemed reluctant to put himself forward and Flick was convinced she heard him groan when his aunt finally nudged him into action. Not that this unwillingness came as any great surprise. Again, thinking back to their first meeting, he hadn't exactly proven himself as the sociable type.

"Hello again," he said.

Staring once more into the greenest of eyes, Flick felt momentarily captivated and, lost for words, she willed herself not to blush. He leaned in to kiss the first of her cheeks, leaving Flick no choice but to breathe in his aroma. Somewhat pleasantly, rather than some fancy aftershave, he smelt clean and fresh like soap. His skin felt rough against hers, the prickle of stubble causing a sweeter sensation than it should have done. *That's enough of that!* she thought, all of a fluster. And suddenly hot and bothered, she immediately stepped back, cutting short this part of their introduction in favour of a formal handshake.

Her sudden change in tack seemed to amuse him. "Nate," he said, accepting the gesture.

"So, you do have a name then," Flick replied.

He picked up a glass of wine from a tray on the console table by his side. "Drink?" he asked, his tickled expression continuing as he handed it over.

Flick took a gulp in an attempt at cooling herself down, before looking to her mum for assistance. However, Brenda was far too busy relishing in the attention being given to notice her daughter's discomfort at being left alone with a handsome stranger. Flick stopped herself from interrupting though. Even if she waited for a gap in the chatter, she realised any complaints on her part would be unfair. It had been a while since her mum had properly relaxed and it was easy to understand why. On top of Dad's death, having the issue of the chateau weighing heavily all this time couldn't have been easy and as she carried on watching her, it felt good to see her mother smiling again.

Instead, Flick continued to just stand there, feeling a tad stupid. Nate might be giving her the odd cursory smile, but he was obviously the strong silent type, a man more interested in everyone else's conversations, as opposed to striking up one of his own.

With nothing else for it, she too tuned in to what the others were saying and it quickly became apparent that she'd been right; everyone did want to know what she and her mum had in store for the chateau. They had so many questions that Flick didn't have the answers to. Unlike Brenda, it seemed, who responded with ease.

"So what big plans do you have for the old place?" Gigi asked.

"Not sure at the moment. We're just enjoying being here for now."

"What do you think of the area?" Jess asked. "Have you had chance to explore yet?"

"Oh, it's wonderful. We haven't had the opportunity to have a good look around, of course, but we will."

"Will you live here full-time? Or flit between France and the UK?" Pete asked.

"Definitely full-time."

Swallowing another mouthful of wine, Flick instantly choked. *Since when was that decided?* This was news to her. Her cheeks reddened as everyone turned. "Sorry. Wrong hole."

She tried to discreetly wipe herself down, at the same time wondering what her mother was talking about. Too busy getting used to the fact that she actually owned the chateau, they certainly hadn't discussed where to go from there. She felt a prod, as an even more amused Nate offered her a tissue and scowling in response, she reluctantly accepted when all she wanted to do was ask him what was so funny. It was all right for him, wasn't it? His life wasn't being dictated by his mother and a bunch of strangers.

"You're welcome," Nate said, reminding her she'd forgotten her manners while clearly trying not to laugh.

As the conversation continued, Flick began to wonder what she was even doing there. Thanks to her mother's quick-fire responses, she wasn't exactly needed.

"I think it would make a fabulous wedding venue," Julia said. Appearing with a silver tray full of canapés, she held it towards the guest of honour.

Flick shook her head; the idea of eating as bad as the host's suggestion for the chateau.

As Julia moved on, Flick didn't just feel overwhelmed, she suddenly felt sick, and needing to escape the discussion altogether, subtly stepped away from the group. With the conversation in full flow, surely no one would notice her slipping out into the garden.

CHAPTER NINE

I n desperate need of fresh air, Flick took a seat at a wrought iron table and as she again breathed in the scent of lavender, she wondered how her life could have gone so off-plan. Looking back, she tried to pinpoint when things had started to unravel. It would have been easy to blame Matthew, she wanted to blame Matthew. But if she was honest, she knew her loss of control began well before her husband's disappearance.

She thought back to when he proposed. Her dad had recently suffered his stroke and although the doctors were cautiously optimistic, no one really knew how well he would or wouldn't recover. Always so strong and healthy, not to mention fiercely independent, seeing him in a hospital bed, so frail and helpless, broke her heart. Naturally her dad suffered the most, but it was a difficult time for everyone. And scary. In fact, Matthew asking Flick to marry him was the one beacon of light in what had, up until then, been a very dark tunnel. A beacon that she'd grabbed hold of and, just like an Olympic torch, ran with.

Not that his proposal was particularly romantic. There was no getting down on bended knee, no roses, or even an engagement ring. Just a simple statement really. Flick had had a busy day at work, every awkward customer possible had come into the coffee shop. Someone's drink was too hot; another's cake was too dry; one individual even had the audacity to complain about the weather in such a way that the rain was somehow her fault.

Ignoring the desire to scream at each and every one of them, she dealt with them all in the same professional manner that she always did. Her positive façade continuing well after closing time when she'd driven straight to her dad's bedside. It couldn't last, of course.

Emotionally, she knew she was reaching breaking point. No wonder the floodgates opened the second she landed back home.

Matthew did his best at comforting her, insisting everything would be all right as he passed her a tissue and a glass of wine. Flick didn't believe him though, how could she? The man in the hospital bed resembled nothing of the giant tower of strength she'd called Dad all her life. That's when Matthew had said it. *I think we should get married.* Six simple words, just like that. Finally, her tears stopped.

She took a deep breath, bringing herself back to the present. "And where are you now, Matthew?" she asked, looking up to the skies.

"You can get locked up for that, you know. Talking to yourself."

Flick turned to see Nate. Despite knowing she couldn't escape for long, she hadn't expected him to be the one to come and find her. After all, he hadn't been very hospitable.

"They're not always like this," he said, nodding towards Julia and her guests back in the lounge. "You're the most exciting thing to happen to this village for a while. It's not every day we get a new chatelaine."

"And I didn't know that was me until I got here." She paused, needing to let the fact that she owned a chateau sink in once more. "So, if you've come to find out what I plan to do with the damn thing, you're asking the wrong person." She looked back at the house. "You're probably better talking to my mother."

Nate laughed, following her gaze. "She is rather enjoying herself in there."

Catching sight of her mum animatedly chatting, Flick couldn't help but laugh too. The woman was obviously getting far too carried away. "She doesn't seriously think I'm going to give up everything in the UK to come here, does she?"

"I don't see why not." Nate took the seat next to Flick. "You only have to look at that lot to see that plenty of people do."

Silence descended and, staring out into the garden, Flick began to feel a little awkward. She could sense Nate's eyes upon her which made her nervous. "What?"

"You should smile more often. It suits you."

Flick scoffed. "You can talk. I've met you twice now and on both occasions you've looked like you'd rather be somewhere else. A girl can start to take it personally, you know."

"Says the woman who recoiled from a perfectly acceptable embrace."

"I did not recoil." Flick sat there indignant. "I'm just not used to kissing strangers." Not about to admit she fancied the pants off him, as excuses went, it was the best she could come up with.

She suddenly fell quiet again, the enormity of her predicament back to taking centre stage. "None of this is funny really," she eventually said. "I mean what am I supposed to do with a blooming great, big chateau? And even if I wanted to do something, have you seen how much money it needs throwing at it? Money I don't have, by the way."

"And if cash weren't a problem?" Nate asked. "Would you be saying something different?"

It was a fair question. One that made her think about how beautiful and full of potential the building was, about her father's love of France, and the reasons he'd bought it for her in the first place. "Yes. No. Oh, I don't know. It's not that easy."

"Believe you me, the best decisions in life never are."

Flick looked back towards the house again, catching another glimpse of her mum deep in conversation with Nate's Aunt Julia and Dee. Flick thought for another moment. The man before her might have a point, but after everything Flick had been through lately *easy* was exactly what she needed.

CHAPTER TEN

The bathroom might look the part, considered Flick, with its giant window, ornately tiled floor and antique roll top bath, but in this instance, it was a definite case of looks being deceiving. Standing there in the cold, it was not a room to luxuriate in.

She stared at the water gushing out of the oversized showerhead, daring herself to just go for it. She knew she didn't have a choice, but bracing herself, Flick also knew what was coming. Quickly letting her dressing gown drop to the floor, she grabbed the bottle of shower gel, holding her breath as she hastily stepped into the tub and under the water. Not that the lack of oxygen flowing through her body was an issue. Exhaling, she still couldn't breathe thanks to the icy shards hitting every inch of her body. She panted, attempting to get air into her lungs, dancing up and down as she smothered herself in non-existent gel suds. Unable to stand it any longer, Flick slammed off the shower and, reaching for her towel, continued to hop from one foot to the other as she dried herself off. "The things I do for this family," she said, yet again wondering what her father had been thinking when he bought the damn chateau.

She donned her bathrobe again and exited the bathroom. Making her way back down the corridor to her bedroom, she shivered. No matter what her mother seemed to think, there was no way Flick could put up with this for the long haul.

She quickly dressed and headed downstairs to the kitchen, the only room comfortable enough to use. Flick immediately appreciated the warmth of the glowing open fire, something her mum had taken to setting every morning, which was a good job considering. Left to her, the two of them would freeze completely.

Brenda looked up from her phone mid-text. "You're up early."

Flick made straight for the coffee. "I thought I might have a wander into town."

"That sounds fun. It'll be interesting to see if anything's changed since your dad and I were last here."

Flick stiffened as she poured her drink. She hadn't meant it as an invite and her mind raced as she tried to come up with an excuse to go alone.

"I'm just telling Linda about the other night," Brenda explained, at the same time resuming her messaging. "About how nice the party was."

Flick shook her head. As kind and welcoming as the other guests had been, *nice* wasn't the word she would have used. She'd spent the entire evening under pressure to discuss her plans for the chateau despite not having any. As well as what a fabulous surprise it must have been to find out she suddenly owned a French castle. *Surprise* being another word she wouldn't have considered.

Everything about that night had been playing over and over in her head ever since. She agreed that the building was, indeed, fabulous, but surely no one really expected her to give up the only life she knew on a whim? Flick recalled her mother's assertion about her moving there full-time, still able to hear the delighted response from everyone present. Flick thought about the way they'd all clambered to give her their contact details should she need any help as she began her new adventure. Her heart sank. Yes, it seemed they did. "About the other night—"

"I know what you're going to say," Brenda interrupted. "And I'm sorry. I shouldn't have jumped the gun, I just got a little bit carried away." She glanced around the room. "It's such an exciting opportunity though and we both know it's what your dad would've wanted."

On the one hand, Flick agreed. The chateau offered countless possibilities for anyone looking for a fresh start. On the other, she'd just been forced to take a cold shower and she was sure her dad wouldn't have wanted his little princess roughing it to this extent.

When he handed over his money, he clearly hadn't realised how much work the chateau needed.

"And even you have to admit this place isn't really a holiday home, it needs someone here permanently."

Of course it did, thought Flick. She just didn't think that *someone* was her. Okay, since Matthew's disappearance she might not have much going on back home in Blighty, but she did have central heating, hot water, and a fire she could turn on with a press of a button. Modern day conveniences she could only dream about were she to stay in France. She thought about the cosy little home waiting for her back in England. Conveniences she would never, ever take for granted again.

Finally, Brenda put her phone down, giving Flick her full attention. Her eyes narrowed slightly, as if sensing all wasn't well. "Anything you want to talk about?"

There was a lot Flick wanted to talk about, but she knew now wasn't the time. She needed to get the morning over with before discussing anything. "Nope," she replied, instead, although as usual her mother knew her too well.

"Look, I understand this has all come as a bit of a shock. Goodness knows I had my reservations when your father suggested we buy you a chateau. I mean who does that? But rightly or wrongly, we did and here we are. And, of course, I'll support whatever decision you come to. I just want you to think long and hard before making up your mind."

"I've done nothing but think, Mum."

"Maybe you need to think some more."

She watched her mother get up to pour herself a coffee.

"Perhaps you should go into town on your own," Brenda suggested. "Get a feel for the local area without me wittering on."

Flick appreciated where her mum was coming from but unless either of them had a cool half a million going spare, which is what it would probably take to make the chateau properly liveable, Flick didn't see the point in getting a feel for anything. *Half a million*, she thought. *And the rest.*

She opened her mouth ready to tell her mum that she'd reached a decision, but the expectation on Brenda's face prevented any words from coming out. Flick felt terrible. The last thing she wanted to do was let her mum down, the woman who'd been there for her every second of every miserable day the last few months. And this, despite losing the man she'd been married to for more years than Flick had been married hours. No, she would get this morning out of the way and then have the dreaded conversation.

She fixed a smile on her face. "Maybe you're right."

*

Flick purposefully parked the car on the edge of town. Her head whirled and she hoped a stroll in the fresh air would help calm her mind. She might have come to a decision about the chateau, but with both her head and heart still arguing over which was right, seeing that decision through felt just has hard as making it.

She made her way along the street, the one road that led in and then out of town. She stopped for a moment at the *Place de la Résistance et de la Déportation*, where a huge, bronze statue of a soldier holding a French flag high in the air commemorated those who died in the two world wars. Flick read the words engraved into its giant marble plinth – *Aux enfants morts pour la France. Pro Deo, pro Patria*. With no translation necessary, it was a sobering moment. Definitely enough to put her own troubles into perspective. "Do I sell my chateau? Do I not sell my chateau?" Yep, her current dilemma was definitely the first world problem of all first-world problems.

She carried on up the street, still mocking herself as she clocked the *Papeterie* on the other side of the road. Crossing, her spirits lifted as she looked in the window before heading inside. Glancing around, it was typical of any stationers, her surroundings as familiar as the tingling sensation she always experienced in shops such as this. It might not be an actual art store, but since meeting Matthew it had become as near as damn it.

"*Bonjour*," said the welcoming young girl behind the counter, her smiling face being a far cry from the surly shop assistants Flick came across in the UK.

"*Bonjour,*" Flick replied.

She headed for the sketchpads, carefully examining the various paper grades and textures and, making her choice, moved on to the pencils. Flick was in artistic heaven, not that she considered herself an artist. Such aspirations had gone out of the window the minute she'd left university. Like Matthew always said, *doodling* didn't pay the bills. She thought back to their conversations about her creative ambitions. He hadn't meant to be so condescending, she was convinced of that. Like he'd said, he was just being realistic.

Flick laid her purchases on the counter, at the same time checking her watch. "*Merci,*" she said, handing over her money.

Back on the street, she continued her stroll and nearing the heart of the town, was pleased to see it was market day. Taking in the numerous stalls, she revelled in the goods on offer – the cheeses, the colourful fruit and veg, the smell of freshly caught fish. French conversation came at her from all directions as locals inspected the wares on offer before handing over their hard-earned cash. Flick almost laughed when she spotted a merchant selling nothing but ladies' housecoats just like her grandmother used to wear. Long sleeved, short sleeved, no sleeves at all, all coming in various colours and patterns. It was like stepping back in time to the 1950s. Flick watched on as neighbours laughed and greeted each other like long-lost friends and Flick's heart suddenly panged. Scenes like this were why her father loved France as much as he did. This was the life he'd wanted her to experience.

Refusing to dwell on her dad, Flick checked her watch again. The place she was looking for had to be around there somewhere. Her eyes scanned up and down both sides of the street and finally locating Jess's little bar, Café Ange, Flick headed over.

A cute little place, it had an outside seating area with little, wooden tables and high-backed ladder chairs, the perfect set up for anyone wanting to watch the world go by, and taking a seat, Flick positioned herself so she could continue to watch the market's comings and goings.

"Flick! What a surprise."

Flick turned as Jess, cloth in hand ready to wipe down tables, appeared at the doorway. Flick watched her look down at her attire and tossing the cloth to one side, hastily run her hands down her jeans. Flick felt embarrassed that Jess was embarrassed. She obviously thought people who owned French castles were posh, which in her own case, couldn't be further from the truth. "Don't mind me," she said, trying to put her host at ease. "You should see the state of me when I'm at work." Although as she put a hand up to the tatty bobble keeping her unkempt hair in place, she realised she didn't fare much better outside of her employment.

It seemed to do the trick and Jess appeared to relax a little as she took a seat at Flick's table. "What is it you do?"

"Much the same as you really. I work in a coffee shop."

"You're joking."

"Nope. It's nothing as nice as this though." She took in the scrolled signage of Café Ange. Set against a pale blue background, its white lettering undulated, perfectly in keeping with the three swirls of the Breton logo. Looking through the window, the interior appeared bright and inviting, the traditional tables and chairs continuing within. "And I certainly don't own the place."

"Ah, but you do own a chateau."

"So, we're equal then," Flick said.

Jess laughed. "If you put it like that. You're probably sick of everyone asking, but any idea what you're going to do with it yet?"

Flick didn't answer. She still hadn't told her mother what she planned, so she wasn't about to tell anyone else.

"If you need any help when you do decide just give me a shout."

"Thank you." Flick appreciated the offer, however, at the same time doubting she'd ever need to.

A harassed-looking Pete suddenly appeared in the doorway. "There you are," he said to Jess. "Oh hi, Flick. Nice of you to stop by. How're you settling in?"

Images of the morning's events in the bathroom flashed through her mind, along with the layers of clothing she'd taken to wearing indoors and the speed at which she threw them on each morning. "Okay, thanks."

"It's great to see life return to the big old place. When I think how long it's been stood empty."

"That explains why nothing works. I haven't had a hot shower since I got here."

"What better way to blow off the cobwebs than standing under a bit of cold water though, eh?" Pete suggested, something Flick couldn't quite bring herself to agree with.

"You're welcome to come and use ours until you get yours sorted," Jess offered. "Your mum too. I can even throw in some dinner, if you like."

Pete turned his attention back to his wife. "Sorry to interrupt, but I need your help. The computer's crashed again."

Jess rolled her eyes. "Technology has never been his thing." She got up from her seat. "So, what can I get you? Tea? Coffee? A beer or wine?"

"A coffee would be nice."

"Just let me sort the computer and then I'll bring it right out."

"You mean you haven't got her a drink already? And you wonder why we don't make any money," Pete said.

Flick all at once felt guilty and reached into her bag for her purse. "It's my fault. I was too busy gassing to order."

Pete laughed. "Relax. I'm only joking, first one's on the house."

"Did I tell you he's a comedian as well," Jess said.

Flick watched them head inside. They seemed such a together couple. *Together*, she thought. There was a time when she'd have said that about herself and Matthew.

Returning her attention back to the market, she wondered what he'd have made of this place. It was a rhetorical question, of course. She knew from experience that Matthew would call it sleepy and boring. Looking back, whenever she suggested a relaxing week away from it all or a romantic getaway, he'd look at her like she'd lost the plot, vetoing the very idea in favour of a beach holiday in some nightclub hotspot. It wasn't that Flick didn't enjoy these vacations, they'd had some fun times over the years. It just would have been nice to simply enjoy one another's company away from the crowds every now and then, something Matthew never seemed interested in doing. Flick scoffed. Maybe the two of them had never been that together after all.

She took out her drawing pad and a pencil and, with one eye on the market and the other on the paper, began sketching the scene before her. With each stroke of lead, an image gradually came to life and she felt her mind ease. Drawing had always had a calming effect and it wasn't long before she lost herself completely.

"Wow!"

A voice over her shoulder suddenly broke the spell.

CHAPTER ELEVEN

"That's brilliant."

Flick quickly closed her sketchpad as Dee joined her at the table. "Just a bit of doodling," Flick said, pushing her notepad to one side.

"That's more than doodling," Dee insisted. "I'd call that talent."

Flick felt herself blush, before quickly realising that she didn't have time to feel embarrassed. Watching Dee immediately delve into her bag and produce an A4-sized folder, it was a case of getting straight down to business.

"Now," Dee said, as if she didn't have a moment to waste. "Let's get started. I've put together a few contacts, all of them highly recommended from our passed purchasers." She opened the folder and looked through its sheets. "I know the building is structurally sound, but I have roofers, builders, plumbers, tilers. All of them speak English. There are even a couple of painters and decorators in here somewhere, although I'm guessing you'll be a dab hand with a paintbrush yourself."

"Sorry?"

"There's no point in paying for work that you can just as easily do on your own."

Wondering what the woman was talking about, Flick didn't plan on paying for anything.

Dee continued examining the contents of her file. "Obviously we don't have to concern ourselves with the gardens for now, although I can give you the details of one or two green-fingered chaps when you're ready. As for any carpentry, if you don't mind I thought I could have a quiet word with Nate?"

"Nate?"

"Yes. Julia's nephew, he was at the party, remember? Funny, I'm sure I saw both of you chatting in the garden at one point and looking very cosy, if I'm not mistaken."

Flick felt herself redden again. Picturing the two of them under the moonlight, *cosy* was exactly how it must have looked. Yes, she fancied Nate, but that was it. The last thing she wanted was people gossiping over nothing. "Excuse me?" she said, needing to set the record straight. "I can't pretend I don't find the man attractive, after all, I'm not blind. But that doesn't mean there's something going on." She tucked her hair behind her ears as she spoke. "And it's probably all one-sided anyway. I mean, I can't imagine he thinks the same about me? For all I know…"

A smile appeared on Dee's lips.

"What?" Flick asked.

"I was teasing."

"Oh." Flick cringed. Thanks to her big mouth, if the locals weren't talking before, they most definitely would be now. "In that case, if we could keep what I just said to ourselves?" Wishing she could take it all back, she had to settle for damage limitation.

Dee chuckled. "Don't worry. Your secret's safe with me."

Flick desperately hoped so, not that she had time to dwell.

"Anyway," Dee carried on with a shake of her head. "As I was saying, he's excellent with wood. An artist like you, in fact. You should see some of his work." She paused. "I'm surprised you didn't already know that, what with him living so close by."

With Dee back to talking thirteen to the dozen and, once again, examining her file, Flick's confusion grew as she struggled to keep up.

"He bought a cottage in the grounds a while ago. In the middle of the woods, can you believe?" She hesitated. "It was supposed to be a holiday home but he ended up staying. Anyway, it's got its own entrance, which probably explains why you haven't come across him. The man does like his privacy."

With her bewilderment increasing, Flick thought it time to intervene. "Dee, why are you giving me all this information? I don't need Nate's help. Anyone's help for that matter. Yourself excluded, naturally."

Dee suddenly stopped thumbing through her sheets of paper. "What do you mean?" she said, her expression quizzical. It was clearly her turn to wonder what was going on.

"I asked to see you," Flick said. "Because I want to sell the chateau, not renovate it."

"But I thought…"

Flick felt bad for dashing what seemed to be *everyone's* hopes, but she had to do what was right for her. Staying on in France just wasn't an option, no matter how many people wished otherwise. "I simply don't have the money to take on a project like this. Or the experience."

"Not in one go, I understand that. But what if you did the work gradually?"

"With what?"

"With that for one." Dee pointed to Flick's sketchpad.

"You're joking. This doesn't pay the supermarket bill, let alone cover the cost of litre upon litre of paint."

"You'd be surprised," Dee said. "Where did you learn to draw like that anyway?"

"Art school," Flick replied, not that she knew what that had to do with anything.

"There you go then."

"There I go what?"

"Do you know how much people pay for painting holidays?"

Flick did, indeed, know. Having previously considered booking onto one herself, she knew exactly how much they cost. And she couldn't afford that either. "But they include bed and breakfast, and evening meals. Plus, they tend to be set in the most gorgeous of surroundings, both inside and out. *Chateau D'Enchantement* isn't exactly in the same league, we both know that." She hated seeing the disappointment on Dee's face, and the prospect of being able to run her own little art school was the stuff her dreams were made of, once of a day. But she had to be a realist about this. "Which brings me back to the beginning, I need to sell."

Dee obviously knew Flick's mind was made up, which was why she began reluctantly gathering up her sheets and putting them back into their folder. "Okay," she said. "Although I can't say I'm not disappointed."

"So, you'll put it back on the market?"

"I will. And I'll speak to the other agents to see if they have anyone looking for this kind of thing on their books."

"Thank you."

"And I'll need to come and take more photos, so it would be great if you don't mind titivating some of the rooms up a bit. Nothing major, you know the kind of thing, a lick of white paint here and there to make it feel a bit fresher in parts."

"Okay."

"Although it might still take a while to find a buyer, you do realise that, don't you?"

"I do."

"I mean it took long enough for your dad to come along and not everyone has his kind of vision."

"I know, but he's not here to see that vision through, is he?"

Tears pricked in Flick's eyes. Refusing to let them come out, she didn't mean to sound harsh. But neither did she deserve to feel guilty for somehow letting down her dad. Talking about her decision had proved harder than she'd thought and with her emotions beginning to run amok, she couldn't help but ask herself if she was really doing the right thing? Especially when despite her complaints she shared her father's view of the chateau. Like him, she saw beyond the aging walls, its dark corridors and lack of up-to-date facilities. In fact, given a real choice, she knew that deep down she'd have gladly thrown herself into restoring the place back to its former glory, plus all mod cons. She grabbed a tissue from her bag and dabbed the corners of her eyes. "I'm sorry. I don't mean to embarrass you."

"Don't be," Dee said, softening. "And you're not embarrassing anyone. I'm sure this hasn't been an easy decision."

Flick managed a smile of appreciation. "It hasn't."

"So how does your mum feel about this?"

Flick couldn't bring herself to answer.

"You have told her, haven't you?"

Again, she remained silent.

"So, Brenda doesn't know about this meeting?"

Flick slowly shook her head, desperately trying to keep herself together.

"Oh, you poor thing." Dee reached out with a comforting hand, an action that Flick appreciated. "It's probably a bit beyond my remit and I wouldn't normally offer, but would you like me to talk to her?"

"No," Flick said, finally finding her voice again. "It's better coming from me." She dreaded breaking the news. "I just hope she understands."

CHAPTER TWELVE

Pulling up in front of the chateau, Flick used the rear-view mirror to stare into the back of the car. Just like when they'd first arrived, she couldn't see out of the window for all the stuff shoe-horned in. Except on this occasion she was looking at litre upon litre of white paint and bag upon bag of everything she'd need when it came to DIY decorating. During her trip to the *bricolage* store, she'd bought a tonne of paintbrushes, wall paper scrapers, wood stainer, countless rolls of masking tape and numerous tubs of filler... the list went on. She sighed. Having loaded it all into the car, she dreaded having to take it back out again, especially when some of it was headed straight up to the dormer rooms. Heavy wasn't the word for ten-litre paint buckets and her arms felt like they'd stretched a couple of inches already.

Unclipping her seatbelt and getting out of the car, she walked round to the boot ready to start unloading. In another case of *déjà vu*, however, a yapping dog made Flick look up to see Rufus rounding the corner, heading straight for her. "Hello, again." He threw himself onto his back and Flick laughed, as she crouched down to tickle his tummy.

"Looks like you have a fan," Nate said, also appearing from the rear of the chateau.

Flick stood back up, hastily tidying herself a little. "He heard the car again?" Trying to appear casual, this was the first time she'd seen Nate since her conversation with Dee and attempting to analyse his expression she just prayed the woman had kept shtum as promised.

"Everything okay?" he asked, obviously wondering what she was staring at.

"Fine," she replied, quickly diverting her gaze. "Why wouldn't it be?"

Nate glanced into the vehicle. "Wow! That's some serious kit you have there."

"Tell me about it. But needs must if I'm going to sell this place."

"You're selling?"

At least his surprise answered her question about Dee, she'd stuck to her word. Flick smiled to herself. Remembering all the gossip back home and the isolation she experienced as a result, it felt good to think there was someone other than her mother around that she could trust. Flick once again took in his expression. "Don't tell me you're disappointed."

Nate laughed. "I'm sure I'll survive." He signalled to Rufus. "But him, on the other hand…"

Catching Nate's eye again, Flick suddenly felt self-conscious. "I suppose I should get to it," she said, her reluctance to move seemingly matching his.

"If you need a hand with anything, feel free to give me a shout."

Acknowledging the work ahead of her, Flick glanced up at the top floor of the chateau and, unable to face carting her wares up the numerous flights of stairs, wondered if it was the time to take him up on his offer. Still feeling the ache in her own arms, she took in the strength in his, before turning to him with a mischievous smile. "You can help me get this lot inside if you like?" she said.

"I'd be happy to. Where do you want it?"

She watched him lift the boot lid and grab the first two paint buckets to hand. She didn't feel too guilty for conning him, he easily swung them out, unlike herself who struggled with just the one. "We need three on the first-floor landing," she said, as they made their way into the hall. "And three on the second."

Nate looked from the staircase to her. "You're joking."

She smiled again, this time trying to appear innocent. "If you don't mind."

Nate shook his head, as if realising he'd been had.

"Unless you're saying you can't manage…?" Flick this time feigned concern.

"Oh, I can manage, all right, but you owe me one."

Flick's tummy danced in response to the way he looked at her, the glint in his eye demonstrating he had a mischievous side of his own. She watched on for a moment, quietly giggling as he began the long walk up with the first of his hauls, imagining exactly how she wanted to pay him back.

Shaking herself out of it, she placed her own paint bucket down and made her way outside for another, surprised to find Nate already nearing the bottom of the stairs for the next lot by the time she re-entered. "I'm impressed." From what she could see, the man hadn't even broken into a sweat.

Picking up the next two, Nate winked before turning straight back around and standing there, Flick easily saw why he wasn't struggling. Taking in his broad shoulders, her eyes moved down to his waist and then to what looked like rather strong thighs. He certainly had the physique for this kind of work, she observed, her gaze drawn to his pert behind. Bums weren't usually her thing, but on this occasion she *had* to make an exception. She heard herself let out a dreamy sigh, a sigh so hard it blew her overgrown fringe out of her eyes. Much to her embarrassment, however, it seemed she wasn't the only one to hear it and Nate suddenly paused mid step to wiggle his hips in response. Flick let out a laugh, knowing it was her own fault for ogling. "Show off!" she said and reminding herself that men, even good-looking ones like Nate, were off the agenda, she headed back out to the car.

Between them, it didn't take long to bring everything inside. Although it would have been quicker if her mum had deigned to give them a hand. She stared at the mountain of DIY materials before her, recalling her mother's response to the fact that the chateau was back on the market, and wondered if she'd be left to redecorate on her own too. She might only be giving a few select rooms her attention, but it still felt like a mammoth task considering the work involved.

She thought about the amount of floral wallpaper that needed tackling, wondering if the papering of ceilings in the exact same design as the walls was a phenomenon peculiar to France? Either way, it had obviously been there for generations and she just had to hope that it wasn't that that was keeping the walls and ceilings up. Regardless, she knew she'd have to do a YouTube crash course in plastering, to then cover it all in goodness knew how many coats of white paint. Wooden floors had to be sanded, treated and re-waxed, as did the wood panelling. Flick felt tired just thinking about it all. Then there was the kitchen with its mismatched cupboards. Another area that was going to need one hell of a makeover and another reason why she needed all the help she could get. "Coffee?" she asked Nate, in an attempt at delaying the inevitable for a little while longer.

He seemed to think for a moment.

"Don't worry," she said, as tempting as it might be. "I won't rope you into doing any more jobs."

Nate smiled. "Okay. Why not?"

With Rufus trotting alongside, Flick led the way down the hall and finding the kitchen empty, continued to wonder where her mother could have got to. "Milk? Sugar?" Flick asked, indicating he should sit down. She got a tray of cups ready.

Brenda suddenly appeared at the patio doors, cursing as she let herself in. "Bloody thing. I've a good mind to put a match to you." Suddenly spotting her daughter and Nate, she appeared surprised to find she had company and thanks to her outburst, blushed. "Looks like I'm just in time," she said, pretending she hadn't just sworn as she nodded to the kettle.

"Put a match to what?" Flick took in her mother's appearance. Covered in a brown liquid substance, she looked like she'd been dragged through a hedge. "Dare I ask what you've been up to? And what is that?" She pointed to the brown stains. "Oil?"

"I've been trying to fix that damn mower."

Flick stared at her aghast. "What mower?"

"I found it in one of the outhouses. I mean, if we're really going to sell this place we've got to do something about those front lawns. We need to give the chateau some, what do they call it?"

"Kerb appeal?" Nate replied.

"Yes, that. Kerb appeal."

"So, you're a mechanic now, are you?" Flick asked.

Brenda looked down at her filthy hands. "Apparently not."

"I can take a look at it, if you like," Nate said. "I can't promise I'll fix it, but I can give it a try."

"Would you?" Brenda asked. "Because I haven't a clue what I'm doing."

"Obviously." Flick turned to Nate, acknowledging the trouble she'd put him to already. "It's very kind of you to offer. But lugging in all that paint was help enough."

He rose to his feet regardless. "It's no problem. I don't mind." He looked to Brenda, gesturing to the door. "After you."

Watching the two of them head outside, Flick thought there was something reassuring about a man who could turn his hand to anything. It wasn't enough that Nate was drop-dead gorgeous, his willingness to get stuck in made him even more attractive. His inclination to help made him seem dependable and safe, as if he'd look after the people in his life. She sighed. Appealing characteristics after everything Matthew had put her through.

Pulling herself together, she insisted that she didn't really fancy Nate. Yes, the man was good-looking, she couldn't deny that, but as was usual of late, her emotions were just playing tricks. His desirability was either the result of some ridiculous crush. After all, she hadn't been in such close proximity to a hot-blooded male for some time. Or on quite a different level, because he reminded her of her dad. He'd been the same when it came to working with his hands. If something needed repairing, he'd repair it. If a garden needed digging, he'd dig it. And if a room needed decorating, he'd decorate it. She smiled as she recalled him tackling every task at hand with gusto.

Unlike her long-lost husband, she remembered, her smile at once fading.

He was the complete opposite. When it came to anything remotely akin to what he considered manual labour Matthew would simply find *a man who can*. After all, why get his own hands dirty when he could pay someone to do that for him? It didn't matter how many times Flick suggested they have a go at updating the décor or build some random piece of furniture, he always claimed they had better things to do. "Better things to do, my arse." Flick would have loved nothing more.

She glanced down the hall at all the paint buckets and bags awaiting her attention, and this time rather than wince at the sight, she felt her eyes light up. "Looks like now's your chance," she said, and taking a leaf out of Nate's and her father's book, for the first time since Dee's suggestion, actually looked forward to getting stuck in.

CHAPTER THIRTEEN

Flick sat at the kitchen table with Dee. Flick watched Dee swipe through the numerous photos on her camera, eagerly awaiting her verdict. Having always considered estate agents a chatty bunch, on this occasion, Dee had proved to be the opposite. She hadn't said much at all as they'd toured the chateau, adding to the already-tense atmosphere floating through the building. There was no immediate feedback on the newly decorated rooms, and even now she wasn't giving much away, causing Flick to wonder if she'd wasted both her time and money trying to beautify the place.

Dee, at last, put down her camera.

"Well?" Flick asked.

The woman smiled. "Well nothing. I love what you've done."

"Really?"

"Really."

Finally, Flick allowed herself to relax.

"Simple yet stylish," Dee continued. "It'll certainly give potential buyers something to think about when it comes to turning this place into a proper home."

Flick glanced around the room. Glad to hear that Dee approved, she too liked the results and despite the long days and blistered hands, had thoroughly enjoyed transforming the various areas of the chateau. So much so, the last few weeks had flown by. She'd also begun to wonder if the building deserved something a bit grander, so it was good to know her efforts had paid off.

"And this kitchen," Dee said. "I can't believe the change in those cupboards. I know I'm supposed to be able to see beyond these things, but I certainly wouldn't have thought to update them. I'd have ripped the whole lot out and started again."

Flick would have liked nothing more, but on her budget, getting rid of almost anything was out of the question, she had to work with what she'd got. She'd also had to search for bargains to get those all-important finishing touches. Not that she minded. If she'd thought scouring the flea markets back in the UK was fun, they had nothing compared to the wares on offer at France's *Vide Greniers*.

"It does look good, doesn't it?" she said, taking in the chunky freshly waxed wooden shelves now home to a variety of jugs and bowls. The newly acquired dresser top and hanging set of copper pans looked very in keeping, as did the much-improved painted dining chairs and pretty floral table cloth she'd picked up for next to nothing. "Of course I would've liked to have decorated more of the place, but it's already cost me a small fortune." She thought about the money she'd spent on rugs, cushions, lamps and knick-knacks to give the chosen rooms a homely feel, not to mention the gallons of paint she'd had to buy. "I can't justify the extra expense when it's for someone else."

"It doesn't have to be." Dee raised her eyebrows.

Flick appreciated the faith everyone seemed to have in her ability to turn the chateau around, but she didn't waver. She knew selling up was her only real option.

"You might want to think about putting that away then," Dee said. With no choice but to accept Flick's decision, she nodded towards the fireplace. "Viewers might not appreciate its significance like you do."

"Oh, Mum." Flick stared at her father's urn, strategically positioned, pride of place on the mantel, not quite sure whether to be annoyed or tickled by her mother's antics. She knew that underneath all the bravado her mum didn't really want her to sell, but to try to play the guilt card, how could she? She returned her attention to Dee, who struggled to suppress her amusement. "Don't worry. I'll find it a more discreet home."

Dee checked her watch. "I should get back to the office." Rising to her feet, she packed her camera away. "I can't wait to see the response once I upload these onto the website."

Flick led the way down the hall to the front door. "I'm glad to be getting rid of this," she said, grimacing as she squeezed past the old scruffy sofa waiting to be moved. "One item of furniture that couldn't be saved."

"I can sort that out for you, if you like. I'm sure there'll be a man with a van somewhere in my list of local businesses."

"That's okay. Jess has already offered Pete's services," Flick said.

"Pete's?"

"Yes, why?"

Dee opened her mouth to say something, before closing it again. "No reason. Right, I shall leave you to it. Say hello to Brenda for me." She paused as she made her way to her car and turned. "Where is she, by the way? I expected her to be here."

Flick recalled her mum's demeanour as she'd donned her coat earlier that morning. Saying that she hoped all went well, her words hadn't quite matched the expression on her face. "She went for a walk, something to do with needing a bit of fresh air. No doubt she'll be back soon."

"She didn't take it very well then, your decision to sell?"

"As well as can be expected." Flick sympathised, of course. Since breaking the news, her mother had tried to be supportive. But Flick knew her heart wasn't in it, that she thought her daughter was making a mistake.

"I'll be in touch," Dee said, climbing into her car.

Flick put up a hand to wave her off. She looked around and, shivering, wrapped her arms around herself as the cool of the afternoon made its presence known. "I'm sorry, Dad, but you do understand, don't you?"

She continued to stand there, despite the cold, unable to bring herself to go back inside.

CHAPTER FOURTEEN

Nate, chainsaw in hand and ear defenders around his neck, strode through the woods. Fallen leaves crunched underfoot and the musky smell of moss and damp soil permeated the air. He smiled to himself as Rufus ran ahead, the little dog barking at anything and everything to announce their arrival. They both didn't just love this place, they knew every square inch of it.

Nate soon spotted the tree he was aiming for and, putting the chainsaw down, assessed its lean. "Definitely more than fifteen per cent, hey, boy?" He could see he was talking to himself, the little dog, by now, far too busy scratting at a mound of earth to listen to anyone. Nate laughed and shook his head, knowing they'd *both* be needing a bath that night. He continued his assessment, stabbing at the ground at the base of the trunk with his foot, putting the lean down to a breakage or weakening of the roots. If he only had himself to think about he'd probably have left it a while longer. But now that he had neighbours to consider, neighbours who might not even notice the danger it presented, the time had come to chop it down.

A part of him still wondered why he was bothering. According to Flick they hoped to be leaving soon anyway, something he had to admit he thought a shame. Not only did he like Flick, but when it came to people living next door, she and Brenda had been perfect. He hadn't seen either of them since he fixed their lawn mower, they hadn't come seeking him out like he'd expected. It seemed they'd failed to pick up on his identity and his privacy had been maintained. Finally, he could start to relax again.

Naturally, he understood Flick's decision. Making a change, let alone starting a new life, had to be a choice, and he of all people knew what it was like to be forced into it. Although in his case there was no denying it had been for the best, especially when he took after his mother a little too much. His life had long been heading in the wrong direction and unlike himself who'd courted controversy, he doubted Flick anywhere near deserved the treatment she'd received. He hadn't meant to pry, but from what his aunt said, it seemed Flick had been burnt in the relationship department too. Not in quite the same spectacular way, of course, but for her it must have been spectacular enough.

A little voice in his head suddenly wondered what was wrong with Flick's ex. As far as he was concerned, she was beautiful, quirky and funny, she teased him. *Boy, did she tease him…* A little voice said that he just as quickly dismissed.

He thought about the night of his aunt's soirée, about how vulnerable Flick had appeared sitting there on her own out in the courtyard. He hadn't intended on going to talk to her, but for some inexplicable reason had joined her anyway. He smiled to himself as he remembered how she'd challenged him on his lack of social skills. In his experience, not many people were so up front when it came to dealing with him. Then again, she didn't actually know who he was. He suspected she wouldn't have been quite so forthright in her comments had she recognised him. In fact, with his reputation, she probably wouldn't have spoken to him at all. His mind moved forward to their last meeting and convinced she definitely wouldn't have conned him into hauling paint about had she known his identity, he felt extra pleased that he remained anonymous. He'd enjoyed the time he'd spent with her. Maybe he'd enjoyed it a little too much?

A twig snapped overhead and Nate looked up as a bird flew from its resting place, enough to tell him he should stop thinking about Flick and get on with the task at hand. He put on his ear defenders, pulled a pair of safety goggles from his combat pockets, and picked up his chainsaw. In one swift movement, he yanked at its chord and the machine fired up ready for action.

Having done it countless times before, he worked fast. Deciding in which direction he wanted the tree to fall, he began with the face cut, efficiently fashioning a V-shaped notch that resembled a slice of cake or wedge of cheese. Turning his attention to the back cut, he checked for Rufus's whereabouts, glad to see him safely out of harm's way as Nate attacked the tree from behind. He used the chainsaw to create a flat, horizontal plane that didn't quite meet the V shaped notch. Instead, leaving just enough of the trunk intact so as to create a hinge. Nate knew full well not to stand directly behind the tree, the potential kickback wasn't worth the risk. Instead, as the hinge began to crack, he hastily retreated to a safe distance at the side just in time to watch it fall. The trunk groaned before slamming itself hard onto the ground, the tree's branches bouncing up and down, tossing leaves in all directions. A job well done, even if he did say so himself. He took off his goggles and ear defenders.

"Well, that was a sight to behold."

"What the...?" Half jumping out of his skin, Nate spun around. Surprised to find he had an audience, he spotted Brenda perched comfortably on a stump left from a previous felling. "Jesus Christ," he said. "You should have told me you were here. If that had fallen the wrong way you could've been killed."

The woman continued to calmly sit there, Rufus by her side. "But it didn't, did it?" she simply said. "Besides, you looked quite the expert to me."

Expert or not, that wasn't the point. Nate moved towards her and, just grateful no one had, indeed, gotten hurt, plonked himself down on the ground at her side. "What are you doing here anyway?" he asked, his heart rate, at last, beginning to slow.

"I needed some fresh air and decided a walk in the woods would do me good." Brenda chuckled. "It's funny how after a while all the trees start to look the same, which is when I realised I was lost." She looked around. "Thankfully I heard your chainsaw and thought whoever was using it could point me in the right direction."

He shook his head. "And risk you getting lost again?" Nate didn't think so. "Come on, I'll take you home." He started to stand up, but halfway to his feet, Brenda still hadn't moved. He sat back down again, wondering what to do next. He didn't want to babysit, but she obviously wasn't ready to go anywhere and he couldn't just leave her sitting there. "I make a mean cup of coffee, if you fancy one?" he eventually said. "Although I do have tea, if you prefer?"

Brenda smiled. "That would be lovely."

Nate finally stood up, glad to see his unwanted guest do the same. "Shall we?" He indicated the way ahead.

They made their way through the trees, Nate pushing aside rogue branches and offering his hand when needed. At last, they reached a small clearing at the side of the lake. "Here we are," Nate said. "My humble abode."

Brenda appeared surprised by what she saw. Then again, he supposed with its not quite square façade, simple slate roof and crooked chimney, it compared more to a child's drawing than a French castle. "Not quite a chateau but I like it."

Brenda turned to him with a warm smile. "So do I."

Nate unlocked the door. "After you." He gestured his guest inside and directed her to a seat at the kitchen table, where Rufus automatically jumped up onto her lap. "Tea? Coffee?" Nate asked, getting on with making the drinks.

"Coffee, please."

He sensed her glancing around the room, no doubt taking in its sparseness, he acknowledged, his sudden embarrassment at the lack of home comforts around the place surprising him. He didn't normally care what people thought of his home, not that he had many visitors.

"How long have you lived here?" she asked.

"Coming up two years." He felt himself tense, wondering where this might lead. "Why?"

"No reason," Brenda replied, much to Nate's relief her voice sounding innocent enough.

Nate handed her a cup of coffee and took the seat opposite. As he watched her take a sip, silence descended and he questioned if inviting her had been such a good idea. "So, what's stopping you from going back?" he asked eventually.

"To the chateau? Nothing."

Nate knew a lie when he heard one.

"We've been so busy decorating, I needed a break from the paint fumes, that's all."

Despite her trying to disguise it, Nate still heard the melancholy in her voice. "How's it coming along?"

"We've finished what we can. Some of the rooms have been transformed. The walls have been white washed, and you should see what Flick's done with the bits of furniture left behind. It's surprising what you can do with a few tins of chalk paint."

"So, what's the problem?"

"Problem?"

Nate gave her a knowing look. He could see she was weighing him up, deciding whether or not to trust him.

She sighed. "I keep wondering if she's made the right decision, that's all."

"You don't think she should sell?"

"No, it's not that. According to her, she doesn't really have a choice."

Nate watched Brenda take another drink.

"I'm probably being daft, but we've only been here two minutes and it feels a bit, well, rash, I suppose. And disrespectful."

"To her dad?"

Brenda nodded. "And I know she's thinking the same, even if she won't admit it."

"She's bound to feel a bit ambiguous, but I'm guessing she knows what she's doing."

Brenda didn't look so sure. "Does she? She's been through so much, I have to wonder if she's thinking straight. First losing her dad and then Matthew, although the less said about him the better… It's a lot to deal with. I'm beginning to wonder if I should have waited a bit longer before bringing her here."

Nate wrapped his hands around his coffee mug. "Things might have still turned out the same. Renovating a chateau is a big responsibility. And costly."

"Tell me about it." She fell quiet for a moment. "I just can't help thinking that once of a day she'd have loved the chance to try something new and exciting. And let's face it, you can't get much more exciting than owning a place like that."

Nate had to agree. Although as he listened, he appreciated her daughter's quandary. The chateau did, indeed, provide Flick with a myriad of opportunities. And yes, she had been quick to make her decision, a decision she may well come to regret at some point in the future. But from what Flick had said she didn't exactly have the means to turn the chateau around, which in her view clearly meant there was no point in trying. Not that he was prepared to remind anyone of this. When it came to mother and daughter relations, no way was he going to take sides, even if that little voice of his wanted to.

"Anyway," Flick's mother said, as if sensing his caution on the matter. "Tell me about you. What brought you here?"

The sudden change in subject surprised Nate. Usually quite prepared when it came to these kinds of questions, words suddenly failed him. He tried to appear laid-back as he took a sip of his drink. The last thing he wanted to talk about was his past and her enquiry felt too close for comfort.

"Living in the middle of a forest must be a far cry from life back in England. I mean what do you do all day?" Brenda continued. "When you're not cutting down trees."

Nate studied her for a moment, watching her gently stroke Rufus's ears as she waited for Nate to answer. She didn't appear to be probing and determining she was only making conversation, he decided there was no need to panic. Still, better to keep any chit-chat in the present, he reasoned, rather than to let it drift back into the past. And what better way to do that than to show her exactly how he spent his time. "You really want to know?" he asked, more than happy to oblige.

Brenda nodded.

He downed the rest of his drink and putting his mug down, rose to his feet. "Then follow me."

CHAPTER FIFTEEN

Ensuring Rufus stayed indoors, Nate led Brenda outside to a wooden outbuilding. He could see Brenda was intrigued, her eyes widening as he opened the door so she could step inside.

"Wow! These are gorgeous." She turned to look at him. "You made them?"

"I certainly did."

She took in the tools of his trade, mainly chainsaws, chainsaw bars, angle grinders and the generator he used to run them. "With those?"

"Yep."

Able to relax again, he smiled at her awe as she looked back at his handiwork, focusing first on the beady-eyed owl sitting on a log and then the cuddly brown bear that had caught a salmon with its fishing cane. "They're so beautiful," she said, approaching another of his pieces, this one the bust of a horse. She reached out, her fingers stroking the long mane that twisted from the back of the horse's head, round to the front and down its chest. "And very life like."

Nate appreciated the compliment. "I should hope so after the amount of effort that went into them."

"And they're each made from a solid piece of wood?"

"Of course."

"No wonder you made such short work of that tree back there." She turned to face him again. "Flick's an artist too. Although drawing and painting are more her thing." Pride seemed to ooze out of her.

"I didn't know that," Nate replied. Impressed, it was nice to know they had something other than relationship woes in common.

"If anywhere's going to get the creative juices flowing it's here. I'll look forward to seeing what she comes up with while I still can."

Brenda let out a wry chuckle. "I wouldn't hold your breath. She doesn't think she's any good. At least, not any more. Saying that, she did pick up a couple of sketchpads and pencils the other day, so you never know."

As Nate watched her continue to admire his creative endeavours, it surprised him to think how much he appreciated her feedback. He rarely spent time with anyone from outside of his inner circle and when he did he always felt uncomfortable. Despite his earlier concern, he felt at ease. Probably because on this occasion he was the centre of attention for all the right reasons.

Even more surprising was the fact that he actually quite liked Brenda, half of him wondering if this was because she was the kind of mum he'd never had. As parents went she seemed conventional, a characteristic no one could ever ascribe to his own mother. Nate's other half insisted it was her daughter that he was interested in, strange considering he was a sworn bachelor. But the more he learnt about Flick, the more attractive she became. More than was admittedly good for him. He recalled their albeit limited interaction, the way her whole face lit up when she smiled and, feeling himself come over all warm and fuzzy, he tried to dismiss his musings, telling himself that firstly Flick was still married, even if it was in name only. And secondly, after his last relationship, he'd sworn himself off women for life.

"Funny how they only ever mention the bad stuff," Brenda said.

Now back in the present, Nate wondered what she meant. Moreover, he couldn't work out if she was talking to him or to herself. Or, indeed, who *they* could possibly be. "Sorry?" he said.

"The papers. They forgot to mention your artistic side in their reports."

Taken by surprise, Nate froze. Searching her face, he told himself he must have misheard. She couldn't really know who he was, could she? If she did, she'd just played a blinder. All that stuff about how wonderful his work was, when really it was all the other crap she was interested in. In fact, he was amazed she'd managed to hold her tongue full stop.

"Not that I believed a word of what they said," she said, matter of fact.

He felt the colour drain from his face.

"About you or your mother."

Nate's heart skipped a beat, he felt nervous, angry and fearful all rolled into one. This couldn't be happening. Talk about him being duped. "How long have you known?"

She turned to look at him. "I recognised you as soon as I saw you."

He tried to raise a smile, to act like the fact that this woman knowing his identity didn't matter. But in truth it did. It meant he no longer had his sanctuary, his safe haven. One word from her and the vultures would, no doubt, swoop in, looking to fill their column inches with yet more scandalous claims. Why, oh why, hadn't he just packed up and left when he'd had the chance? He felt so stupid for letting his guard down, especially when he knew better. "And Flick?"

Brenda let out a short sharp laugh. "Flick? Goodness no, she hasn't a clue."

At least that was something. The mother might have fooled him but thank goodness the daughter hadn't, *her* treatment towards him had been genuine. "So, what now?"

"What do you mean?"

He raised an eyebrow. She wouldn't be the first to play the innocent then turn out to be anything but.

"Don't worry," she said. "Your secret's safe with me."

"Really?" Suspicious of her motives, Nate struggled to believe her. "Then why even bring it up?"

"Don't you think if I was going to blab, I'd have done it by now?"

Her question hung in the air. Nate didn't know what to think. Her words might be small comfort, but he supposed she had a point.

"I would like your help with something though?" She looked at him directly. "But you can't tell Flick. She'd kill me if she knew I was intervening like this."

Nate narrowed his eyes. *Here we go*, he thought.

"I just want her to have a choice. A proper choice, before she goes and does something I know she'll regret."

Nate stared at her. Her determination to help her daughter might be admirable, but the woman clearly wasn't as conventional as she had him believe. "You do know this is blackmail, right?"

CHAPTER SIXTEEN

Coming to, Flick willed herself back to sleep. She'd lain awake for hours the night before, mulling things over and over in her head, and could have done with a few extra zeds. Her brain was having none of it though and she opened her eyes. Yawning, the crisp white bedding and brand-new duvet felt luxurious compared to the sleeping bag she usually woke up in. And no longer zipped into a confined space, she stretched her limbs out in all directions, simply because she could.

She thought about the day ahead. With as much decorating as she could afford done and Dee on with finding that all-important buyer, it felt strange not having a long to-do list of jobs to tackle. But at least she could relax and have the holiday this trip to France was meant to be. She threw back the covers. "Starting today."

Getting out of bed, she put on her dressing gown and approached the window. Looking out and down the long driveway, she still couldn't believe that all this was hers, albeit, only in the short term. She felt a pang of envy that someone other than her would be waking up to this every morning. Not that there was any point in feeling envious, she knew that. She just had to make the most of the time that she had left.

Heading downstairs to the kitchen, as she made her entrance, Brenda was busy texting again. Going off her mother's gravitas, she was, no doubt, giving her friends an update, letting them know she'd be back in the UK sooner rather than later. Flick watched her click the send button, her mum's serious expression continuing well after placing her phone down on the table. "Everything okay?" Flick asked.

"Sorry?"

Flick nodded to the discarded mobile. "Is everything okay?"

Brenda shook herself out of her reverie. "Fine. Why?"

Flick joined her at the table, concerned. Her mum might be saying all the right things about her decision to sell the chateau, but that didn't mean she was one hundred per cent behind it. Flick knew she was only going along with things for her sake, but what choice did either of them have? "I know what's happening is difficult for you. I'm not finding it particularly easy myself. But there isn't much else we can do, Mum."

Her mother seemed distracted again and Flick's concern grew. "Are you sure you're all right?"

"Can you excuse me for a minute? I just need to make a quick call."

She watched her mum get up and leave the room.

Within seconds, she was talking to someone and Flick strained her ears, trying to tune in to the conversation. The thick chateau walls muffled the sound, however, and she couldn't make out the words. Although thanks to the tone, she had a pretty good idea her mum would be on the phone to Linda, her go-to person in times of need.

Having known each other for years, the two of them were like sisters, there for each other through good and bad. Linda had been a tower of strength when Flick's dad died, although it wasn't one sided, her mother had been there for Linda during her times of need too. *That's what friends do*, thought Flick, realising that apart from her mum, she herself had no one; a fact made more than clear upon Matthew's disappearance.

Their friends turned out to be his friends, all of whom happily followed his lead and vanished, never to be seen again. On a good day, Flick tried to forgive them. After all, what do you say to a jilted bride? Her supposed friends were probably as embarrassed as she was by the whole affair. But still, it would have been nice if at least one of them had hung around to help her pick up the pieces.

Brenda's voice suddenly got louder, grabbing Flick's attention once more. Still not clear enough for her to understand, she couldn't help but wonder what on earth the two of them were discussing. She just hoped that whatever the issue, it wasn't as serious as it sounded.

The conversation ended and Flick tried to appear indifferent as her mum re-entered the room. "Everything all right?"

"What? Yes, of course." The woman was obviously lying.

"And Linda?"

"Linda's fine. Why wouldn't she be?"

Flick decided not to pry any further. Knowing her mum, she'd share when she was ready. "Just asking," she said instead.

"Anyway, getting back to earlier, what was it you were saying?" Brenda asked, retaking her seat.

"I was telling you that I understand your reservations about me selling this place."

Brenda reached over and patted Flick's hand. "You don't have to explain, although I can't deny I wish things were different."

Flick followed her mother's gaze as it moved to the stone mantel above the fire. She wasn't surprised to see her father's casket of ashes back to sitting there. Following Dee's visit, no matter how many times Flick put it away, her mother kept getting it back out again.

"Do you think if you had the money you'd decide differently?" Brenda asked, returning her attention to her daughter.

"But I don't have the money."

"What if you did though?"

Flick thought for a moment, recalling Dee's comment about the chateau making a great art school. The suggestion had sparked not just Flick's interest but her artistic passion; a passion that she'd long since buried – something else she could blame Matthew for. She didn't think it had been his intention to dampen her ambition, but she certainly couldn't say he'd been encouraging. Rather, he'd made her artistic endeavours seem trivial and unworthy.

Naturally, his inability to support her dreams had gradually eroded her own desire to succeed, something she thought she'd never get back. Thanks to this place though, it was as if a flame had been rekindled and as she looked around the room, she knew she had the perfect environment in which to fulfil any potential she might have. "If I had the money then I suppose I'd at least consider staying on." She knew it was a pipe dream, of course. "But as things stand…"

Besides, she had more important things to think about. Her immediate future for one.

"Plus, there are things I need to sort out." Flick returned her attention back to her mother. "Like the situation with Matthew. Whether that means a divorce or an annulment, I have to do something. You said it yourself, I need to move on with my life."

"And when you get your divorce or annulment, then what?"

"I don't know. Maybe I'll start painting again." She watched her mum sigh, as if resigning herself to the fact that Flick wasn't going to change her mind about selling.

"At least that's something."

A banging on the front door interrupted their conversation. "Oh no. What time is it?" Flick looked at her watch. "That'll be Pete coming to collect the sofa. I can't believe I forgot." She pulled her dressing gown tight across her chest as she made her way out to let him in. Opening the door, she suddenly found herself speechless.

"Isn't she a beaut?" Pete's chest swelled with pride as he turned to admire his new car.

"She's certainly something." Flick's eyes fixed firmly on the vehicle parked in front of her. She recognised it as the hearse from outside Julia's house on the night of the soirée. Having made the decision not to enquire at the time, she hadn't been the only one who'd failed to mention it, which is why in the end she'd put its presence down to pure coincidence.

"The repatriation business is a bit slow at the moment," Pete said, his attention back to Flick. "Which is why I'm now seeing it as a multipurpose vehicle."

"Repatriation?"

"Oh, yes. Didn't Jess tell you? It's my new venture." His pluming continued. "To be honest, I'm surprised no one's already doing it. I mean how many expats are there out here? But hey ho, I suppose that means more business for me."

Flick smiled. She didn't have the heart to tell him that rather than a gap in the market, a lack of service provision could indicate there wasn't a market to begin with.

"Anyway, until things pick up, there's no point having this little lady sat around doing nothing."

Little, thought Flick. The damn thing was humongous.

"So here we are." Back to business, he looked over her shoulder. "That's what you want moving, is it?"

Flick followed his gaze to the dusty brown sofa. With its once-comfortable seats resembling giant used teabags, and its former plush velvety fabric all worn and threadbare, she supposed making its final journey in a hearse was quite apt considering the state of it.

She spotted her mum appearing at the far end of the hallway.

"Don't leave the poor man at the door," Brenda called out, just as quickly disappearing again. "Bring him in, I've put the kettle on."

Pete rubbed his hands together. "Don't mind if I do, seeing as we're still waiting for reinforcements."

"Reinforcements?" Flick asked, as if she didn't feel self-conscious enough in her current attire. If she'd known this was going to be a party, she'd have showered and dressed before coming down stairs.

"It's a two-man job," Pete said. "I haven't got a coffin trolley yet, you see. I'll need help loading it in."

Flick almost laughed as images of the old sofa being solemnly stretched out and into the back of Pete's hearse flitted through her head.

"And I didn't want to presume you'd be happy to help. If you're anything like Jess…" He lowered his voice as if not wanting to offend his car. "You won't want to go anywhere near her."

As Flick stood aside to let Pete in, she continued to stifle her amusement. "Straight ahead," she said, indicating down the hall to the kitchen. The man might not have much by way of business sense, she silently giggled, but at least he was considerate. She took another look at the hearse. *To everyone and everything.*

CHAPTER SEVENTEEN

Nate suddenly awoke and shot up into a sitting position. He grabbed his phone off the bedside table and checked the time. "No!" he said, unable to believe he'd slept in.

As he jumped out of bed, he could have sworn he'd set his alarm. Then again, had he? He'd been so wrapped up in his dilemma with Brenda, he couldn't actually remember. Nate cursed to himself. *Of all the mornings to be running late, why did it have to be this one?*

He quickly threw on some clothes and headed to the bathroom to sluice his face with water and give his teeth a cursory brush. He'd have to sort himself out properly once he'd got this morning out of the way. As he raced downstairs, Rufus was already bouncing up and down at the door, his accompanying yap telling Nate that he wasn't the only one that needed to go out. "Okay, okay," he said, reaching for the dog's lead. "We're going."

He made his way through the woods and as Rufus darted this way and that way ahead of him, the Jack Russell's excitable movement caused Nate's head to spin. Despite waking up with a start, he still wasn't ready to join the land of the living. Over the last couple of years, his mind and body had gotten used to a more gradual approach to the day, one that involved leisurely sipping on a coffee as he looked out onto the lake. This had to be followed by a second cup and then a third, taking the latter out to his studio to drink as he organised his tools ready for work. Still, he reassured himself, after such a rude awakening, the day could only get better.

At least he hoped it could only get better.

Since moving to France he'd forged a new life for himself; a life that once again felt in jeopardy thanks to Brenda. He let out a dry laugh as he pictured her. She didn't look like a blackmailer. But then again, who did? He supposed he could call her bluff and refuse her request, however, the ensuing chaos that'd result wouldn't just affect him. Aunt Julia and his friends would experience the fallout too. And was this a risk he was prepared to take? He wasn't sure. He could disappear, he considered. Quietly pack his bags and head off into the sunset. That would certainly foil Brenda's plan. But where would he go? And how long before he'd be forced into moving on again? "Thanks, Mum," he said, wondering if he'd ever truly be free of her.

It felt like a no-win situation. Even if he gave in, who was to say Brenda's demands would stop there. Didn't blackmailers always come back for more?

Rufus's yapping interrupted Nate's thoughts. "It's far too early for this." Nate sighed, deciding it wasn't the hour to be considering whatever options he did or didn't have. If pushed, he'd just have to insist on more time to think things through.

Continuing on his way, he found himself thinking about Flick, wondering what kind of a morning person she might be. Was she like him? Lacking immediacy? Or a whirlwind like Rufus? On the move the second her feet touched the bedroom floor? If she were staying, he would have liked to have found out. *If...* a predicament that seemed to rest on his shoulders.

The woods began to clear, finally revealing the chateau. Making his way round to the front, he couldn't believe he was doing this. He let out a wry laugh, wondering if his aunt would have volunteered his services to help Pete had she known the predicament Brenda had put him in. Then again, taking in the vehicle he was confronted with, he began to question how she could offer his services at all. Even she had to see that helping Pete squeeze furniture into the back of a hearse was only encouraging him. He just hoped his friend didn't expect him to accompany him to the tip so he could assist in unloading it as well. He could feel the embarrassment. Pete might not have any shame, but he certainly did.

With the chateau's front door wide open and no sign of Pete, Nate hesitated, wondering what he should do. Realising he couldn't just stand there, he approached the entrance. "Hello," he called out, tentatively stepping inside. Chatting sounded from down the hall. "Hello," he repeated.

Brenda appeared at the far end, beckoning him forward with the wave of a hand and a welcome smile. "Nate. Lovely to see you."

I bet it is, he thought, determined to get in and out of there as quickly as possible.

"Come on in," she continued.

He took a deep breath before doing as he was told and making his way down the hall, following her into the kitchen.

"Glad to see you could make it," Pete said.

Nate smiled, trying to mask the awkwardness he felt. "Think yourself lucky I'm here at all," he replied, a message meant for Brenda as much as it was Pete.

He turned his attention to Flick. Thanks to her mother, he knew he should distance himself, but just the sight of her seemed to lift his spirits.

"Morning." Nate watched her put her hand up to her hair and quickly tuck a few rogue strands behind her ear. She appeared as self-conscious as he felt, although as far as Nate was concerned, she needn't be. Even in her dressing gown, she looked stunning. However, she obviously didn't agree, leaving Nate a tad disappointed when she suddenly rose to her feet.

"If you'll excuse me," she said. "I think it's time I got myself showered and dressed."

"Not on my account, I hope."

She blushed. "Of course not."

Nate smiled as he watched her go, forced to stop himself from laughing out loud when she suddenly paused in the doorway to wiggle her hips. Payback for when he'd done it to her, no doubt.

"Would you like a coffee?" Brenda asked, thankfully, like Pete, oblivious to Flick's action.

Coming from his blackmailer, Nate knew better than to accept. He needed to get the sofa loaded up and then he could leave.

"Of course he does," Pete said, jumping in before Nate could decline. "It's not like we're in any rush."

Cheers, mate! he thought. With no other choice, Nate tried to ignore his discomfort, telling himself he'd be fine. After all, with his friend in the room Brenda wouldn't dare press him for an answer, that would mean giving her game away. Reluctant, he took a chair at the table as she placed a mug in front of him, although as he savoured the rich aroma, he had to admit he was ready for this.

Pete suddenly plonked his empty cup on the table and rose to his feet.

"Oh, come on," Nate said. Being left alone with his blackmailer was the last thing he wanted. "Seconds ago, you said we weren't in a rush."

Pete put up a staying hand, signalling that his friend should remain seated. "We're not. I'm just gonna get started on sizing up the sofa," he said, pulling a tape measure out of his pocket.

"Good idea," Brenda replied.

Nate flashed her a look. *She* would say that.

"There's no point even trying to move it if it isn't going to fit," continued Pete, heading out into the hall. "Honestly," he called back. "You take your time. We've got plenty of it."

As Brenda took the seat opposite, Nate felt cornered. Cautiously taking in her demeanour, she had a determination about her and seemed to be waiting for him to speak, her silence making him feel even more ill at ease. Fidgeting in his seat, he wished he'd just gone with Pete, regardless of any protests and glancing around the room he tried to come up with a suitable conversation, one that didn't involve her blackmail attempt. "I'm impressed," he said, keeping his tone casual as he took in all the changes. "You've done a great job in here."

At last, Brenda seemed to relax. "Flick did most of the work," she replied proudly. "I mainly kept her fed and watered while she got on with it. But I agree, it does look good, doesn't it?"

Nate took another drink of his coffee.

"I was telling Flick she's not the only one around here with a creative streak," she carried on. "That you sculpt out of wood with a chainsaw of all things. I thought it would be nice if she could see some of your work before we leave?"

Her use of the word *leave* surprised him and his eyes narrowed as he wondered if this meant he was off the hook. Her accompanying smile seemed to indicate that he was, resulting in such a wave of relief that he could have hugged her. Glad to hear she'd seen the error of her ways and decided against extortion, he told himself that he'd known all along she wasn't the criminal type. She was simply a mother looking out for her daughter. He let out a long grateful sigh. At last, he could relax again. "You're more than welcome to come over. I'll even return the gesture." Nate held up his mug.

"That's *if* we leave."

Nate froze and, with his mug still mid-air, life as he knew it again flashed before his eyes. The woman was good, he'd give her that.

"Have you managed to think about my proposition?" she asked. "My silence for your help."

Nate scrutinised her expression, hoping for a hint of weakness, something to show she was just trying her luck. But her face remained steadfast, telling him nothing at all. *If this woman doesn't play poker*, he thought, *then she bloody well should*. "Let's just say I'm still thinking about it," he said, trying to match her in the stakes.

"Well don't think for too long, I've already put the papers on speed dial."

"I don't believe it," Flick said from out in the hall, her voice an octave higher than usual.

Nate swung his head round as she suddenly burst into the room all of a fluster. His heart raced. Surely she hadn't overheard.

"You'll never guess who that was," she said. Holding her mobile aloft for all to see, her face broke into a smile. "It was Dee.

We only have ourselves a viewing!" She squealed, struggling to contain her excitement.

Nate sighed, struggling to hide his relief.

"Finally," Flick carried on. "I can sort my life out once and for all."

Nate wondered if this meant an end to Flick's mother's scam. One more look at the woman, however, and he knew all he needed to know.

CHAPTER EIGHTEEN

Flick sat on the wall outside the *boulangerie*. Staring in at the delicious pastries and breads on display, her stomach felt like her throat had been cut. It was her own fault. Having spent the last few days scrubbing down every inch of the chateau, she couldn't risk messing up the kitchen. One of the most important rooms when it comes to selling houses, the last thing she wanted was a rogue croissant or forgotten cereal bowl putting off the buyer.

Flick shifted slightly, no longer able to feel her backside thanks to the cold stone surface it rested on. Although at least a numb bottom stopped her focusing on her grumbling belly, even if it didn't quell the nervous anticipation surrounding that day's viewing. She checked her watch, wondering how it was going. If all went well, she could, at last, get back to life as she knew it. She paused in her thinking. Was that really what she wanted?

She turned her attention to her mum inside the shop. Laughing and joking with Gigi, she seemed to be sampling everything the *boulangerie* had to offer. Not that Flick and her stomach could blame her. Her mother had been forced to go without breakfast too.

Finally, the two women appeared to be saying their goodbyes and Flick jumped down off the wall in readiness. "You took your time," she said, as her mum made her exit.

"We're not in any rush, are we?" Brenda held up a bag of newly acquired goodies with a smile. "For later."

Flick looked at her watch again. The viewing would be well underway by now. "Coffee?"

"I thought you'd never ask."

Flick rolled her eyes at her mother's cheek. They could have been on their second cup had she not spent so much time with Gigi. Flick led the stroll down the high street towards Café Ange, her mother admiring the quaintness of the town as they passed *La Poste* and the *Salon de Coiffure*.

"This place has everything you could need," Brenda said.

Flick couldn't help but admire her mother. She'd expected a morning of silence on her mum's part, broken up every now and then with the odd woeful sigh. Instead, the woman at her side seemed chirpy, as if the sale of the chateau was no longer an issue. Flick wished she could feel the same, but her mind wrestled over whether or not she was doing the right thing. "I must say you're taking this all very well."

"Am I?"

"Well, yes." She thought about her own anxiety, a kind of hopeful anticipation mixed with a strong sense of guilt. It was strange how a single decision could feel both so right and so wrong at the same time. "You seem to be handling it better than me, in fact."

Brenda smiled. "Maybe I just don't see the point in worrying about something that hasn't happened yet."

"You don't think we'll get an offer?"

"I think we should sit down and have that cup of coffee I'm desperate for."

Realising they'd reached their destination, Flick decided to let the matter drop. Thanks to that day's viewing, she supposed they'd be doing lots of talking soon enough.

"Hello, you two," Jess said, appearing to serve them. "How lovely to see you both."

The customary round of cheek kissing began, something Flick still found strange, unlike her mum who continued to relish every second.

Jess's face crumpled slightly as she stood back. "I promised I wouldn't say anything, but I can't believe you want to leave us."

Brenda gave her a motherly smile. "Like I was saying only a moment ago…"

"There's no point worrying over something that hasn't happened yet," Flick said, imitating her mother's voice.

Jess laughed. "Sorry. That was unfair. Everyone knows how hard it must be for you, what with your dad and all that. I should have kept my mouth shut. Now what can I get you?"

"Two coffees, please." Flick's stomach rumbled again, much to her embarrassment and everyone else's amusement, loud enough for them to hear.

"Do you have a microphone attached to that?" Brenda asked, nodding at Flick's belly.

Flick flushed red. "Sorry," she said to Jess. "We missed breakfast."

Jess giggled, her laughter continuing as she headed back inside to get their drinks.

Along with her mum, Flick took a seat and as both of them fell quiet for a moment, she was just content to soak up the autumnal sunshine. Determined to make the most of it while she could, she knew she'd be confined to the indoors once they got back to rainy old England.

"How do you think it's going?" Brenda asked.

Flick shrugged. "Dee said she'd phone once it's over." Flick checked the time, telling herself it was no surprise that there hadn't been a call yet. There were, after all, three floors and rather a lot of rooms to get through. She wondered what the prospective buyer thought of *Chateau D'Enchantement*. Did it live up to its name for him too? Did he like the building's architecture and original features as much as she? Of course he did. As far as Flick was concerned, he'd be mad not to. She felt a sudden resentment. Ridiculous considering she'd never even met the man, her only knowledge being that he had the cash to turn the chateau around while she didn't. She sighed, consoling herself in the fact that it had at least been hers for a little while. "Thank you," she suddenly said to her mum.

"For what?"

"For the chateau." Flick might not be able to keep it, but that didn't mean she couldn't show her appreciation. She looked around. "And for all this. For showing me there's light at the end of the tunnel after everything that's happened." She considered the existence she was going back to. The TV dinners for one, the lonely evenings, and the sleepless nights. Although to be fair, she did enjoy her job at the coffee shop. And they'd been really good about her having time off at short notice, insisting she take as much as she needed. "For showing me there's another life waiting for me when I'm ready." She suddenly laughed.

"What's so funny?" Brenda asked.

"I was just thinking about work."

"So, they know you're going back soon?"

Flick nodded. "I rang them."

"Did you tell them about the chateau?"

"I did."

"And?"

"And they wanted to know everything about it. How old it is, how many rooms it's got, exactly where in Brittany we are. Just like you, they think I'm barmy for not staying on."

Brenda raised her eyebrows. "And that surprised you?"

"Not really." Flick continued to smile. "That lot will say anything for a cheap holiday."

"Here we are, ladies."

Flick turned to see Pete appearing with their coffees. No sooner had he set them down when Jess arrived carrying two plates, one for Flick and one for her mum.

"What's this? We didn't order any food." Flick looked down at a golden pastry parcel, next to a bed of rocket and cherry tomatoes. Not only did it look good, it smelt divine.

Jess happily handed over their cutlery. "Just a little something seeing as you missed breakfast. I hope you like it."

"It seems a shame to break into it," Brenda said, looking from her plate to her hosts.

More than ready to tuck in, Flick felt no such concern. Slicing into the filo crust, her mouth watered as a creamy mix of Camembert, bacon and caramelised onions oozed out of its shell. She paused before scooping a forkful into her mouth, making sure to savour the taste before swallowing. "I'm in foodie heaven."

"Me too," Brenda joined in.

"Now will you listen?" Pete said to his wife. He looked to Flick. "I keep telling her we should put together a menu, but will she have it?"

"And I keep telling you, I'm just a home cook," Jess said.

"I don't think so, dear," Flick's mum said. "I'm a home cook and I couldn't produce anything as good as this."

"She's right," Flick said. "And I have to say, I agree with Pete, you should do a menu."

Jess shook her head and smiled, pleased with the compliment. "Well, I'll leave you to enjoy it," she said, as more customers arrived to divert her attention. "Come on, Pete. We've got work to do."

"*Bon appetite*," he said, before doing as he was told.

Flick was happy to continue eating in silence. She couldn't remember the last time she'd eaten something so delicious. "Wow!" she said, finally setting down her knife and fork. She pushed her plate to one side and flopped back in her seat. "I'm stuffed."

"Me too," Brenda said, following suit.

"I'm always saying this place should be a restaurant," an unexpected voice said.

Flick looked up to spot Dee staring down at their empty plates. Automatically sitting up straight, this was the last person Flick expected to see.

Dee plonked herself down in a chair. "I was just on my way back to the office when I spotted you both. And I thought why ring when I can talk to you face-to-face?"

With her nerves making a sudden reappearance, Flick looked to her mother for reassurance before speaking. "How did it go?"

"Very well."

Much to Flick's dismay, rather than continue, Dee spent the next few seconds trying to catch Jess's attention. A fruitless task, considering the proprietor was still busy serving customers inside.

"In fact," she said, at last, only to falter once more as she again tried to catch Jess's eye. Thankfully, this time she was successful and as she mouthed her coffee order Jess put her thumb up confirming she understood. "Sorry about that," she said. "You know how it is when the caffeine levels get a bit low. Now, about the viewing."

Flick held her breath, steeling herself for the outcome.

"He loved it."

Flick exhaled, her relief there for all to see.

"I thought you'd be pleased," Dee said.

"Enough to put an offer in?" Brenda asked, clearly less enthusiastic.

"Indeed." Dee tilted her head and knitted her brow, indicating it wasn't all good news. "Although it's a little bit lower than what you and your husband paid, I'm afraid."

"How much lower?" Flick asked. Planning on paying her mother back every penny, she had hoped to at least break even.

"Sadly, not everyone appreciates a building's history. Developers tend to—"

Flick jumped in. "The viewer is a developer?"

"He most certainly is. And a very successful one, by all accounts. From England. Anyway, buyers like that don't want to pay a premium when they're just going to rip a place apart."

"What do you mean?" Flick didn't like the sound of this.

"He wants to turn it into apartments," Dee said. "Subject to planning permission, of course."

"You mean he's going to carve it up? But he can't."

"He can do whatever he wants," Brenda said. "If he owns it."

Flick suddenly felt sick. She flopped back in her seat again. "I expected the next owner to love the chateau for what it is. A beautiful building that just needs bringing back to life." She looked to her mum who seemed equally as saddened.

"Naturally, you don't have to accept the offer, not straight away," Dee said, maintaining an air of professionalism. "Especially if you feel that strongly. However, I wouldn't take too long to think about it if I were you. Not if you're serious about selling."

CHAPTER NINETEEN

While Rufus rummaged about outside, Nate sat on a stool in his workshop staring at the giant lump of wood in front of him. His chainsaw lay silent at his feet. He knew he should get started but he couldn't bring himself to pick up the bloody thing. His heart wasn't in it. All thanks to the sense of foreboding that had enveloped him since he'd made the decision not to help Brenda. It was the right decision, of course, he knew that. Even if he hadn't gotten around to telling the woman yet. Like a coward, he was delaying the inevitable, trying to cling on to the calm around him for as long as he could.

Except he didn't feel calm. His insides continued to churn, his innards going around and around like a pile of laundry in a washing machine.

His mobile vibrated in his pocket, its buzzing interrupting the silence. Getting up from his seat, he pulled out the handset and checked the number before answering. "Aunt Julia," he said, not really in the mood to chat.

"Nate. Thank goodness." She sounded as miserable as him. "Have you heard?"

"Heard what?" Nate struggled to join in with her gossip at the best of times, let alone when he had his own problems to deal with.

"About the chateau?"

Nate rolled his eyes. Whatever news she had, he didn't want to know. As far as he was concerned, that place had caused him enough grief already. "What about it?"

"Someone's made an offer."

"Really?" Nate said, all at once interested.

He suddenly felt the need to sit down, telling himself that maybe there was a god up there, after all. If the offer was a good one, Brenda might forget all about her threat. It could mean he was home and dry. "How much for?"

"What do you mean, how much for? That's not really the point."

In Nate's view it was. Brenda was obviously cash driven and as his aunt's news continued to sink in, he closed his eyes for a second, a small smile of relief spreading across his face.

"What matters," Julia continued. "Is that we don't know who we're going to get next. As chatelaines go, Flick was perfect."

Nate found himself silently agreeing, although admittedly his opinion had nothing to do with her role at the chateau. Not that his feelings mattered. Thanks to the buyer, she was leaving town and that was that.

"She might be new to the land-owning game," his aunt carried on, "but at least she'd have kept the building in one piece instead of turning it into a block of flats."

Nate's smile vanished. "Excuse me?"

"Exactly."

He jumped back onto his feet. "Did I hear that right? *Flats*?"

"Flats, apartments, who cares what they're called. Oh, Nate, I could cry when I think about what's going to happen to it. *Chateau D'Enchantement* just won't be the same once workmen and their sledgehammers move in. Because believe you me, this developer might claim to admire the building's original features, but that won't stop him ripping them out and selling them on to the salvagers. It's the way of the world. Where do you think I got what I needed to turn my little abode back into what it once was?"

Pacing up and down, Nate struggled to take in his aunt's ramblings. His brain was still stuck on the words *flats* and *developer*, both sending him straight into panic mode. If he thought Flick's mother had shattered his sense of peace, goodness knew how many residents a building that size could accommodate and, once identified, news of his presence would spread like wildfire.

Then he really would be in trouble. It would be like living in a goldfish bowl.

He stopped. Putting his hand up to his forehead, he needed time to think. "Look, I've got to go."

"But you can't. We need to come up with a strategy to prevent this."

Like Nate needed telling twice.

"I'll speak to you later, yeah?" he added, silencing his aunt with the end call button.

Nate sat back down on his stool and dropped his head in his hands. Giving in to Brenda felt wrong. And even if she had specified how much money she actually wanted, he couldn't just hand over a great wad of cash, which is what it would take to turn the chateau around. He thought back to their conversation, not even sure if she even wanted money. The only thing she'd asked for was his help.

As if sensing something was awry, Rufus appeared at Nate's side. He reached down gently stroking the dog's back as he tried to formulate a plan. If the sale of the chateau went through, life as they both knew it would be gone. There'd be no more roaming around the woods at will. They'd be prisoners in their own home, too scared to go out in case they were seen. Even when necessity meant they'd have to leave the house, Nate knew he'd be constantly looking over his shoulder. "What are we going to do, boy?"

He straightened himself up. There had to be some way to assist Flick and Brenda. A way that didn't directly involve him or his wallet.

He looked at the phone still in his hand, suddenly knowing exactly what he needed to do. It pained him, after all, he'd be selling his soul to the devil. But steeling himself ready to dial the number, what other choice did he have?

CHAPTER TWENTY

Flick wandered from room to room. She absorbed the chateau's calming atmosphere as she took everything in. The beautiful claw foot baths, the never-ending coving that flowed from one space to another, the stonework and the beautifully worn wood flooring, what wasn't there to like? The views from every window were spectacular.

Her admiration continued as she made her way downstairs, fully understanding why the building was a developer's dream. It was obvious that turning it into *units* rather than selling it on as a *lot* would make them a shed load of money. *But what about the chateau's soul?* Surely money wasn't everything.

She scoffed. Of course it was. Wasn't money the very reason she was selling on? Thinking about it, if cash weren't an issue, she knew she'd be planning an art school by now. After all, ever since Dee had suggested it, the idea had continued to grow in its appeal. Flick stopped for a moment and glancing around again, it seemed unfair to think her dream was so near yet so far. "Why did you do this to me, Dad?" she said, looking up to the heavens before continuing on her way.

Her heart knew exactly why her father had done it. It wasn't just that she'd been his little princess, he'd wanted her to experience his love affair with France for herself. He'd wanted her to broaden her horizons, having constantly said as much. Most of all though, he'd wanted her to paint and what better place to be inspired?

Her head, however, insisted she needed to be realistic and accept the offer. Falling for some romantic notion was all well and good, but she had to be sensible about this. The last thing her dad would want is for her to be a martyr to his cause, especially if that meant being penniless.

Flick paused in her thinking. When it came to words like *realistic* and *sensible*, was that really her talking? Or was it Matthew?

She headed to the kitchen, stopping short in the doorway when she spotted her mum sat in front of the fire, staring into the flames. She was so engrossed in her thoughts, she obviously hadn't heard her daughter come in and Flick thought it a shame to disturb her. Maintaining the quiet, she picked up one of the table's chairs, carried it over and sat down at her mum's side.

"There you are," Brenda said. "I was beginning to wonder where you'd got to."

"You okay?" Flick asked.

Her mother smiled as she patted Flick's knee. "More to the point, are you okay?"

Flick sighed. "Not really." She fell silent, her mind still whirring over what to do for the best. The offer for the chateau had been on the table for a few days and she knew the developer would be wanting his answer soon.

"It's not just a building, is it?"

Flick knew it was a rhetorical question. She also knew exactly what her mother meant. Everywhere she looked she didn't just see bricks and mortar, she saw her father. Although with his casket of ashes *again* staring back from the mantelpiece, she supposed it was hardly surprising.

She suddenly felt an urge to get out into the fresh air. "Fancy a walk?" she asked, rising to her feet.

"Around the grounds? Why not?"

Flick went to fetch their hats and coats. "We'd better wrap up warm," she said, handing over her mother's. "Looks like the clouds are coming in." Hoping the fresher weather would help clear her head, she zipped up tight and led the way down the hall and out through the front door.

"Who's that?" Brenda pointed down the driveway. "Looks like a sports car."

Flick turned, her gaze following that of her mother's. As it drew nearer, she squinted, failing to recognise either the vehicle or its driver. "I haven't a clue."

"It could be the developer. Maybe he wants a second viewing?"

"I wouldn't have thought so. Not when he's already made an offer." Flick continued to watch his approach, her eyes narrowing as her suspicion grew. "Unless he's come to pressurise us into accepting." She felt her hackles rise. It wouldn't be the first time a property developer had resorted to bully boy tactics.

She observed the car coming to a standstill before the driver disembarked. "What's he doing now?"

"Beats me."

Professional-looking camera in hand, he took photos of his surroundings.

"The cheek of it," Flick said. "Like Dee hasn't supplied him with enough pictures already."

Finally, he got back into his vehicle and manoeuvred it forward again until he reached the chateau entrance. "*Bonjour*," he said. Getting out of the car once more, he held out his hand to greet them, maintaining eye contact and a suave smile.

Listening to his accent, Flick knew an Englishman when she heard one, although admittedly the UK number plate on his vehicle helped. She took in his expensive suit, recognising the quality thanks to Matthew's equally expensive tastes and oozing confidence and style, the man looked to be around her mother's age. Like Dee had said, the man before her was clearly successful and, no doubt, used to getting his own way. Flick remained unimpressed however. Standing there waiting for his spiel, it would take more than a flash car, an outstretched palm, and a bit of French to get around her. She leaned into her mother. "Leave this to me."

Tempted to give the property developer a piece of her mind, she told herself to play it cool. "Can I help you?" she asked, keeping her hands firmly by her side.

"I'm looking for the owners of this chateau."

Flick gave him a no-nonsense stare. "That would be us. But before you ask, we haven't come to a decision yet."

"Excuse me?"

The developer appeared confused, although Flick could see why. With her and her mother trussed up in their winter coats and hand-knitted bobble hats, they didn't exactly exude ownership status.

"We do have a lot to think about," Flick continued. "Especially when you intend chopping the place into pieces. I mean look at it, it's beautiful." Directing his attention to the chateau's exterior, with its tired stonework and flaky paintwork, she quickly wished she hadn't. "In a haunted kind of way. And you have to understand my father bought it to be lived in just the way it is."

"Your father?"

"Yes."

"So, he's the owner?"

Flick frowned. "No, my dad's dead."

The man's bewilderment appeared to grow. "I'm sorry to hear that."

"Thank you, Mr…" Brenda joined in, clearly happy to pick up Flick's mantel.

"Richardson. Rob Richardson."

"Thank you, Mr Richardson. But even with your condolences, we still have a lot to discuss." Her mum smiled as she folded her arms tight across her chest, as if letting him know that they wouldn't be swayed. "So, I'm afraid you'll just have to be patient a little while longer. We'll let the estate agent know once we've had chance to properly reflect on your offer."

"Estate agent?"

"That's right," Brenda said. "The woman who showed you around the other day, remember?"

"Showed me around?"

Flick felt her own frustrations growing. The developer might not be getting the message, but did he really have to keep repeating everything her mother said?

He stepped forward. "I think there seems to be some mistake."

"Mistake?" Flick asked. For God's sake, it seemed even she was at it.

"I'm not here to buy the place."

Upon hearing this, Flick's heart didn't know whether to sink or sing. "You're not?" she asked, wondering what had made him change his mind.

"No."

"Then what are you here for?"

"To hire it."

"Dee never said anything about hiring." Brenda turned to Flick. "Did she say anything to you about hiring?"

Flick shook her head. "Nothing at all."

"I don't know any Dee," the man said.

"She's the estate agent," Flick explained.

"I don't know any estate agent."

Flick looked from him to her mum. "I think we need to start again," she said, realising no one was getting anywhere fast.

"I think we do," the man replied.

Brenda leaned in to her. "So, he's not the property developer then?"

Flick shrugged. "It would seem not."

Taking Flick at her word, the man stepped forward, his hand outstretched ready to formally introduce himself all over again. "Rob Richardson at your service."

"Pleased to meet you." This time Flick accepted the handshake, telling herself it was the least she could do if she wanted to get to the bottom of this. "I'm Flick. And this is my mum, Brenda."

"Pleased to meet you both."

"Now what can we do for you, Mr Richardson?"

"Please, call me Rob."

"Okay. What can we do for you, *Rob*?"

"Like I said, I'd like to hire this chateau."

Flick looked at the building's exterior once more, wondering why on earth anyone would want to do that. "As you can see–"

"Don't worry," he interrupted, as if reading her mind. "I'm not looking for a wedding venue."

That's a relief, thought Flick. Even if the place had been suitable, she couldn't have stomached that.

"I was hoping you'd let me use it for a video shoot." He pulled a business card from his inside jacket pocket and handed it over. "You'll be paid, of course, and the money's not bad. More than worth it if you don't mind the intrusion."

Flick read the details on the card. *Robert Richardson, Location Manager.* It looked genuine enough, as did the man before her, now they'd gotten any misunderstanding out of the way. Still not sure what to make of it all, however, she passed the card to her mother. "What kind of shoot?"

"For a music video."

"Anyone we know?" Brenda asked.

Flick watched him take in her mum's duffle coat and woolly hat.

"Probably not," he replied.

Flick almost giggled. He obviously didn't know her mother.

"Try me," Brenda insisted.

"Argon Fire. They're an old-school rock band. Obviously not quite your thing musically. Anyway, they're experiencing a bit of a resurgence and..."

Her mother reached out, using Flick's arm to steady herself. "Not *the* Argon Fire?"

Obviously impressed by her knowledge, Rob stared in disbelief. "What? You've heard of them?"

"I haven't," Flick said.

"Felicity," Brenda said. "Everyone's heard of them."

Flick looked to Rob. "Did you know of them before you were asked to help with their video?"

He scrunched up his nose as he spoke. "I'm afraid so. They have been around for quite some time."

Brenda scoffed. "Only since forever."

"Anyway," Rob continued, almost laughing as he got back to business. "This place would be the perfect backdrop. We're looking at an abandoned mansion kind of theme, nothing too scary considering their new fan base. Don't ask me why, but today's kids love them."

"Because they've got taste, that's why." Brenda turned her attention to her daughter. "I've always said that the youth of today don't get enough credit."

Flick rolled her eyes. Her mother had never said anything of the sort.

"Although I suppose none of this matters now anyway," Rob continued. "Not considering you're selling up."

As intriguing as his request sounded, Flick didn't know how to respond. After all, the man did have a point.

"Not necessarily," Brenda said.

"What do you mean?" Flick asked. Of course they were selling. "In case you've forgotten, we don't have a choice."

Brenda lowered her voice. "We're only considering an offer. We haven't accepted it yet, have we? And you did say that if you had the cash you'd think about staying on."

Much to Flick's annoyance, her protests went ignored.

Instead, her mum returned her attention to the location manager with a smile. "This video shoot of yours, how much money are we talking about?"

CHAPTER TWENTY-ONE

With her mother busy messing on her phone, Flick got on with making them a sandwich. Usually such a straightforward if not mundane activity, that day organising lunch gave her a warm fuzzy feeling. To think, she could be eating real French baguettes, smothered in creamy French butter, packed with genuine French cheese, every day if she wanted to. She could enjoy a rich red Merlot, or a crisp white Chablis with her midday meal for the foreseeable future. She could cook her evening dish on the giant range... And not just in any old French chateau, of course, in one that she owned.

She knew she was getting ahead of herself. She'd been doing that all morning. Unlike on previous occasions, when she'd gone from room to room burdened with the prospect of letting her father down, she seemed to float through the building.

Instead of feeling heavy, her heart sang with possibility. She allowed herself to imagine how the place would look once she'd filled it with antique whites, misty greys, country creams and rustic ochres, giving it the grandeur of an old-world chateau. Not that her renovations would be too extravagant, of course. At least not straight away. What with faulty pipework, no doubt, a new septic tank, and goodness knew what other hidden delights to consider, she knew she'd have to make any money coming in stretch. Flick let out a wistful sigh. She could have hugged herself. Not even thoughts of dodgy plumbing could spoil the day's reverie.

"Wow!" Brenda said.

Flick turned to see her mother's eyes widen as she scrolled through some website or other.

"At these rates you'll be a millionaire."

"What rates?" she asked, wondering what her mum found so interesting as to risk losing her eyeballs.

Brenda held up her phone. "It's an agency specialising in renting out properties for film and television. They have everything from two-up two-downs to great big mansion houses. And Mr What's-his-name wasn't lying when he said the money's not bad. I'm thinking we should give them a ring to add this place onto their books. They'd love it."

"They've put a special call out for abandoned-looking chateaux then?"

Brenda laughed. "It won't always look abandoned. A couple more bookings and you'll be able to turn this place around in no time."

It was Flick's turn to laugh. She carried their sandwiches over to the table. "You mean today Argon Fire. Tomorrow *Downton Abbey*?"

"Exactly!"

Taking a seat, Flick wished she could share her mum's confidence.

"Argon Fire. Can you believe it? I keep pinching myself to make sure I'm not dreaming."

She also wished she could share her mum's excitement. "That we'll soon have a group of ageing, has-been, rockers in our midst? No, not really."

"I'm surprised, even if you're not."

"Mum, you're talking to a woman who's just inherited a chateau. A chateau she didn't even know existed until a few weeks ago." Flick took a bite of her sandwich. "As surprises go, I doubt anything could ever top that."

"I still can't believe you've never heard of them. They were massive in their day." Brenda came over all nostalgic. "Just wait until Linda hears about this. We're going to be mixing with rock star royalty."

"Like I said, ageing has-beens. Probably drug addled too."

"They certainly had their moments," Brenda said. "Then again, what band from way back when didn't?"

"Sex, drugs and rock 'n' roll. Wonderful. That's just what we need."

Brenda giggled. "Not any more. These days, as far as Argon Fire are concerned, a cup of tea is as exciting as it gets."

"How do you know?" Flick asked. Although with most of the rooms still in need of refurbishment, even if her mother was wrong Flick supposed it didn't matter. They couldn't do much damage anyway.

"Because I like to keep myself abreast of these things. Unlike some, I read the papers."

"Gossip pages, more like."

"Those too."

"But why? When nothing they print is true anyway?"

"Why not?"

Flick shook her head and smiled. Her mother had no shame.

"So, what did Dee say?" Brenda asked, coming over all serious as she too began eating her lunch.

"Dee?"

"When you turned down the offer?"

Flick picked up the second half of her sandwich, but thanks to the change in subject put it down again, her appetite starting to fade.

"You have phoned her, haven't you?"

"Nope."

"Why not?"

"Because I'm not turning it down."

"What do you mean?"

Flick pushed her plate away, her desire for food all but gone. "We don't know how this video shoot is going to pan out, do we? What if it's more hassle than it's worth? It could take months before another buyer comes along, so what's the point in burning our bridges just yet?"

"You worry too much."

"So you keep telling me."

Flick pushed the crumbs on her plate into a neat little pile. She knew her mother was right. But as much as she was prepared to enjoy the moment, as much as she wanted to believe this was a golden opportunity, it all seemed a little too easy; as if it were only a matter of time before something went wrong. She was being daft, of course. Her fears, no doubt, a legacy left behind by Matthew when he vanished. However, even though Rob had insisted the chateau was perfect, that little voice of experience insisted he could also change his mind and decide to use a different location. Just like on her wedding day, her dreams could shatter in front of her very eyes.

All at once Brenda rose to her feet. "Where's your phone? I'd say use mine but I don't have the number."

Flick looked up. "Whose number?"

"Dee's, of course. You need to at least tell her what's going on. It's only fair you keep her in the loop."

Flick sighed. As usual her mother was right.

"Then we need to have a talk."

"About what?"

"About the call I had from Linda the other day."

Having known her mum would open up when she was good and ready, Flick had almost forgotten about the phone call she'd tried and failed to listen in on. Her stomach churned as she took in her mother's seriousness, recalling the last time the woman had suggested they needed to talk. On that occasion she'd ended up the proud owner of a chateau and Flick dreaded to think what she was about to hear next.

"She rang to tell me about Matthew," her mum explained. "It seems he's back in town."

CHAPTER TWENTY-TWO

Nate observed his aunt. He had hoped their trip into town would cheer her up. She usually loved a stroll up and down the main street; breezing into the *boutique de fleuriste* for a selection of fresh flowers, before popping into the *boulangerie* for pastries and a catch up with Gigi, to then check out the seasonal produce at the *magazin de fruits et legumes*. These little excursions were, according to her, all the more enjoyable on the very rare occasions that he joined her; trying to lift her spirits being the only reason he'd offered to tag along on this occasion. His ploy seemed to have failed, however, and he was forced to watch his aunt with a mix of hilarity and bewilderment.

Her trip always finished up at Café Ange, where she'd insist Jess tell her all the latest in gossip. That day though, there was no such conversation. Instead, the only sound emanating from Aunt Julia was a periodic sigh as she nursed her coffee, opening her mouth to say something one second, only to close it again in the next. Turning his gaze on to Jess, Nate considered her just as bad. Slowly circling her cloth as she wiped down tables, she was nowhere near her typical jovial self.

He struggled to contain his amusement. Anyone would think someone had died the way these two carried on.

Pete appeared in the café doorway and Nate nodded, acknowledging his presence. He chuckled as his friend rolled his eyes at the two women's demeanour.

"Come on, ladies," Pete said. "This is a bit of an overreaction, don't you think?"

"Well said." Nate was glad to know he wasn't alone when it came to maintaining a sense of perspective.

Of course it was easy for him to say; he knew something they didn't. And while he felt guilty for keeping his plan to himself, he didn't see the point in raising his aunt's hopes, raising anyone's hopes for that matter. At least, not until something concrete happened.

"How can you say that?" Julia asked, defending her position.

Nate scoffed. "Because it's true."

"Some of us think Flick and her mum were the most exciting thing to happen around here in years. Some of us were looking forward to seeing that chateau brought back to life."

Jess approached the table. "I was just hoping Flick and I could be friends."

"Oh, sweetheart," Pete said, coming to her side with a grin. "She can still be your friend."

"What? Like a pen pal?"

Pete struggled to keep a straight face. "A pen pal's better than no pal."

Nate chuckled as he watched Jess flick her cloth against her husband's chest. Nate sympathised with her. Whereas he didn't have many friends through choice, he preferred to keep people at a distance, Jess's small circle came down to a lack of confidence on her part. A characteristic that Nate had never quite understood. In his view, Jess was funny, smart, pretty, and in a great relationship. Yes, Pete might threaten their financial stability from time to time, but emotionally their life together was solid. Nate often felt envious of what they had.

Pete cupped his wife's face and planted a kiss on her forehead, enough to make Nate feel that familiar pang of envy. Not that there was any point in being jealous. His single status was another conscious decision he'd made way back when. And no matter how many favours he called in to prevent it, the only woman to pique his interest in years could still be about to disappear as quickly as she'd arrived.

"I suppose none of us should be surprised that you're okay with this turn of events," Julia said. "Welcoming newcomers has never exactly been your thing, has it?"

"That's true," Jess said.

Even Pete nodded sagely, showing his agreement.

"That's hardly fair." Nate straightened himself up in his seat. Thanks to Mummy dearest, when it came to keeping his distance from strangers it wasn't as if he had a choice.

"Don't get me wrong, it's not a criticism," Julia continued. "I, of all people, understand your reasons. We all do. It's just–"

"Actually," Nate interrupted. "I quite like Flick. I'd be more than happy for her to stay."

"You would?" Jess asked.

"Really?" Pete added.

For once, Julia was speechless.

Taking in their expressions, Nate could have kicked himself. Despite his and Flick's periodic banter, he didn't have a clue what she really thought of him and he'd hate for any of this lot to start playing matchmaker. The embarrassment he'd feel if she didn't feel the same, he should have kept his mouth shut. "And her mum too," he hastily added. "To stop the developers moving in, of course."

He watched Jess's face break into a smile. Then she broke into song. "Nate and Flick, kissing in a tree."

Nate shot her a warning look, but she continued anyway. "K.I.S.S.I.N.G."

He supposed their shock at hearing this shouldn't come as any great surprise. In all the time he'd been in France, he'd done his damnedest to keep himself to himself. He certainly hadn't been tempted on the romantic front. Until Flick came along.

He felt his cheeks redden. Without her realising, Flick had managed to put a chink in his invisible armour. But regardless, he didn't plan on acting on this chink, either then *or* in the future. Having been burned in the past, it was an experience he had no intentions of reliving and he certainly wasn't about to chance rejection. He looked at each of the group, paying particular attention to the two women. "Not that any of us need mention this again," he said.

Jess nodded, heeding the warning. Pete smiled a wry smile. Julia, however, continued to just sit there quiet. Nate could almost see her cogs turning, no doubt, trying to hatch a plan to get him and Flick together. As well as rebooting her nephew's love life, she probably thought such scheming might be enough to make Flick choose France and her chateau over the UK. Talk about killing two birds with one stone.

Still, at least everyone's silence meant the conversation could move on.

"Thank you for your understanding," Nate finished.

Images of Flick popped into his head. He smiled to himself. In some ways, she seemed to lack confidence like Jess. Flick clearly didn't know how beautiful she was and she had this vulnerability that Nate supposed understandable after everything she'd been through. Every now and then though, a quiet determination had shown itself – a quality she obviously got from Brenda.

He thought about Brenda's unwavering request for help. Did he really think she would broadcast his whereabouts once she got back to England? Was his plan really about protecting himself? Or had his growing interest in Flick somehow informed his decision to step in? He had to admit that deep down he'd been as disappointed as everyone else when he learned of her decision to sell up and leave. Not that he supposed any of this mattered. When it came to being blackmailed, thanks to the developer, it turned out he didn't really have a choice. Flick's mother seemed the lesser of two evils.

He remembered his own mum's adage about keeping enemies close. For what good it did her; when it came to friends and foes, she never did have the right judgement to tell the difference. If anything, she seemed to have a knack of attracting the wrong people, something that Nate had to admit he too had been guilty of in the past. But whereas he liked to think he learned his own lesson, he wished more than anything that he could say the same about his mum.

Dee suddenly appeared at the café. "Why all the weird faces?" She plonked herself down in a seat at the table and, looking around at everyone, waited for an answer.

Nate jumped in before the others had chance to pull themselves together. "They're commiserating the new chatelaine's departure."

"Even more so now we know Nate fancies her," Jess said.

Nate threw her a look. How could she?

"Really?" Dee placed her bag on the floor. "Now that is interesting."

"It's a bloody shame," Julia said. "That's what it is. So, if you've come bearing more bad news, I suggest you keep it to yourself."

"I come with nothing of the sort actually. Unless you count the hordes of screaming teenagers about to descend on the place. Along with a mass of ageing groupies of which I have to admit I'm one."

Realising this could be the 'concrete' he'd been waiting for, Nate's interest grew, unlike that of his aunt who was clearly in no mood for games.

"What are you talking about now?" she asked.

Dee turned her attention to Pete. "Be a love and get me a cup of coffee, will you? I'm parched."

"Well?" Aunt Julia persisted.

Nate too wanted an answer. If he was right, his plan was, at last, coming into fruition and he willed Dee to continue. Unfortunately, the glint in her eyes, as she waited for Pete to return with her coffee, told him she much preferred a more teasing approach when it came to disclosing what she knew.

"You might want to sit down for this," she said, refusing to continue until everyone, including Pete, was seated. She looked around to make sure no one else was listening. Taking a sip of her drink, she then leant forward, bringing her voice down to a whisper. "It seems there's been a development."

"What do you mean?" Jess asked, intrigued.

"What kind of development?" Julia asked, straight to the point.

Dee appeared unsure, as if she'd said too much already.

With his future at stake, even Nate's impatience grew thin. "Come on, Dee. You're an estate agent not a doctor. There's no such thing as client confidentiality."

"You'd be surprised." Dee took another sip of her drink, but try as she might, maintaining her professional façade didn't last long. "Oh, okay then," she said, her whole body crumpling thanks to her need to reveal all. "I suppose I've started, so I may as well finish." She took a deep breath. "It would seem the sale of the chateau is on hold for now."

Julia smiled. "Really?"

Dee nodded. "Apparently, someone wants to use it for a video shoot."

"Who?" Pete asked.

Thank goodness, thought Nate. Having stuck to his part of the bargain, Brenda would have to stick to hers.

Dee pursed her lips, evidently doing her best not to appear too excited.

"Well?" Julia pushed.

"A music band."

"Anyone we know?" Jess asked.

"Yep," Dee replied, her voice suddenly rising an octave. "That's the best bit." She looked around the group. "It's only bloody Argon Fire."

"No," Jess said.

"Blimey," Pete said.

What the…? Nate thought.

"Is that so?" Julia asked. Taking in the group, her eyes rested on her nephew. "I wonder how that came about?"

Feeling her stare, Nate shifted slightly in his seat. Refusing to give her his full attention, he was as shocked as she to hear this.

"I know, isn't it great?" Dee grinned.

"Great? It's bloody fantastic," Pete said.

"You can say that again," Jess added.

Nate raised a smile, trying to join in with their excitement, as did his aunt, but he could sense that she was as unhappy about this turn of events as him. Continuing to feel the weight of her stare, he wondered if he should have given her the heads up, after all?

More to the point, he wondered why, out of all the bands Bruce could have chosen, he had to pick Argon Fire?

CHAPTER TWENTY-THREE

The drive back to Aunt Julia's house was difficult, the tension palpable. Much to Nate's frustration, his aunt was back to opening her mouth to say something in one moment, only to close it again before any actual words came out. Every time he tried to speak, she put up a hand to silence him. He couldn't tell if she was annoyed at his having kept secrets from her, or because Argon Fire was coming to town. After one sigh too many on her part, he gave up on his attempts to explain, choosing instead to stare out of the passenger window.

Hearing their name had been as much of a surprise to him. Having shut them out of his mind years earlier, they were a blast from the past Nate could have done without. He questioned why Bruce would do this to him. Yes, their relationship was tenuous, but wasn't it enough that he'd sold his soul and agreed to take part in the celebrations Bruce had planned for his mum? Nate felt manipulated. The two events had to be linked.

He decided not to think about it, but his curiosity bone began to niggle and he found himself wondering what the band might be like these days. Were they still throwing television sets out of hotel windows? Clichéd antics even back then. Not that he cared one way or the other, he insisted. As far as Nate was concerned, they could all go to hell. Lenny could go to hell.

Pulling into the courtyard, his aunt stopped the car, pausing to look at him as she switched off the engine. Words failed her once more and shaking her head, she simply undid her seatbelt, before getting out of the vehicle. Left sitting there, Nate felt tempted to just go home and leave her to it. But he knew they'd have to sort things out at some point, and he supposed sooner was better than later. Deciding to follow her, he got out of the car and headed towards the house.

Once inside, he watched her move straight for the drinks cabinet and pour herself a whiskey from the decanter. She downed it in one. "Right," she said, turning her eyes on Nate. "I'm ready. Hit me with it. Tell me what's going on."

"Do you mind?" Also approaching the drinks cabinet, he too poured himself a glass and plonking himself down on the settee, he took a long hard swig before speaking. "I'm doing Brenda a favour," he finally said.

"A favour?" his aunt asked, as if not hearing correctly.

"Yes."

Nate took in her concern, acknowledging that she had a right to be worried. As good deeds went, this one did seem to have taken on a life of its own.

"Nate, a favour is lending a neighbour a cup of sugar. A favour is not inviting your mother's ex-boyfriend round to film a video shoot." She perched herself on the opposing sofa.

Ex-boyfriend, thought Nate. If only things were that simple. In his view, Lenny had been more than that. He'd been the father figure he'd never had, either before or since. And although far from perfect, after all, the man did love his drink, Nate had gotten used to having him around. They'd had fun. Lenny taught him to play the drums, how to make the perfect Bloody Mary, and he even tried to give Nate the sex talk when he got his first girlfriend. A bit too descriptive in content, Nate was lucky he hadn't been put off sex for life.

But then one day Lenny was gone.

"Nate, this is Argon Fire we're talking about," his aunt continued. "They're trouble. Whatever it is you're up to, it's more than simply helping someone out."

He appreciated where she was coming from. Despite their complicated relationship, Aunt Julia had always been protective of her sister. And thanks to their well-publicised exploits, it was easy to see why she blamed the band, or more to the point, Lenny, for Nate's mum's spiralling problems. But in truth, his mother had been on a slippery slope well before Argon Fire came along. Up until then, she'd just been better at hiding it.

"It's not like I knew they were going to be involved," Nate said. "I'm as shocked as you. I'm guessing it's Bruce's idea of a joke, although not a very funny one, I'll give you that."

"Bruce? Where does he fit in with all of this?"

"It's complicated."

Julia got up from her seat, poured herself another drink, then retook her position on the sofa. "Try me."

Nate sat forward, ready to start at the beginning. "Brenda recognised me."

"Really? She didn't say anything to me."

"Nor me at first. In fact, she kept quiet until Flick decided, once and for all, to sell up. That's when Brenda asked for my help."

Julia's eyes narrowed. "When you say help? What do you mean?"

"That's the thing, she didn't talk about anything specific. And she certainly didn't ask for money. She just wanted Flick to have a proper choice with regards to the chateau, I suppose, and asked if there was anything I could do."

"What? That's it."

Nate shifted in his seat. "Not exactly."

"Meaning?"

"Meaning, if I refused to help her, she'd reveal my whereabouts to anyone and everyone who'd listen once she got back to the UK."

"No!" His aunt put a hand up to her mouth but Nate knew she was only feigning shock, that her action had more to do with hiding the beginnings of a smile.

"It's not something I'd make up."

"So, she's blackmailing you?"

As her eyes widened, he sensed her smile getting bigger. At least someone found his predicament funny.

"Looks like it."

"Well, well, well," his aunt said, finally letting her hand drop. "Doesn't it show how images can be deceiving. I mean, the woman looks so normal, nothing like your typical extortionist."

Nate raised his glass, finishing off the last of his drink.

"Then again, who does?" Julia continued. "They don't exactly wear a uniform, do they?" She thought for a moment. "I suppose you have to admire the woman."

Nate scoffed, unable to quite believe what he was hearing. "Says who?"

"And we shouldn't really be surprised," his aunt carried on. "Mothers do fight hard when it comes to their children."

"Not all mothers," Nate said.

Julia stopped dead and suddenly serious again, she looked him directly in the eye. "Yes, Nate. All of them. Even yours."

He let out a short sharp laugh. "You almost sound like you mean that."

She frowned, clearly failing to appreciate his attitude. "Your mum and I might not have seen eye to eye on a lot of things, young man, but I don't doubt for one minute the love she had for you." She sighed, as if reflecting on her long-lost relationship with her sister. "She just had so many issues. Issues that affected everyone, not just her."

Nate shook his head. As far as he was concerned, his mother didn't deserve such sympathy.

"Leaving you was probably the hardest decision she ever had to make. It was her way of setting you free from all the drama she caused."

"You make it sound so poetic." Nate knew she thought him harsh, but when it came to discussing his mother he couldn't seem to help himself. Yes, his mum had had her problems, but she also had choices. The help was there, she just didn't take it and he was left paying the price. A little voice reminded him that the apple didn't fall far from the tree; that he too had made bad decisions. The shenanigans he'd gotten up to had garnered as much negative attention as his mother's had in her day. But unlike his mother, he counter-argued, he'd made a change. Besides, she was wrong for abandoning him like she did. For leaving him to fend for himself, no matter the consequences. Because when you stripped it all back, got rid of the excuses, that's exactly what she'd done.

A part of him felt guilty for not being able to fully understand his mum's actions. Maybe one day he would see things from her point of view. However, that day was still to come.

"You're going to have to deal with it at some point, you know?" His aunt stood up and taking his glass, poured him a refill.

"So you keep telling me."

"Does Flick know who you are?" she asked, handing him his drink before retaking her seat.

"According to Brenda, no."

"At least that's something."

Nate watched Julia's expression turn quizzical.

"You still haven't told me about Bruce," she said. "And what he has to do with any of this."

Nate sighed, wishing he had nothing to do with anything at all. But the fact was, out of everyone he knew, Bruce had been the only person in any real position to help him out. Nate drank a mouthful of whiskey. It galled him to think about what he had to do in return.

"Initially I decided to keep out of it, I thought I'd take my chances and let Brenda do her worst. But talk about timing, she couldn't have picked it better considering what year it is. Her telling the press about me would just give them another excuse to plaster Mum's face all over the papers." He scoffed. Like they needed an excuse. "And mine."

"There is that," his aunt said.

"Then a developer turns up intent on turning the chateau into a posh block of flats and we both know I couldn't let that happen, that I had to do something to try to stop it." Nate took another drink. "And because I couldn't just hand over a great wad of cash to Flick's mother, I mean, what might that lead to, I did the next best thing."

"Which was?"

"Come up with a plan to help them raise their own money."

"Enter Bruce…"

"Exactly. I told him about my predicament and asked if there was anything he could do without letting Flick and Brenda know I'm involved."

"And the catch?"

Nate rolled his glass between his palms, first one way and then the other. "I take part in his documentary."

"And you agreed?"

Nate shrugged. "What choice did I have?"

"Wow!" She obviously didn't see that coming.

"Believe me, if there'd been any other way."

"Still, it's a big thing that he's asking of you. Are you sure you're up to it? Because from how you seem to feel about your mother, I'm not so sure."

"I didn't say I'd compromise myself. I only said I'd take part."

"Oh, Nate," his aunt said, clearly sympathising. "Why didn't you come to me first? I'd hate for you to make a bad situation worse."

"And what would you have done differently? You'd have picked up the phone and called Bruce just like I did and the outcome would have been the same."

"I wouldn't." She thought for a moment. "All right then, maybe I would. I don't suppose we'll ever know now, will we?"

"I don't suppose we will."

"Brenda's not stupid though, she will realise it's all down to you. After all, we're talking about Argon Fire here. The connection between them and your mum is common knowledge to anyone of a certain age."

"Maybe."

"I'm only surprised none of the others have made the connection."

Nate wasn't one hundred per cent sure his friends hadn't. For all he knew, they could have done their research when he'd first landed in France and were just too embarrassed by what they read to admit it. Thanks to his mother, his story wasn't exactly dinner party conversation, especially when acknowledging the good, meant acknowledging the bad.

"And what about Flick?" his aunt asked.

Flick, thought Nate. She was the only good thing in what was turning out to be a complete almighty mess.

"What do you mean?"

"What if she finds out what you and Brenda have been up to? Have you considered the fact that she might not want your help? She hasn't exactly had an easy time of it of late, what if the last thing she needs is you conning her into doing something you think is for the best, and then just like her husband, regret your involvement later on?"

"Why would I regret it?"

His aunt tried to appear relaxed, coming across to Nate as anything but. "Like you've already mentioned, there's the price you're having to pay for one. It's a big secret you've been keeping and you're still angry about it. What if you let slip? Then there's what you said today. You liking Flick doesn't have anything to do with this decision of yours, does it? Because if it does, it could all backfire, particularly if she doesn't feel the same way. You'll still be neighbours, remember."

Nate had hoped that, after everything they'd discussed since, she'd have forgotten all about his earlier admission. "She isn't going to find out though, is she? I'm not going to say anything. Her mum certainly isn't going to say anything. That only leaves you…"

He could see his aunt felt uncomfortable. If there was one thing she hated, it was being put in a position.

"Don't worry," she said. "She won't hear anything from me."

Relieved, Nate smiled slightly, glad of the support. "Thank you."

"And Lenny?"

"What about him?"

"How are you going to deal with him?"

Nate found her question strange. "Why would I have to do that?"

"He's going to have an idea you're around here somewhere. Bruce isn't exactly known for his tight lips now, is he?"

"Bruce can say whatever he wants. As you well know, I'm pretty adept at hiding myself away when needs must."

CHAPTER TWENTY-FOUR

Flick yawned. Pouring a much-needed coffee, she could feel the weight of the bags under her eyes and wanted nothing more than to just go back to bed. "Chance would be a fine thing," she said to herself, and thinking about the morning ahead, she yawned once more.

"Good morning."

Flick observed her mother's cheeriness as she breezed into the room. At least one of them had gotten the prerequisite eight hours. "Is it?"

"You didn't sleep very well?"

"Nope."

"Because of Matthew?"

Flick scoffed. "Who else?"

Brenda approached and gave her a hug. "Oh, love, I am sorry. Maybe I should have kept my mouth shut."

"Don't be. I might be knackered, but I'm glad you told me."

"Really? Because the last thing I wanted to do was upset you."

As her mother also helped herself to coffee, Flick leant against the kitchen counter. "That's the thing. I'm not actually upset. It wasn't just the wedding day that had me tossing and turning all night, it was lots of things. And the more I think about it, the more I realise he only asked me to marry him to stop me focusing on Dad. Instead of helping me through the pain of having to deal with what Dad was going through, he thought *I know, I'll propose, that'll stop all her whinging*."

"That's a bit harsh, isn't it? I might not be the man's biggest fan, but still…"

"Not really. Now I've had time to reflect, it's pretty obvious that Matthew didn't do anything unless there was something in it for him. So, thank you. If you hadn't have told me he was back in town I'd still be wondering *why* and *what if*. And I'd definitely still be feeling sorry for myself." She felt her mother's comforting hand on her arm as she took a sip of her drink. "It's as if, finally, I can see our relationship for what it was. One-sided. I suppose some things never change, eh?" She let out a mocking laugh. "I mean, come on. To turn up out of the blue and expect me to be there waiting for him like some sort of sap, especially after everything he's put me through. Thank goodness that location scout turned up when he did."

"What do you mean?"

"If he hadn't, we'd probably be back home by now. Matthew would be turning on those puppy dog-eyes of his, because that's what he always did when he wanted his own way. And, like some fool, I'd be crumbling, because that's what *I* always did." She turned to her mother. "I don't know who I'm annoyed with more. Him for being so selfish? Or me for being so soft?" She downed the last of her drink. "From now on I'm gonna do what's right for me without *any* interference from anyone else. I refuse to be manipulated and woe betide anyone who tries."

She took in her mother's concerned expression, an expression she supposed understandable considering her outburst. "I'm sorry, Mum, I don't mean to sound so aggressive. I'm just tired. And ready to get on with my life, only for real this time." She put her cup down on the counter and checked her watch. "Which reminds me, I suppose we should get a move on."

Flick led the way down the hall, grabbing their coats and bags off a hanger by the door. "Although I'm still not sure why we're doing this."

Brenda smiled. "We're doing it because apparently it's the done thing here in France."

Flick laughed. "Doesn't make it any less embarrassing though, does it?"

Once wrapped up, they made their way out to the car and got in. Her mum seemed pensive during the drive into town but Flick didn't mind the silence. She was happy to enjoy the moment. She felt empowered. Admittedly still tired as well, but the lack of sleep was worth it. She hadn't just spent her waking hours addressing issues with Matthew and their relationship, she'd done a mental check list of the pros and cons of her life in the UK compared to how it could be here in Brittany. Brittany was in the lead. And not just for the weather, food and wine. Thanks to Matthew, her life in the UK had come to a standstill. In France, she had a chance to start again. She crossed her fingers. That's if all went well with the video shoot.

Last night had also given her the opportunity to consider her new-found friends and how encouraging they'd been. As far as they were concerned, there didn't seem to be any doubt that she was up to the challenge of renovating a chateau. Running an art school of some sort was deemed more than a possibility – a dream that Flick had long since forgotten about. She smiled, thanks to the unwavering support she'd received. It felt good to know it wasn't just her mum that was rooting for her, her neighbours were too. She reached out to squeeze her mother's hand. Flick hadn't felt this lucky in a long time.

Approaching the main street in town, Flick felt nervous. She was about to take a big step and, despite not quite being in a position to say she was categorically staying, it was still nerve-wracking to know the odds were leaning that way.

She pulled the car into a space opposite the *Mairee*, taking in the building before her. For a mayor's office, it didn't look anything like the official structures she was used to in England. Back home they tended to be modern, cement constructions. In contrast, this one was pretty and hospitable; homelier, she supposed. Built from natural stone, flower boxes sat on all the window ledges, the last of the season's colourful geraniums contrasting nicely against the dark grey paintwork. But regardless of its welcoming façade, she still couldn't stop the bumblebees buzzing around in her stomach.

Flick watched her mum rummage in her handbag for her compact and lipstick, using one to expertly reapply the other, before snapping it shut and putting it away again. How could her mother be so calm? "Does this not feel, at least, a bit awkward to you?" she asked, glancing at the building once more. "And embarrassing? I mean what are we supposed to say? What if he doesn't speak English, because we certainly don't speak French?"

Brenda turned to face her and smiled. "That's why we have back up."

"What do you mean?"

At that moment, a car pulled up alongside. And much to Flick's surprise, Nate's Aunt Julia excitedly waved from behind the wheel before turning off the engine and getting out.

Brenda laughed. "What? You think I'd let us humiliate ourselves in front of a dignitary? You don't mind do you, but even I knew we needed a translator and when Julia offered..."

"I don't mind at all. In fact, I'm relieved."

Flick and her mum got out of their vehicle and the usual *faire la bise* commenced.

"Thanks for helping out," Flick said, greetings over with. She took a deep breath, steeling herself ready for the formalities ahead.

"Yes, thank you," Brenda said.

"Don't be silly, I'm more than happy to assist. I remember what it was like when *I* first landed. I didn't speak a word of French... talk about muddling through. And there weren't that many Brits here back then. Believe me, I had no choice but to pick up the lingo. Anyway." She turned to Flick. "Can I just say, I am so glad you've decided to stay."

"But..." Flick wanted to explain that everything rested on the video shoot, however, Julia was on a roll.

"And don't look so nervous. We're just popping in to say hello. It's customary, that's all." Julia paused to produce a bottle of single malt from her bag. "As is this. It's always good to come bearing gifts and the French do love their whiskey." Handing it over, she raised her hand, indicating to the entrance. "Shall we?"

Flick took another deep breath as she and Brenda followed her inside.

"Sophie," Julia said to the receptionist. "*Ça va?*"

The two women chatted easily and going off their interaction, it was clear to Flick that they knew each other well. Not that Flick understood a word of what was said and as she continued to listen, she knew that if they were serious about a new life in France, the language would be one obstacle they'd definitely have to overcome. Just the thought of trying, however, made her brain hurt. And unlike Julia all those years earlier, she couldn't imagine either her or her mum ever conquering that particular mountain.

Conversation over, the receptionist finally picked up the phone to let the mayor know they'd arrived, causing Flick to grip the neck of the whiskey bottle even tighter, as she and her mum began following Julia down a short corridor.

"Ready?" Julia asked. Stopping, she gently tapped on the door in front of them.

Flick, again, looked to her mum for reassurance as all three entered the room.

"*Bonjour,*" said the mayor, rising to his feet to greet them.

A handsome man about the same age as Julia, he wore smart trousers, a crisp white shirt and a tie. Approaching their interpreter first, he seemed warm and welcoming, although watching their exchange, Flick thought him a bit too friendly on that front. She wondered if she were imagining things. The way he spoke, the way he looked at Nate's aunt, and the way she played with her hair in response – Flick had to ask herself if there was more to this relationship than anyone had let on. She might not have understood their words, but the subtleties in their interaction pointed to a lot more than that of a public figure meeting a member of his community.

Flick took the opportunity to scan the room. Piles and piles of files lay stacked across the floor and there were two desks, one home to yet more mountains of paperwork, the other obviously kept clear for meetings such as this. Taking in all the mess, she questioned how on earth anyone knew where anything was, the phrase *organised chaos* automatically springing to mind. Faded out-of-date event posters adorned the walls, with a presidential portrait taking pride of place amongst them. And there was a small drinks table upon which sat a half-full decanter of wine plus four glasses; one of them used, she noted. Alcoholic beverages aside, the whole place reminded her of the headmaster's office at the local comprehensive school she'd attended as a girl.

"Right," Julia said at last, turning her attention to Flick and her mother. "To business." She began the formal introductions. "*Monsieur le Maire, voici Flick et sa mère...* Ladies, *Monsieur le Maire.*"

He stepped forward, greeting both women with the usual cheek kisses. Flick blushed, unlike her mum who, as always, enjoyed the moment.

"Oh." Flick suddenly remembered the whiskey bottle in her hand. She thrust it towards the mayor. "For you."

"*Merci.*" He smiled, happy to accept the offering and, checking out the label, raised an appreciative eyebrow. He placed it on the drinks table and poured each of them a glass of wine. "*S'il vous plaît?*" He indicated for everyone to take a seat then settled himself behind his desk, taking a moment before commencing. "*D'accord.*"

Julia translated as he welcomed Flick and Brenda to his little town, adding that he hoped they'd both be happy there. Apparently, he was as delighted as everyone else to see the chateau occupied again and was intrigued by their plans for it. Julia must have already told him about the video, Flick realised, as he took no prompting at all when it came to discussing the band starring in it. Like everyone else, the man was clearly a fan of Argon Fire, leaving Flick wondering if she were the only person on the planet to have never heard of them. She nodded regardless, making sure to say *oui* and *non* in all the right places, while politely sipping on her wine.

After a while, the mayor and Julia rose to their feet, leaving Flick and Brenda no choice but to follow suit. It seemed the meeting had come to an end and as they said their goodbyes, Flick breathed a sigh of relief. It felt good to have the mayor's support, as if she had one less hurdle to overcome. *Or to put it another way*, she thought, *I'm now one step nearer to a brand-new life.*

"Do you have time for a coffee?" she asked Julia, as they made their way outside. "My way of saying thank you."

"I'm way ahead of you, my dear." She checked her watch. "It looks like we got out of there just in time."

"Sorry?" Flick asked.

Her mother smiled. "Come on, you'll see."

Flick looked from one woman to the other. Clearly that morning wasn't just about meeting the mayor and she wondered what else her mother had gotten up to behind her back.

CHAPTER TWENTY-FIVE

Flick had an idea they were going to Café Ange when they headed up the main street on foot rather than driving to their destination. What she didn't expect, however, was the welcome party waiting to meet them. She felt lost for words.

"*Ma cherie.*" Gigi jumped from her seat to give Flick a hug.

Flick couldn't help but laugh at the speed at which the old lady moved, telling herself that with any luck, she'd be equally as spritely when she reached that age.

"How did it go?" Dee asked, also rising to her feet.

Flick wondered what they were all doing there. But thanks to everyone's eagerness, not to mention the round of *faire la bise* that ensued, her bewilderment got lost in all the excitement.

"Let me get you a drink," Jess said, as usual the consummate *hostess with the mostess.*

Pete appeared in the doorway, a bottle of wine and tray of glasses at the ready. "No need."

Flick took in the group of smiling faces. She suddenly felt ambushed, without knowing the reason why. "What's going on?" she asked, finally finding her voice.

"First thing's first." Pete proceeded to pour the drinks.

As he handed them out, Julia indicated they should all sit down. Once seated, she raised her glass. "Cheers, everyone. *Salute.*"

"Cheers. *Salute,*" they replied, including Flick, who despite her obliviousness, felt compelled to join in.

"Right, shall we begin?" Nate's aunt continued.

Glad they were finally getting to the point, Flick watched her pull a posh looking notebook and a pen out of her handbag.

"You've probably realised by now, my dear, that we're all aware of this up and coming video shoot?"

Taking in the excited faces looking back at her, Flick knew she'd been a fool not to have realised. She glanced at Dee, who flushed red. Of course, the poor woman wouldn't be able to keep something like that to herself. Not if the band involved was as famous as everyone seemed to claim.

"Sorry," said the estate agent. "I couldn't help it. I mean come on, it is Argon Fire."

"And you're probably also wondering what that has to do with any of us," Julia carried on. "Let me start by saying that we understand what a big opportunity it is for you and that we're all here to help."

Flick could see the willingness amongst the group and she appreciated the offer, despite not knowing why an offer had been made in the first place. According to Rob's emails, the video crew and band would arrive, do their thing, and then leave. If all went to plan, it should be over and done with come evening time. Even Flick didn't have a role in the event, a position she'd positively welcomed. The people in front of her, however, seemed keen to get involved and Flick felt terrible at having to let them down. "That's very kind of you all, but completely unnecessary. According to the location manager there's nothing for me or anyone else to do."

"Under normal circumstances I'd agree," Julia said. "But in this instance, I think there's a lot we can do."

The group eagerly nodded in response, telling Flick they'd obviously put a lot of thought into this. She, however, simply sat there confused. She looked to her mother, hoping for some enlightenment, but rather than clarify, Brenda silently encouraged her to listen. With no other choice, Flick turned her attention back to Nate's aunt.

"I suppose what I'm trying to say is that this video shoot could be the start of something big for you. Which means, you need to milk it for all you can."

"Okay," Flick said.

"That means showing them what a wonderful venue *Chateau D'Enchantement* is."

"And not just for bands," Jess joined in. "But for film and television too."

"Even advertising," Pete said.

Flick's mother gave her an enthusiastic nudge. "Remember what you said? Today Argon Fire, tomorrow *Downton Abbey*?"

"But that was a joke, Mum." Flick couldn't believe anyone had taken that seriously.

"It doesn't have to be," Dee said.

Flick admired their commitment but doubted any of them knew what they were talking about. "So how do you all suggest we do this then?"

"By providing them with a great wrap party," Julia said.

"Like they do in Hollywood?" Flick asked. Talk about getting ahead of themselves.

"*Exactement!*" Gigi said. "You provide great food, fine wine, everything France is famous for."

"Then they go back and tell everyone what a great time they had and what a great hostess you were," Julia said.

"And we all know that the film industry isn't about what you know, but who you know," Brenda said.

"Do we?" Flick wondered where her mum's sudden expertise had come from.

"And everyone's trying to hit the big time," Julia continued. "Music directors, advertising directors. In fact, some of them already have. Do you know how much money directing a commercial can bring in?"

Flick shook her head, half expecting her mother to come up with the answer.

"A lot, I can tell you. They might say they just want to keep busy when they're in between films, but it's really about the cash."

"Is it?" Flick asked.

Julia nodded. "Remember the Chanel ad for their Coco Mademoiselle perfume? That was directed by Joe Wright who also did *Pride and Prejudice* and *Anna Karenina*. Baz Luhrmann did one for Chanel No.5 and David Lynch did an ad for Clear Blue pregnancy tests, can you believe?"

"Really?" Flick said, incredulous. "How do you know all this?"

"I'm not the only one who reads the gossip columns," Brenda said.

"Which is why between us, we can put *Chateau D'Enchantement* on the map," Jess said.

"*Exactement!*" Gigi said again.

"So, are you up for this, Flick?" Brenda asked.

With talk of big things, big directors and big budgets, Flick thought it all a bit scary. Then again, she needed a big budget all of her own considering the amount of work that needed doing on the chateau. If she really was serious about a fresh start in France she couldn't live on nothing, she'd have to bring money in somehow and this was the best chance she'd have at providing for herself. At least initially. She took a deep intake of breath, daring herself to just go for it. "Yes. I am."

Brenda heaved a sigh of relief, while Gigi sat clapping her hands in delight.

Jess squealed. "This is so exciting." She patted her husband's arm. "Isn't it, Pete?"

"It certainly is."

"I might even sell extra houses on the back of it," Dee said, ever the professional.

"Okay then," Julia said with a smile. Eager to get down to business, she looked around the group, her pen and notebook at the ready. "So, who wants to start?"

"Obviously I can provide the bread," Gigi said to Flick. "No French meal is complete without it. I can also offer pastries and cakes. And my son-in-law can give us some *Cidre*. A Breton speciality, of course. I can also bring cheese, thanks to my sister. As you can tell, we are a family of artisans."

"We can provide the wine," Pete added. "Beer, cold drinks, whatever you need. We can even have a go at your infamous cocktail list, Julia."

"And after everyone's eaten I can do a more detailed tour of the building, selling both it and you," Dee said.

Thanks to their generosity, Flick sat there wide-eyed and grateful. She also felt embarrassed as she didn't have the cash to pay for any of this, something she'd have to explain before their plans grew even more extravagant. She felt herself blush. "This is very good of you and it all sounds fabulous, but I can't really afford any of these things."

Everyone returned her gaze, appearing aghast at the mere suggestion that money might exchange hands.

"We don't want paying," Julia said, sounding almost affronted.

"We just want to help," Jess said.

"I might leave a few business cards lying around though," Pete said. "To let them know about Café Ange. You never know they might call in."

"And to be able to say we cater for events such as this will only add to our reputation," Gigi said.

"And I've already said how I'll benefit," Dee added. "House hunters will be lining up to buy property around here once word gets out."

Listening to them, Flick felt almost tearful. She looked from the group to her mum who, full of excitement, beamed back at her. "Thank you," Flick said to them all, wishing she could find the words to say more.

"You're welcome," Julia said. "Now…" Reading through the notes she'd taken she was obviously keen to get back to the task at hand. "Where were we? Oh yes, the food. Who do we think should take charge of that?"

Everyone's eyes automatically fell on Jess. Her cheeks reddened at being the centre of attention. "I don't think so."

"Why ever not?" Dee asked. "You're a great cook."

"Just not a professional one." Jess looked to her husband for support, but he simply shrugged, clearly agreeing with everyone else.

"Your food's as good as any chef's I've ever tasted," he said.

Jess laughed nervously. "You're biased."

"I'm not."

"No, he isn't," Dee said. "But don't take our word for it. What do you think, Flick? You've tasted her food, haven't you?"

Flick felt a little uncomfortable being put on the spot, especially when she could see Jess wasn't keen on the idea. But in considering the mouth-watering lunch Jess had previously made, just thinking about the Camembert dish made Flick salivate. "I think you'd be perfect for the job."

"I think so too," Brenda added.

"Really?" Jess said.

"As do I," Julia said, scribbling something in her notebook. "So, that's settled then." She looked up with a smile. "Jess is on food."

Their enthusiasm for the video was clearly catching, as even Flick felt a frisson of excitement over the whole thing. She considered which room they could use for the post-shoot gathering, the information she'd have to get from Rob to make sure they were catering for the right number of people, and where they could source cheap tables and chairs. "We can focus on getting the chateau ready. Can't we, Mum?"

"And I'm more than happy to act as liaison officer," Julia said. "To coordinate everything."

If her actions up to then were anything to go by, Flick couldn't think of anyone better.

Nate's aunt continued to make a few more notes, before finally putting down her pen. She smiled. "Okay then. Let the preparations commence."

CHAPTER TWENTY-SIX

Since listening to Nate's aunt, Flick had put on her business head. She knew it wasn't enough for the video crew to remember the chateau long after they left, she wanted them to keep talking about it too – the very reason why she'd decided to hold the wrap party in one of the front reception rooms.

Thanks to Nate's mechanical skills, he'd fixed the mower and the view out onto the expansive lawns and sweeping drive was memorable for all the right reasons. Certainly worthy of discussion, the freshly cut lawns gave the chateau a real sense of grandeur; an extra selling point that could very well help with future bookings.

"So, what do you think?" Flick asked her mum, turning her attention back to the room's interior. As Flick looked at the line of pasting tables that cut through the centre of the space, she wished she could say they were as befitting of the building as the vista from the window proved, but in truth, they just looked pathetic.

"I've already told you," Brenda replied. "I think we should hold it in the kitchen. Not only is there a perfectly good table in there, that room is right next to the lake."

"And like *I* said, Mum, we've all heard stories about band members and late-night skinny dipping. The last thing we need is an aging rocker drowning amongst the lily pads. That lake might not look anything like a swimming pool to you and me, but after a couple of Julia's legendary *Amour a Mosas*, who knows what Argon Fire will see."

Brenda laughed, ready to say something.

"I know, I know, they're all teetotal these days," Flick butted in. "I'm just not prepared to take any chances. This event is far too important."

Flick took in the pasting tables once more. Her heart sank. "Let's hope Julia's as good at table dressing as she is at making cocktails."

Again, Brenda laughed. "Remember her place the night of the soirée? I doubt a woman with that good an eye for detail will let you down." She looked at her watch. "Anyway, I'm more interested in what time Jess is going to be here. I can't wait to find out what's on tonight's menu."

"Me too. That fennel and blue cheese *tarte tatin* was to die for." Her stomach grumbled just thinking about it. Despite Flick arguing to the contrary, Jess had insisted they sample her wares before she decided on a final *carte du jour*, something Flick's waistline was, no doubt, paying for. "And those *gougères*, who'd have thought cheese puffs could be quite so good."

"Not exactly the finger buffet we're used to, eh?" Brenda said.

"*Aperitif dinatoire*, if you don't mind." It was Flick's turn to laugh. "Everything sounds so much more refined in French, don't you think?"

A rickety old van coming up the drive caught her eye. Her brow furrowed as she failed to recognise it, although she frowned even more when she finally clocked the driver. "What's he doing here?" she asked, curious, although she couldn't deny she was pleased to see him.

Exiting the room to find out, Flick saw that Nate had already brought the van to a standstill and climbed out by the time she and her mum got there to greet him. Flick smoothed down her attire as she watched him walk round to the passenger door, open it and pull out a large cardboard box.

"For you," he said, bringing it over. "From Aunt Julia."

"What is it?" Flick asked.

"Oh, that'll be the table linen." Brenda stepped forward to relieve Nate of the box. "I forgot she said she'd pop some round. I can't wait to see it."

Flick watched her mum head back inside, leaving her and Nate to it. "Thank you. I haven't forgotten my manners, even if Mum has."

"Just following orders. So how are the preparations going for the video shoot?"

Flick found his interest surprising. He seemed to have steered clear of her and the chateau of late. Whereas everyone else had thrown themselves into helping with the wrap party, he seemed to have done a disappearing act. "I didn't have you down as a rock fan."

"I'm not. Just making small talk."

Flick smirked. She knew an excuse when she heard one.

"That's what neighbours do, isn't it?" he continued. "Chat about the latest goings on."

Flick smiled. She liked the sound of that. "Neighbours. Who'd have thought it, eh? I still haven't properly got my head around all this yet. I keep pinching myself to make sure it's real."

"Oh, it's real all right."

"Anyway, seeing as you've asked, I don't think my hands can take another round of cleaning." She looked at the dryness of her fingers and palms, the bleach having taken its toll on her reddened skin. Unable to find a decent scrubber anywhere, she'd had no choice but to resort to good old chemical warfare. "It's like painting the Golden Gate Bridge keeping on top of this place."

"I can see why." Nate glanced up at the building.

"And I'm going to have to do it all over again once they've finished filming." Flick paused. "Consider yourself invited, by the way."

"Parties aren't my thing."

"Parties are everyone's thing."

"Not mine."

Flick ignored his adamant tone. "But what if I said I wanted you to come?" She saw his eyes light up at her question and for a second, she thought he might change his mind.

"Honestly, I'll be far happier at home with Rufus. Mingling with a bunch of people I have no interest in isn't really my idea of fun."

Admittedly, Flick felt disappointed and an awkward silence descended. But rather than taking this as his cue to head off, Nate seemed to be waiting for her to fill the quiet. Flick wondered if she should invite him in, but as she was about to do just that, he turned to leave and the moment passed.

"I'll let you get back to it then," he said, making his way towards to his van.

Flick's disappointment continued. Although with so much to do, she supposed his departure was for the best.

"Unless you fancy a couple of hours off," he suddenly called back.

Despite still having a long list of jobs, Flick couldn't deny that she felt more than a tad tempted. Regardless of their dodgy beginnings, she enjoyed spending time with Nate. And having scrubbed the chateau, first for the viewing and then for the video shoot, she had to admit that a break from the housework was just what she needed. "What do you have in mind?"

"What if I said it's a surprise?"

Flick's face fell. She didn't like surprises.

"You don't have to look so worried. It's something you'll enjoy."

She reminded herself that she was supposed to be forging a new future in France, one that embraced life, not one that shied away from it. Whatever Matthew had done to her was in the past, his actions certainly shouldn't prevent her from enjoying the present. After all, not every surprise was bad and she only had to look at the chateau for proof of that. Flick's smile returned. "It sounds wonderful."

"Great." Nate stepped forward again.

Flick's shoulders slumped as she remembered her prior engagement. "I've just realised, Jess is meant to be calling round. She wants us to okay her cuisine before finalising the menu for the shoot."

Nate laughed. He obviously didn't see a problem. "Have you sampled Jess's food before?"

"Have I." Flick's mouth salivated at the mere thought.

"Then you know that whatever she makes it's going to be good. Besides, I'm sure your mum would be happy to step into the breach."

Flick thought back to all the other food-tasting sessions. She hadn't been the only one to tuck in with gusto, her mother had wholeheartedly thrown herself into them too. "And with me out of the way I suppose it's only more for her to enjoy."

"Exactly."

"Which means when you think about it, having a couple of hours off would be doing her a favour." Flick responded to Nate's growing smile with one of her own. "Sold. Let me get my coat," she said, before turning to head back indoors.

"And you'll need your wellies!" Nate called out.

CHAPTER TWENTY-SEVEN

As expected, Brenda was more than pleased to take full responsibility for sampling Jess's fayre, leaving Flick to escape the pressures of the video shoot for a short while. Closing the front door behind her, bag and coat in hand, Nate had already started the van's engine by the time she returned.

"Ready?" he asked, as she opened the passenger door and climbed in.

"I most certainly am."

As they set off down the drive, Flick took in the vehicle's interior. She'd never seen the inside of an old Citroën van before, not that there was much to look at. The dashboard, if you could call it that, consisted of nothing more than a speedometer and a petrol gauge. Next to that was a shelf from which the gearstick poked out, an odd positioning that Flick knew she'd find confusing were she the driver. And the steering wheel was ginormous. In fact, from the seating to the pedals to the windscreen wipers, everything about the vehicle appeared basic. A continuous detail that, no doubt, included the van's tyres.

Passing through the chateau's large iron gates and under the canopy of tree branches, the Citroën bumped in and out of every pothole going, causing Flick to bounce around equally as uncontrollably. *Something else I need to add to my renovation list*, she told herself, gripping the sides of her seat. *Resurfacing the chateau entrance.*

"You okay?" Nate asked.

Flick nodded, choosing to ignore the smile written across his face.

As they pulled out onto the main road, Flick could, at last, relax. She still felt every loose-lying bit of tarmac under the vehicle's wheels, but at least she could travel hands free.

As they continued on their way, she decided that meandering along lots of French country lanes in a vintage van was actually quite nice, romantic even. Romantic in the broader sense of the word, of course. "Are you ready to tell me where it is we're going?"

"What? And spoil the surprise?"

She gave him her best puppy-dog eyes. If it worked for Matthew, why shouldn't it for her?

"If you must know," Nate said. "I thought as a fellow artist you might like to see *La Vallée des Saints*."

Her eyes went from puppy-dog to questioning.

"It's a feudal mound linked to the priests and monks who came here from the UK hundreds of years ago. Be it in celebration or out of respect, sculptors began creating giant granite statues. A gathering of saints, if you will. They all look down on the valley."

"Really?"

"Yep. It's a practice that continues to this day."

"How interesting." Flick tried to imagine the oversized effigies and she looked forward to seeing them. "Mum said that you're a sculptor yourself."

"A chainsaw artist, yes."

"I'd love to see some of your work. Mum also said what you do is amazing, by the way. How did you get into it? Did you have to train? It's not exactly something anyone can do, is it?"

"I don't see why not," Nate replied. "All I did was watch a tonne of YouTube videos and then give it a go."

Flick laughed, thinking about her own artistic endeavours. "Like it's that easy."

"I didn't say I was any good back then. Like everything else, practice makes perfect."

"Maybe when I get my art school up and running you could teach a course?"

"I don't think so."

"Or you could do some sort of demonstration?" She pictured him with his broad chest and flexed muscles, expertly wielding a chainsaw as he attacked a huge trunk of wood. She smiled, further imagining a sea of appreciative students. "That would certainly pack in the ladies."

"Would it now?" Nate asked, eyebrows raised.

Flick flushed red, wondering how she could think something like that, let alone say it out loud. "I'm talking from a purely business point of view, of course."

"Of course." Nate grinned.

He obviously didn't believe her and looking out of the passenger window, Flick focused on the woods that lined the roadside until her blushes waned.

"So, what brought you to Brittany?" she finally asked, ready to move on the conversation. "We all know why I'm here. But why are you?"

Nate appeared to think for a moment. "I fancied a change of scenery."

Flick turned in her seat to face him. "Meaning?"

"Meaning just that."

Seeing his hands tighten around the steering wheel, she narrowed her eyes as she addressed him. It didn't take a genius to realise there was more to this guy than he was letting on. "You don't give much away, do you?"

"In relation to…?" Staring straight ahead, he was clearly refusing to look at her.

"Yourself."

"Maybe there's nothing to tell."

Flick disagreed. "There's always something to tell."

He continued to focus on the road ahead. "Maybe some people just have boring lives."

"Rubbish. Most people are happy to talk about lots of things. Like their brothers and sisters, for example."

"If you must know, I don't have any. Although I'm happy to pretend and make a couple up if you'd prefer."

Flick smiled to herself. He might be an unwilling participant in this conversation, but at least she was getting somewhere. "Most people chat about where they come from."

"Then in my case that would be London. Which tourist destination would you like to discuss first?"

Flick considered not so much his words, it was his tone that she found intriguing. He seemed to have zero enthusiasm when it came to his old life. But surely it couldn't have been that bad. "They also drop their parents into the conversation once in a while," she carried on, regardless.

Nate turned his head in her direction. Something in her tummy fluttered as his intense green eyes stared straight into hers. God, he was gorgeous. He seemed to search her face, but whatever answer he hoped to find, she could tell by the way he looked back at her that he wanted to say something. And whatever that *something* was, it was clearly important.

"If you must know," he said.

Flick caught a glimmer of something in the woods just ahead. "What's that?" she asked, momentarily forgetting their conversation.

"What's what?" Nate moved to follow her gaze, but he was too late.

"Look out!" she said, as something darted out in front of them.

A huge mass of brown fur charged from left to right, attempting to cross their path. It had a long pig-like snout, small pointy ears, and at almost a metre high, it was like nothing Flick had ever seen.

"Shit!" Nate slammed on his brakes.

Flick gripped her seat with one hand and clung on to her seat belt with the other. Tyres screeched and everything seemed to move in slow motion as the car refused to stop. Struggling to hold on, gravity suddenly flung her forward. Flick automatically threw her arms out and, fear surging through her body, she reached for the dashboard. Her seatbelt locked and her whole body jolted back again as the van finally came to a standstill.

Flick sat there, her heart still racing as she stared at the road in front of them. "Talk about an adrenalin rush. What was that?"

"*Sanglier.*" Nate took a sharp intake of breath and ran a hand through his hair as he exhaled.

Flick was still none the wiser. "And that would be?"

"Sorry," Nate said, obviously still recovering from their near miss. "Wild boar."

"Really?" Flick struggled to hide her excitement. "I've never seen a wild boar before."

"Lucky you. They're a bloody nuisance. And vicious. I'm guessing that one was escaping the *chaise.*"

Again, Flick needed a translator.

"The hunt. It's that time of year."

Flick's eyes widened. "You mean someone was going to shoot it?"

"Don't look so horrified."

"With a real gun?"

"That's country life, for you. Besides, France is over-run with them. Some would argue they need a good culling."

Unable to believe what she was hearing, she opened her mouth to protest but Nate got in there first.

"I'm not saying I agree. But when it comes to issues like these, things are more complex than we townies appreciate. Anyway, enough about that boar's welfare. Are you all right?"

Flick looked at him. His lack of concern for a wild animal was in stark contrast to that which he appeared to have for her. "I'm fine."

"You're sure? Because that was one hell of an emergency stop."

Suddenly nervous, she stared into his eyes. She didn't know if it was his gaze that was making her hot and bothered or the after-effects of nearly hitting that poor beast. Whatever the reason, she couldn't bring herself to look away. And neither, it seemed, could he.

Her pulse quickened once more as his face began slowly moving towards hers. She knew he was going to kiss her. Damn, she wanted him to kiss her, and feeling the warmth of his breath, she parted her lips, tilting her head slightly in readiness. "Ouch!" she said, suddenly grimacing.

Nate pulled back. "What is it? Are you okay? Oh God, I'm sorry."

Flick put a hand up to her neck. "I think I've got whiplash."

CHAPTER TWENTY-EIGHT

Flick stood at her bedroom window looking down on the activity below. Watching the scene before her, she took in what could only be described as organised chaos. Rob, the location manager, had warned her about the hectic nature of a video shoot. He'd talked about set builders, directors, cameramen, lighting chiefs, key grips, props people, hair and make-up, costume... Flick hadn't banked on these also having assistants, and as they all milled around, unloading large vans ready to set up for the day ahead, Flick felt as excited as the young guy amongst them taking photos of everything.

She guessed he was from the band's fan club. He didn't appear as professional as everyone else and Rob had mentioned that someone might tag along. Apparently, these trips were offered to keep fan clubs sweet and were a nice way of saying thank you for their loyalty over the years. "Years." Flick realised Rob was right about Argon Fire's new fan base. Focusing on the lad concerned, he looked such a baby face. No way was he around when the band first hit the music scene.

Flick shook her head as she returned her attention to the crew, realising they were, in fact, all a tad youthful. Everyone seemed so busy and the noise level as numerous people called out instruction after instruction easily penetrated the closed windows. She didn't mind the clamour though. It was good to experience the chateau coming back to life.

"This is it," she said to herself. "The beginnings of a new start." She imagined her dad looking down on events alongside her, a big smile across his gentle face as he cheered on her venture. She felt exhilarated yet daunted at the same time. Daunted because she wasn't just leaving Matthew and her so-called marriage behind, she was saying goodbye to everything she knew.

She pictured herself back in the UK, continuing in a dead-end job, albeit enjoyable, with nothing in particular to look forward to. And, thanks to her mother's revelation that Matthew was back in town, spending her days looking over her shoulder in case she inadvertently bumped into him. It was bound to happen at some point, they lived in such a small place. In fact, it wasn't much more than a village. Staying in France gave her the time and distance she needed. It meant she could deal with him when she was good and ready, as well as on her own terms.

Flick laughed at herself. She couldn't believe how much she'd hesitated over her decision to give things here a go. For anyone else it would have been a no-brainer. It was clear that in the UK she'd be existing, whereas in France she had a future.

Thoughts of Nate formed in Flick's mind. Where did he fit in to her new life? She recalled the two of them together in his car, the concern on his face after the wild boar incident, their almost kiss. In that moment she'd so wanted their lips to connect and could still feel the disappointment when they didn't. On the other hand, she supposed she should be glad that she'd pulled her neck out. Since then, Nate hadn't just withdrawn, he'd gone in to hiding, as if what passed between them had been nothing but a huge, embarrassing mistake. "Maybe he's right." Flick looked around the room. With so much to do to the chateau, embarking on a relationship would only complicate things. Flick let out a long wistful sigh. She would've still like to have kissed him though.

She pulled herself away from the window and headed downstairs, forced to pause at the bottom as a crew member lugged a big black chest across the hall. Flick spotted her mum at the front entrance chatting on her phone.

"Don't worry," Brenda said, her tone serious. "I'll give you a ring when the coast is clear. Okay. Bye." She appeared startled by Flick's approach and immediately clicked off her phone.

"Anyone I know?" Flick indicated her mum's mobile.

"Just Julia."

"And?"

"And nothing. She wanted to know what time the band are leaving."

Flick laughed. "Leaving? They haven't even arrived yet."

"It's nothing sinister."

Flick frowned. "I didn't say it was."

"She wanted an idea of when she and the others should mobilize. There's a lot to do for the party. There's furniture to move, tables to lay out…" Her mother seemed to be garbling. "Yet more cleaning to do thanks to this lot." She pointed to the crew. "They just want a head start."

Thinking about their workload, Flick couldn't disagree. But still, she knew her mother and something didn't feel right. "Everything is okay though, isn't it?"

"What do you mean?"

"You just seem a bit on edge."

"I can't think why. I'm fine."

"And Julia?"

Brenda played with her wedding ring, twisting it around her finger. "She's fine too."

Flick scrutinised her mum's face. "So we're not becoming a bit of a nuisance? As if we're expecting too much?"

"From Julia?" Brenda asked. "Whatever gave you that idea? She's happy to help, she just doesn't want to see the band."

Flick scoffed. The way everyone else had gone on she found that hard to believe. "Why not?"

Brenda drew her mouth into a straight line. "Not everybody likes Argon Fire, Felicity. You of all people know that."

Despite not quite believing her mother, Flick tried to dismiss her unease.

"Look," Brenda said, suddenly relaxing over the whole thing. "All Julia wants out of this, is for you to succeed. And if I knew of something that would prevent that from happening, don't you think I'd tell you?"

Flick nodded. "I suppose."

"So, does this mean we can stop worrying about other people and just enjoy today's event?" Her mum offered a tender smile, encouraging Flick to cheer up with a gentle shoulder bump. "Please?"

Flick took a deep breath. What choice did she have? "It does."

"That's the spirit."

Brenda returned her attention to the crew. "Apparently this shoot has created quite a stir," she said, her enthusiasm reignited. "According to Julia, the mayor's been fielding off calls all morning. Apparently, everyone and their dog spotted the convoy of vans passing through the village. They're all dying to know what's going on."

Flick followed her mother's gaze. "I can understand the curiosity. That's a big workforce and a whole lot of equipment."

"I know. And isn't it exciting?"

Flick took in her mum's reinvigorated demeanour. The glint in her eyes and the smile on her face were as bright as a child's on Christmas morning. Despite it still being early, such was her anticipation, she'd already donned her best clothes and applied her lipstick, enough to make Flick feel bad for almost spoiling things. "It certainly is."

Brenda appeared wistful. "Do you think I'll get to meet them?"

"The band?" Like Flick needed to ask.

"I'm not talking about any of this lot, am I?"

Flick stepped back to make room for yet another crew member hauling goodness knew what kind of equipment inside. Flick apologised, not wanting to get in anyone's way; after all, this shoot was as important to her as it was to them. Unlike her mum who sought to be around to meet the infamous Argon Fire, Flick was simply showing her face should anyone need anything. She laughed at her naivety. Continuing to observe the organised chaos, both she and her mother might as well have been invisible.

She thought back to Rob's visit, appreciating why everyone here seemed to know which direction to go in and with what.

Rob had taken a tonne of photos and even sketched floor plans for people to work from. According to him, this was a role normally undertaken by someone else. On this occasion, however, time had been of the essence so he'd had no choice but to cut out the middleman. She pondered his actions for a moment; he never did explain why the rush.

"Who do you think is in charge?" Brenda asked.

"The director, I suppose."

"And that would be?"

Flick didn't have a clue. She scanned the group in front of her, her eyes resting on one particular individual. Placing her in her twenties, the woman exuded confidence and seemed to be the one doing most of the organising. "That woman there, I guess," Flick said, pointing her out.

All at once, Brenda stepped forward, setting off on a march.

"Mum, where are you going?" Flick asked, to no avail. She cringed. What on earth did her mother think she was doing?

Flick shook her head as she watched her mum accost the director. Rob had suggested they might want to go out for the day and she could see why. Her mother hadn't exactly kept quiet about her love of Argon Fire when he'd visited. He must have known from experience that she wouldn't be able to keep herself from interrupting events.

Her actions clearly didn't go down very well and Flick stifled a laugh as the director took a firm hold of her mum's arm and began leading her back to the chateau. "Perhaps you could go and have a cup of tea or something," Flick overheard her say.

It sounded more like an order than a request.

Nearing the entrance, the director turned her attention to Flick. "We still have a lot of setting up to do and the last thing I want is for someone to trip over a rogue cable."

"I understand. I'll keep her out of your hair." Flick tried to give her mum a gentle push towards the kitchen, but much to her embarrassment she refused to budge.

Thankfully, the director didn't notice. Instead she held out her hand as she introduced herself. "I'm Claire, by the way."

It was a gesture Flick was happy to accept.

"I don't know what it is about this band," the director continued. "I've never known fans like them, talk about obsessive."

"I *am* still here," Flick's mother said.

Flick had to admit that she didn't get the fascination either, forced to laugh when, as if on cue, the club photographer suddenly appeared snapping on his camera.

"And here's another one," said the director, fixing a smile on her face as he took yet another photo.

"Don't worry," Flick said, when the young chap had moved on. "I'll lock mine in if I have to."

Her mum opened her mouth to protest again, but Flick didn't give her the chance to speak. She lowered her voice and leaned in. "We're supposed to be creating a good impression, remember," she said, her eyebrows raised.

Brenda may have got the message, but she refused to hide her disappointment. Instead, she let out a long hard sigh as she turned, dragging her feet like a wronged teenager as she headed down the hall. Flick rolled her eyes. "Anyone would think I was the parent."

"I don't mean to be awful," said Claire, trying to hide her amusement. "But the quicker we get set up, the quicker we can get done." She checked her watch. "Although it looks like we're not the only ones running late." She looked at Flick. "What is it they say? Never work with children, animals and old school rock bands."

"I'm sure they'll be here soon," Flick said. "As for Mum, no doubt, she'll get over it."

Claire looked up at the building. "It's a gorgeous place you have here. I'm actually quite envious."

Flick smiled in response.

"In fact, I can't wait for the party when I can have a proper, more relaxed, look around. Anyway, I better leave you to it."

As Flick watched Claire get back to work, she felt a warm glow in her tummy. She let out a nervous giggle. Who'd have thought it? A bona fide video director feeling envious of her.

CHAPTER TWENTY-NINE

Nate stood at his living room window staring out at the lake. He half expected to see a few die-hard Argon Fire fans sneaking past to get nearer to their idols. Instead, everything was as it always was. Peaceful, quiet, uninterrupted – just the way Nate liked it.

His gaze settled on the rear of the chateau beyond and he imagined the activity taking place within its walls. It might still be early, but he knew from experience these things took a lot of setting up. The work that went in to three minutes of video footage was inconceivable to the average Joe. Sat in front of their screens, all most viewers wanted to do was enjoy the end product that came with their favourite band's latest release.

Nate wondered how Flick was coping. Was she revelling in the new experience? Or struggling with the intrusion? After all, according to Lenny video shoots were nowhere near as glamorous as some might think. He recalled when, back in the day, Lenny would complain about having to reshoot scene after scene until the director was satisfied, to the point that come the end of filming, he was sick of hearing his own song. Nate shook his head and sighed. Lenny seemed to have no idea that he'd been part of the problem. A make-up artist might have the skills to cover up the visual impact of too much sex, drugs and rock 'n' roll, but he or she certainly couldn't improve a star's resulting performance.

It felt weird to think that Lenny was just across the lake. It would be so easy to pop over and say hello, long time no see. Nate scoffed at the very idea. Despite any curiosity, it was something he had no intentions of doing. That part of his life was over. It ended the day Lenny walked out.

Nate's frustration over the whole situation rose, although he knew he only had himself to blame. He should have found another way to meet Brenda's demands. Turning to Bruce for help had never been the answer. He thought back to their last conversation about Argon Fire and the day's event.

"Does this have anything to do with Mum and that documentary?" Nate had asked. "Are you hoping to get us playing happy families again?"

"Of course not. What do you take me for?"

Bruce's denial came as no surprise.

"If you must know, it was all Lenny's idea. Argon Fire needed a location and you had one. That's all there is to it."

Why couldn't the man just be honest for once?

"You didn't exactly give me much notice, Nate. What was I supposed to do? Wait around in the hope that someone else came forward?"

Nate's back went up. "So now it's my fault?"

"What can I say? It's certainly not mine."

Nate realised he was getting nowhere, that their discussion was pointless.

"If either of you think I'm about to join in with your game, you can think again. I mean it, Bruce."

The sudden silence on the line confirmed that that had been his intention all along.

"Shit, man. When I asked for your help I told you there'd better be no funny business."

"Nate, mate. You've got this all wrong."

What else was Bruce going to say? He'd always been a manipulative bastard, there was only Nate's mother who couldn't see it. He clamped down on his jaw before he said something he'd regret, as angry at himself as he was at him.

"You are still in though, aren't you? You're not pulling out on me? I mean I did stick to my side of the bargain."

Hearing the panic in Bruce's voice was of little comfort. Unlike him, Nate had always been a man of his word. "I said I'd do it, didn't I?"

Rufus barked, but Nate continued to stand there, wrapped up in contemplation. He knew deep down that it was too easy to blame Bruce for this situation; hell, he could even blame Brenda if he wanted to. But he, alone, had to take credit, for thinking he could keep his past hidden come what may, buried away like some dirty secret. Maybe he was more like his mother than he cared to admit. Like her, he'd run away from his problems, instead of facing up to them.

A knock on the door made Rufus bark even louder and, glad of the reprieve from his thoughts, Nate turned. "Quiet, boy." Wondering who it could be, he wasn't expecting any visitors.

Opening the door, he immediately froze and unable to find his voice he stared at the person in front of him. "Lenny," he eventually said.

"In the flesh."

Nate swallowed hard. It didn't matter that his aunt had suggested something like this might happen, the man's presence still came as a shock and he continued to stand there, rooted to the spot.

"Aren't you going to invite me in?"

Remaining silent, Nate stepped aside. Almost on automatic pilot as he allowed his unwanted guest over the threshold, his mind raced as it tried to catch up with what was happening.

Nate had often played this moment out in his head, deciding what he'd say and do if he ever came face-to-face with Lenny again. He'd tell him exactly what he thought of his disappearing act all those years earlier, then explain how, as a child, Nate had blamed himself for it. He'd outline how he'd spent days, weeks and months looking back on his own behaviour, trying to pinpoint the exact action or word that had made Lenny walk out. Because in his younger mind, it had to have been his fault. Why else would Lenny not even bother to say goodbye? Nate swallowed again. Being honest, the little boy inside of him still thought he was responsible, no matter how much Nate the adult insisted otherwise.

He watched Lenny take position in the centre of the room and observed him absorb his surroundings. The man looked surprisingly well. Not just sober, but healthy. He was also a lot smarter in appearance than Nate remembered. His hair was neat and cut short, not like back in the day when it fell into a scruffy mess below his shoulders. The tight jeans had been replaced with a more comfortable and less revealing fit. Getting older suited him. It was more than his image that had changed though. Standing there, he seemed humbler, and he even had the decency to appear as awkward about this situation as Nate felt.

"Nice place," Lenny said.

Nate recalled the plush interior of his childhood home. This was nothing like it.

"I admire you," Lenny carried on, failing to disguise the nervous edge to his voice. "Sometimes I think of escaping myself, disappearing."

Nate folded his arms across his chest, wedging his feet hard against the floor. "Wouldn't be the first time, would it?" he replied, in no mood for small talk.

Lenny shot him a pained look. "I suppose I deserved that."

"What do you expect? More to the point, what do you want?"

"Straight talking, I like that."

Nate didn't care whether he liked it or not.

His guest indicated to a chair at the table. "May I?"

Nate nodded.

Taking a seat, Lenny rested his arms on the table and clasped his hand. "In answer to your question," he said, forced to clear his throat. "I'm here to make sure you're okay. And to say I'm sorry."

Nate let out a burst of mock laughter. After all this time, did Lenny really expect him to believe that? "I warned Bruce not to pull a stunt like this."

"Bruce?"

Nate glowered. Did the two of them actually think he was that stupid?

"What? You think he's the reason I'm here?"

Yes, it would seem they did.

"Isn't he?" Nate asked. "Him with all these grand plans for Mum in the pipeline and you who just happens to have a new album or whatever it is to promote. It all seems a bit too convenient to be anything else, wouldn't you say?"

Lenny looked at him directly. "You know me better than that, Nate."

Nate held his gaze. "Do I?"

"Look, I don't expect you to make this easy for me, but you can at least sit down and hear me out." Lenny gestured to the seat opposite. "Please?"

Nate approached the table and sat down. He watched Lenny take a deep breath as if preparing some grand speech that Nate didn't want to hear.

"I know I shouldn't have run out on you like I did. I should've tried to explain what was happening, but..." His words trailed off.

"Go on."

"Oh I don't know, I was a different person back then. Immature, selfish, too out of it to know any better, call it what you want." He kept his eyes on his fidgeting hands throughout. "But I did love you and your mum, you have to know that."

Nate sneered.

"It's just that things were always so volatile between me and her. We weren't always good together."

Nate didn't need reminding. He easily recalled how much of a pendulum their relationship had been. Everything fun and frolics, as if life was one big party as it swung one way. Only for things to turn nasty as it swung the other. The insults and accusations that were traded, the glasses that were thrown. At times, it was like living in a war zone and they were both as bad as each other. Nate took in Lenny's pathetic manner. If he wanted sympathy he'd come to the wrong place. "That's because you were both drunks."

"Tell me about it." Lenny's expression turned even more pensive. "We did agree to go to rehab. A few times, in fact. We even got as far as booking ourselves in. Not at the same place, most centres don't allow that. I often wonder if that's the reason your mum always refused to go in the end. As if she didn't have the strength to fight it alone."

Nate felt his hackles rise. "So you're blaming her?"

"No, no, of course not. You misunderstand." Finally, Lenny lifted his gaze to look Nate square in the face. "But surely you remember how bad things became. Neither of us could take much more, someone had to do something. Anyway, I got it into my head that the two of you would be better off without me. I thought with me out of the way, your mum would get the help she needed."

"Yeah? And look how well that turned out." Nate knew he was being flippant, but he couldn't seem to help himself. He let the room descend into silence for a moment, before speaking again. "And me? What was I? Collateral damage?"

Lenny sighed. "The way I saw it, you needed your mum. But she could never be there for you while she still drank, not properly." He fell quiet, as if drifting back into the past for a moment. Then just as quickly he was back in the present. "I suppose given everything that's happened, then, yes, Nate. That's exactly what you were."

Whatever response Nate had expected, he hadn't anticipated one quite so honest and Lenny's words stung like a slap in the face. His bluntness stunned him into silence.

"You have to understand," Lenny carried on. "I wasn't thinking straight back then. Jesus, the amount of crap in my system I'm surprised I could think at all. I loved you both so much, you have to believe that. I'd have done anything for you."

"Except stay."

"If I could turn back the clock I would." Lenny leaned back in his seat. "I wrote you a letter, you know. More than one actually."

"Really? Because I didn't get them."

"That's because I didn't post them. I felt too ashamed for abandoning you like I did, leaving you to pick up the pieces." Lenny sat forward again, talking more to himself than Nate. "You were just a child, that wasn't your job."

"You mean the job of putting my mother into the recovery position night after night because she'd passed out? Or making sure I didn't fall asleep after the fact, so I could step in if she started choking on her own vomit? You're damn right, it wasn't."

Nate could see the guilt on Lenny's face. He could see his embarrassment at not knowing how to respond. Maybe he was sorry, after all. Not that Nate supposed it mattered. Whatever it was that Lenny wanted from him, he wasn't prepared to give. As far as Nate was concerned, this was all a bit too little, too late. "So why now? Why come here?"

Lenny shrugged. "Bruce put the word out that you needed some help and I saw an opportunity, a chance to say sorry. I figured if I didn't do it now, I probably never would. Call it fate, call it coincidence, call it collusion, it doesn't really matter. I've said my piece."

Nate watched him rise to his feet.

"And now I shall bid my farewell. The quicker we shoot this video the quicker we get back to the UK. Like you said, we have a song to promote."

He smiled, but Nate could see it wasn't a happy gesture. His face was tinged with a mixture of sadness and hope. Not that Nate responded to either of his guest's feelings. With his own emotions all over the place, how could he? He simply joined him on his feet and accompanied him to the door.

"Don't ever be a fool like me," Lenny said as he opened it to leave. "If you're lucky enough to fall in love, make sure you hang on to it, no matter what. Leaving you and your mum is something I'll always regret. I often think about what could have been."

"You've never moved on?"

He let out a hollow laugh. "Have you?"

Nate didn't answer. He simply watched Lenny head for his car.

Opening his vehicle door, Lenny stopped before climbing in. "Have you heard the new song, by the way?" Without waiting for an answer, he reached inside and pulled out a CD, before tossing it in Nate's direction. "You should listen to it."

Seeing it hurl towards him, a reflex action kicked in and Nate automatically reached out to catch it.

"Nice save," Lenny said.

Nate continued to stand there as Lenny got behind the wheel, started the engine and drove away.

Any frustration Nate felt turned to melancholy. He never thought he'd feel almost as sorry for Lenny as he did for himself.

He looked down at the CD in his hands, surprised to see a picture of his mum looking back at him. He took a deep breath. "Do you have any idea about the hurt you've caused?"

CHAPTER THIRTY

With the party looming, Flick undertook a final check of the chateau in readiness. She soaked up the atmosphere as she went, which felt in stark contrast to that during the video shoot. With no mass of people racing around, no stacks of equipment crowding the place and no music blaring, it was as if the band and crew had never been there. Everyone had left the building exactly how they'd found it, to the point that anyone would think she'd imagined the whole thing.

A calmness had settled and she felt at peace as she wandered along the upstairs landing. Entering one of the bedrooms, she wanted to believe that it was her father's presence surrounding her, that he was there somehow, enjoying the adventure alongside his wife and daughter. Of course, the video shoot shenanigans weren't over just yet, she acknowledged, they had to get the evening out of the way before they could truly relax and plan for the future. And catching sight of herself in one of the mirrors, she just hoped that she looked the part of chateau owner even if she didn't quite feel it yet.

She smoothed down her crimson woollen dress and checked out her matching kitten heels, examining her reflection face front, before turning side on and then back again. For once, Flick actually liked what she saw. For the first time in a long time, she felt confident and, ready to give the evening her all, she was glad she'd ditched her usual black. She took in her red attire again. It felt symbolic, as if she'd come out of mourning. It was a statement to say she'd finally moved on. "What do you think, Dad? Will I do?"

Making her way downstairs, she popped her head into the reception room where she planned to serve the food and drink.

Flick still didn't like the idea of using pasting tables but thanks to Julia's crisp white linen, at least they were well hidden. And, naturally, once Jess's delicious food was in place everyone would be too busy eating to notice anything else. "As long as they don't miss the view." Looking out of the window, Flick almost pinched herself. Was this really all hers? Was this new life in France really happening?

Flick's ears pricked as the sound of voices filtered down the hallway and heading to the kitchen, she wasn't surprised to find Dee fully prepared and ready for action.

"Good, you're here," she said to Flick. "Let's get started."

Flick watched her pull out a ream of A4 sheets from her bag, happy to accept as she passed one each to both her and her mother.

"These are the details of the chateau, complete with photos, which we'll give to anyone and everyone who'll take them. I find it's always good for potential customers, in this case yours and not mine, to have something to keep referring to."

Flick looked down at Dee's handiwork. "These are stunning."

"The place looks gorgeous," Brenda said.

Dee dismissed the compliments with a wave of her hand. "Now when you're talking to people, focus on the room sizes, the original features et cetera. And if anyone dares to go down a negative route, after all, we can't hide the fact that this place isn't exactly *Versailles*…"

"Not yet, it's not," Brenda said.

"Simply point out that the building is a blank canvas. Draw their attention to this…" She held up an A4 sheet. "And tell them that if it looks this good now, imagine how fabulous it could look once one of their set directors gets their hands on it."

Flick giggled. It was clear why Dee was good at her job. "Remind me never to go house-hunting with you." Flick turned to her mother. "No wonder you bought this place. You and Dad didn't stand a chance."

Dee paused to look at her audience. "So, we all know what we're doing?"

"We do," Flick replied.

"Definitely," Brenda said.

"Good." Dee suddenly relaxed, her eyes full of eagerness as she put her professionalism to one side. "Now tell me about the video shoot. How did it go?"

Like Brenda needed asking twice. "It was great fun," she said, coming over all animated. "I'm surprised we didn't see you yesterday though. I'm surprised we didn't see any of you."

"Oh, we all tried to get in on things, believe you me. Only to be thwarted at every turn thanks to that mayor of ours."

Flick looked to her mum, glad to know she wasn't the only one who didn't have a clue what Dee was talking about.

"You mean no one told you? He closed off the road. Apparently, he had so many calls from people wanting to know what was going on, he didn't want to risk a bunch of gatecrashers turning up."

"That was kind of him," Flick said.

Dee shot her a look. "Kind is not the word I used."

Flick laughed. "Trying to keep this one under control was enough for me." She indicated her mother.

"I wasn't that bad."

"Mum, we had to more or less lock you in the kitchen. Goodness knows how much disruption you would have caused otherwise." Flick turned to Dee. "Honestly, she wouldn't settle until she'd met every single band member. Talk about embarrassing."

Dee gasped. "You talked to them?" She scrambled for a seat at the table. "Sit," she said to Brenda. "Tell me everything."

With her mum happy to oblige, Flick rolled her eyes and left the two women to it. Checking her watch, Jess and Pete were due to arrive so she headed down the hall ready to greet them.

Much to her surprise, they were already unloading the hearse by the time she opened the front door.

"Just in time." Pete pulled a box of wine bottles from the back of the vehicle. "Where do you want this?"

"In the hall please, the room on the right."

"You two look very smart," Flick said to Jess, taking in their matching white shirt and black trouser dress code. "But you didn't have to come up with a uniform, you're not the hired help."

"It wouldn't hurt for people to think we are, though would it?" Jess said. "Besides, it was either these or a couple of Café Ange T-shirts that Pete was all ready to get printed up. I know they'd already been mentioned, so I made him settle for a few business cards to pass around."

Flick laughed. "That's fine, although the T-shirts would have been okay too."

Jess handed her a large foil-wrapped tray of delicious smelling goodies before grabbing another one to carry herself. "Anyway, what about you? That dress is stunning, red is definitely your colour."

Appreciating the compliment, Flick took a peek inside the car. "How much stuff have you brought?" she asked, before leading the way inside.

"Too much," Pete said, passing them on his way back out for another crate of wine.

"You can talk," Jess said. "There's enough alcohol in the back of that thing to run a pub."

Flick continued to help unload the hearse. By the time the three of them had finished, it was clear they could forget the public house, they'd brought enough sustenance to feed and water a small army. "I can't wait to see what's on these plates," Flick said, taking in the sea of foil that covered the line of tables.

"Me too," Nate's aunt said, suddenly appearing in the doorway.

Flick smiled. "Julia, lovely to see you."

"I hope you don't mind me letting myself in, but the door was open." She bobbed her head back out into the hall, stretching her neck as if checking out who else was there, before beginning a round of *faire la bise*.

Stepping forward, to say this was a custom that Flick usually found uncomfortable, that day it felt nothing of the sort, her own willingness to participate coming as a pleasant surprise. Julia's responding hug felt tense, however, and her smile appeared strained, causing Flick to yet again wonder if she'd expected too much from her.

"*Bonjour. Il y a quelqu'un?* Is anybody home?" Gigi suddenly entered the room carrying two huge baskets of breads and pastries. "*Pour toi*," she said to Flick.

Distracted from her concerns, Flick stepped forward to retrieve them. Each baguette still felt warm and smelled divine. "*Merci*. That's what I call freshly baked."

"I have *fromages* in the car," added Gigi. "The best cheeses *Bretagne* has to offer." She looked to Pete, tilting her head slightly. "*S'il te plait*. Would you mind?"

"Not at all," he replied, heading straight out to get them.

"And I have glasses and crockery to bring in," Julia called after him.

"On it."

"Now where are the others," Julia continued. "Gossiping over the video shoot, no doubt. Or should I say singing the praises of that band."

Still troubled, Flick noted the disdain that accompanied her words. "In the kitchen," she replied, directing everyone down the hall.

As predicted, Dee and Brenda were still discussing Argon Fire.

"But I was so hoping to meet them." Dee sighed like a lovelorn teenager.

"The band will not be here?" Gigi asked, stopping short.

Jess also paused, disappointed, and tutting at the very idea of them being a no show, she plonked herself down in a chair at the table.

"They have back-to-back interviews and appearances scheduled," Flick's mum said then looked to Julia. "They're on their way back to the UK."

Her mother's pointed tone told Flick there was more to the statement than a simple explanation, forcing her to again to wonder what was going on between the two. She looked from one woman to the other, her eyes narrowing as she took in Julia's response; her shoulders seemed to slump a little, as if she could finally relax. "Is everything all right?"

"Fine," Brenda replied. "Why?"

Julia fixed a smile on her face. "What could possibly be wrong?"

"I don't know. That's why I'm asking."

"I'm sorry," Julia said, finally coming clean. "You're right. All hasn't been well lately."

Flick knew it.

"Although as it turns out, I've been fretting unnecessarily. It's just that we all know how important tonight is and while dealing with the crew is one thing, having to cope with a rock band like that... Who knows how the night would have gone?"

"I suppose," Flick said, not quite sure whether or not to believe her.

"Honestly," Julia continued, as if determined to make her point. "Things will be so much more relaxed without Argon Fire here."

"But not half as much fun," Dee said.

"I agree," Jess said.

"Me too," Gigi said.

"Now, where are we with the preparations?" Julia asked, ignoring all three.

As everyone began discussing what still needed to be done, Flick continued to feel as if there was something her mother and Nate's aunt weren't telling her. But whatever it was, much to her dismay, they were determined to keep it to themselves. She told herself to let it go. After all, she knew she wasn't the only one under pressure, everyone present had invested something in that night's event, and were probably all a bit stressed as a result.

Or maybe you're simply being paranoid? Flick thought, which she considered understandable. The last big occasion she'd been a part of was her wedding day and look how well that had turned out.

CHAPTER THIRTY-ONE

As Rufus lay sleeping in front of the blazing wood burner, Nate sat in silence at the table. He stared at the discarded CD in front of him, an unwanted gift from an unwelcome visitor. Nate sneered. Even without the photo of his mum gracing the front he would have known the song was about her. Why else would Lenny suggest Nate listen to it? Sliding it out of arm's reach, that was the last thing he planned on doing.

He wished he'd handed Brenda a wad of cash instead of trying to be clever. She hadn't asked for money, but it would've made his life a whole lot easier if she had. He wasn't just tied to Bruce's up and coming plans, Nate's past had invaded his home, his sanctuary.

He got up from his seat and headed for the window. The nights were certainly drawing in. It might still be early, but it was black out there, the only hint of life being the bright lights of the chateau. Lit up against the darkness, it looked stunning, like an image in one of the fancy calendars sold to visiting tourists.

He wondered how it was all going over there. Were the video crew so enamoured by their hosts and the venue, that they couldn't wait to get back and tell all their colleagues, friends and family everything about the place? He hoped so. Otherwise the predicament he found himself in would all be for nothing. The property developer would move in and his home would become a prison. Not only that, Flick deserved some success after everything she'd been through. He was definitely cheering her on.

Thinking back to when he'd first met her, Nate laughed at his own stupidity. He should have known the second he clapped eyes on her that his life would never be the same again. She didn't look at him the way most people did. There was no awe in her eyes, no wondering, and there certainly weren't any pound signs. There'd been a hint of recognition from somewhere in the back of her mind, but she didn't push it. She didn't question his feeble explanation, she accepted it. She took him how she found him. As the man he'd become, not the man he once was.

He thought about what Lenny had said about holding on to someone, recalling his warning to never let love go once he'd found it. Flick had certainly made an impact that he'd never experienced before. But was it love? Having kept people at a distance for so long, he couldn't be sure what his emotions were telling him. When it came to Flick, they seemed to be all over the place, getting to know her both enlivened and scared him. And what about her? Did she feel anything for him?

He felt a sudden urge to go and see her and, before he could change his mind, he raced over to the door, grabbing his jacket and a torch off a coat hook. He knew he was taking a risk, but for the first time in a long time he didn't care if someone recognised him. He didn't care about the protective wall he'd built around himself. As far as he was concerned, if he and Flick did have feelings for each other, there was only one way to find out.

Rufus lifted his head at the commotion.

"Stay, boy," Nate said to the Jack Russell, before letting himself out into the night.

Making his way through the trees, Nate didn't have a clue what he was going to say to Flick once he found her. And the nearer he got to the chateau, the more his heart galloped in anticipation.

Finally approaching the building, he headed round to the front door. It was open and he paused, the consequences of being outed beginning to dawn. He took a deep breath and composed himself. Having come this far, there was no point backing out now. "Come on, Nate. You can do this."

Another breath later and he stepped inside.

A crowd had gathered in one of the front reception rooms and standing in the doorway, he had to stretch up onto his toes to scan the faces within. He felt nervous as he waited for someone to recognise him. The disdain he felt for the people in front of him. These were the professionals who'd ruined his mother's life, documenting and commentating on her meteoric rise and magnificent fall, milking every last detail for their own ends. His growing discomfort turned physical. Beginning to feel a tad hot, even from his position, he could feel the heat in the room thanks to the mass of bodies within. Flick was worth the anxiety and rising temperature though and as his eyes continued to search in an attempt to locate her, he continued to go unnoticed.

Unable to quite believe what was happening, for the first time in years he felt invisible. A broad smile spread across his face. He felt like a nobody.

Finally, he spotted Dee, her arms gesticulating as she chatted to some chap who appeared to hang on her every word. Knowing her, she was giving him the hard sell and as with most of her buyers, he was falling for it. "Good on you, Dee," Nate said to himself.

"Excuse me," said a female voice that Nate couldn't quite place over the noise.

Whoever it belonged to, it came with an accompanying nudge, a physical request for him to step out of the way. He dropped from his toes and turned round, pleased to find it was Jess trying to get through with a tray of fancy-looking canapés. "Those look good," he said. Despite enjoying the anonymity, he felt glad of the friendly face.

"Nate. What are you doing here? Everyone thought you weren't coming."

"I didn't intend to."

She proffered the tray, her expression suggesting he might try one of her wares, but he declined with a shake of his head. As delicious as its contents looked, he felt too nervous to attempt eating. He took another look around the room. "It seems to be going well. Everyone certainly looks happy."

"So far, so good. I'm just keeping everything crossed it stays that way." She smiled, giving him a knowing look. "If you're hoping to see Flick, she's in the kitchen."

"Is she?" Nate tried to appear cool, calm and collected. "I suppose I should go and say hello, this is her party."

"I suppose you should," Jess replied, her accompanying grin letting him know he wasn't fooling anyone. "And I'd better get back to it," she added, still smiling as she headed into the melee.

Nate watched her for a moment, at the same time listening to snippets of the conversations taking place around him. From what he could hear, it was clear the party was having the desired effect, everyone seemed to love the chateau. He smiled as he made his way down the hall to the kitchen, it looked like Flick was staying.

Entering the room, his ears immediately pricked thanks to the sound of Brenda's voice. He couldn't see her through the hoi polloi, but she was definitely coming through loud and clear. She seemed to be outlining some ambitious plan to host big budget films and remembering the last time she'd been in this position, Nate laughed. It felt like a case of *déjà vu*, making him wonder if Flick knew about these grand plans too.

He scanned the crowd and spotted Julia also busy talking to one of the guests. Taking in her broad smile and confident stance, she was no doubt another one giving it the hard sell. But where was Flick? Quickly casting his eyes over the rest of the room, she didn't seem to be anywhere in sight.

"Nate!" his aunt suddenly called.

Re-catching his attention, she appeared to make her excuses before joining him. "What a surprise. Is everything okay?"

"I thought I'd come and see how things are going." It was as good an excuse as any.

Aunt Julia leaned in to give him a hug, making sure to lower her voice as she spoke. "Don't worry, you're safe. The band isn't here."

"I know. Lenny said they were shipping out early."

Julia pulled back. "You've spoken to him?"

As soon has his words were out Nate could've kicked himself. Yes, he'd fully intended on telling her about Lenny's visit. He looked around. Just once the excitement of the party had died down. "He turned up at the house wanting to talk things over."

"When?"

"Just before the video shoot."

"And you didn't ring me?"

"At the time? What would've been the point?"

As much as she tried to hide her strength of feeling, his aunt fumed. "I told Bruce to keep him away. If he's upset you..."

"He hasn't. I'm fine." He could see she didn't believe him. "Honestly. If anything, I ended up feeling a bit sorry for the bloke."

"Sorry? For him?"

"Sounds daft, doesn't it?" Nate's gaze wandered as he resumed his search for Flick. Although he still didn't have a clue what he was going to say once he'd found her.

"Nate, are you sure everything's all right?" Julia asked, his sudden lack of attention failing to go unnoticed.

"Look, I know it's important, but can we talk about this later?" He watched his aunt's concern turn to bemusement. "I'm here to see Flick."

A glint suddenly appeared in her eyes and as was the case with Jess, a knowing look swept across Julia's face. "I see."

Nate shook his head. What was it with these women?

His aunt laughed. "If you must know, she was heading for the courtyard the last I saw."

"Thanks." Nate kissed her cheek. "And don't worry about Lenny, I'll catch up with you in a bit, yeah?" Nate didn't wait for an answer. Instead, he left his aunt standing there as he squeezed his way through the crowd to the patio doors.

As Nate slipped outside, the cold night air hit him full force. As did the image of Flick. Standing at the wall that separated the chateau from the lily pad lake, she looked beautiful under the moonlight, stunning, in fact, and so deep in thought he wasn't sure if he should disturb her. Watching her, he shivered and realising that without a coat she must be freezing, he took off his jacket. "Flick," he said, sounding his arrival.

She smiled as she turned. "Nate, what are you doing here? I thought parties weren't your thing."

He stepped towards her. "Here," he said, holding his jacket aloft. "Put this on." She appeared reluctant to take it, but he left his arm outstretched until she did as she was told.

"Thank you," she said, placing it over her shoulders. "It is a bit chilly out here, isn't it?"

"Everyone seems to be having a great time though." Nate indicated inside.

"Thankfully. Mum's having an absolute ball."

Nate laughed. "I heard." He watched her smile fade slightly and he suddenly felt concerned. "And you? Are you enjoying all this?"

"To tell you the truth, I'm finding it a bit nerve-wracking. I'm probably worrying over nothing, I mean everyone's saying the right things. And Claire, she's the director, has even mentioned something about an agency she knows that specialises in locations. Apparently, the chateau would make a great addition to their books."

"Sounds promising."

"But what if she's just being kind? What if they're all just being kind?"

"In that industry? You've got to be kidding."

Flick smiled and Nate wondered if she thought he was simply being kind too.

"Time will tell, I suppose," she said, returning her attention to the lake.

A companionable silence descended as they stared out at the water; the quiet only broken up every now and then by the tooting of an owl. Standing there, Nate knew he should say something, talk to her about how he felt, but summoning up the required courage proved harder than he'd imagined.

"Still think you've made the right decision?" he eventually asked.

"I do, yes. This place is what I needed. A clean break, a challenge."

"Well you certainly have one of those." He looked back to the building. "Although considering how long it's been stood empty it's in surprisingly good nick."

"The neighbours aren't bad either."

Despite them being under moonlight, Nate still saw her blushes. He liked that. Looking down at his feet, he also liked the fact that he was blushing too.

"I thought you might be avoiding me," she carried on. "After the other day."

She was right, of course, that's exactly what he'd been doing. He'd wanted to call round, but every time he considered it embarrassment took over. He'd picture himself, head tilted and lips poised in anticipation, only for the moment to be ruined by a sudden squeal of pain instead of a pleasurable moan. He might be out of practice, but when it came to such advances that wasn't the kind of response he was used to. Then again, Flick wasn't the kind of woman he was used to either.

"Obviously you wouldn't be able to avoid me altogether," Flick carried on. "We're neighbours, so we're bound to come across each other once in a while..."

As he listened to Flick's ramblings, Nate once again felt a desire to kiss her. Indeed, if he was honest, the desire had never left him.

"I just thought you might be avoiding this." She turned to face him, indicating to the small gap between them. "You know, just you and me."

"How is the whiplash, by the way?"

His interruption finally silenced her. She put a hand up to her neck. "It wasn't whiplash," she said, caressing her skin. "I'd just pulled a muscle."

Nate felt his pulse quicken. She really did have the most beautiful neck.

"The pain only lasted a couple of days..."

She also had the most mesmerising eyes.

"And it was gone."

As she looked back at him, Nate held her gaze as he gently lowered her hand. "I'm glad to hear it," he said. Stepping forward slightly, he shut down what space there had been between them. "Shall we try again?"

Suddenly silent, Flick nodded, appearing as nervous about this as he felt. His hands shook as he raised them to cup her face, before slowly bringing their now-parted lips together.

What began as tentative, soon became passionate, before their tongues settled into a perfect rhythm. He wrapped his arms around her. Her lips were as soft and luscious as he'd imagined. It was a kiss that Nate and his body never wanted to end.

CHAPTER THIRTY-TWO

Flick had spent the last few days walking on air. The video shoot was a success and the feedback from the wrap party had been excellent; everyone present exclaimed how much they loved the chateau. They'd all gone back to the UK ready to tell anyone who'd listen about the wonderful venue they'd found, and Claire, the shoot director, had certainly been true to her word. Much to Flick's surprise, the agency Claire had mentioned had already been in touch and seemed very keen to move things forward.

Then there was Nate.

Flick could still see the intensity in his eyes as he gazed into her own. No one had ever looked at her like that before, not even Matthew. She could still feel Nate's hands as they touched her face, then his muscular arms as he wrapped them around her. And that kiss. She so hadn't wanted it to end. Little wings flapped around in her tummy. She couldn't wait to see him again…

"Earth to Flick," Brenda said.

Flick snapped out of reverie, in time to see her mum, notepad at the ready, put down her pen. "Sorry?"

"I can probably guess what's on your mind. Or more to the point, *who*."

"That obvious, eh?" Flick smiled, letting out a long dreamy sigh. "He's asked me on a date, you know."

Brenda jolted, suddenly extra attentive. "And I'm only just hearing about this?"

Flick laughed. "When have I had the chance to tell you anything? We've been so busy with this place, cleaning up after the party, answering emails… Plus trying to come up with a schedule of works for all the jobs that need doing around here." She indicated to her mum's notepad. "The money from the video shoot might be good but we still have to prioritise." She could see that her mother knew she was lying, that she'd actually chosen to keep this snippet of information to herself. But she didn't care. She felt like a teenager who'd gotten her first boyfriend. Every time she thought about Nate she came over all warm and tingly. It was a feeling she'd wanted to keep to herself for a while, as if she needed to protect it.

"And do you plan on going on this date?"

"Of course, why wouldn't I?"

Brenda frowned. "Are you sure that's a good idea?"

Her mother's response surprised her. The woman had been banging on for months about Flick needing to move on with her life. She'd assumed her mum would be pleased that Matthew and her non-existent marriage had been consigned to the past.

"Don't get me wrong, I like Nate, I really do."

"So, what's the problem?"

Brenda took a deep intake of breath, as if getting ready to say something only to decide against it. She suddenly smiled. "There isn't one. Don't mind me, I'm worrying over nothing. As long as you're happy, that's all that counts."

Flick's phone rang. Checking the number, it was one of her co-workers from the café back in the UK. Rather than answer she set her mobile to silent, preferring to let it ring out as she returned her attention to her mother. "I am happy. For the first time in a long time."

"And when is this date?"

Flick grinned. "Saturday. Although I have no idea what he's planning, which means I haven't a clue what to wear. Do I go formal? Do I go casual?"

Brenda smiled and shook her head. "I'm sure you'll find something suitable."

Flick paused before speaking again. "Thanks, Mum."

"What for?"

"I know I keep saying it, but for everything. None of this would be happening if it weren't for you and Dad."

Brenda reached over and squeezed her hand. "Shall we?" she said, letting go in favour of her pen. "This jobs list isn't going to write itself."

As Flick and her mum settled down to get on with the task at hand, a loud knocking on the front door interrupted them. "Who could that be?" Flick asked, getting up from her seat.

Brenda shrugged. "We're not expecting anyone, are we?"

Flick left her mum hovering in the kitchen doorway. As she walked down the hall, she secretly hoped it was Nate, as keen to see her as she was him. She looked down at her appearance, wishing she'd tidied herself up a bit just in case. But opening the huge wooden door, her smile immediately froze. She felt the colour drain from her face as she stared at the unexpected caller. "Matthew?" she said, not quite able to believe her eyes.

"Flick."

CHAPTER THIRTY-THREE

S tanding at the door staring at Matthew, Flick's mind raced with questions. What did he want? How did he know where to find her? She hadn't seen or heard from him in months, so why seek her out now?

"Aren't you going to invite me in?"

Flick turned to look at her mum, who appeared equally as stunned at the sight of their unexpected guest. However, not knowing how best to respond, Flick simply trained her gaze back on Matthew. Keeping her silence, what she wanted to do was slam the door in his face, but she felt too shocked to move let alone speak.

Not that any of this seemed to matter to him, as rather than wait for an answer, Matthew stepped straight over the threshold.

"Can we talk?" He looked at Flick's mum and then back to her. "In private."

Even from Flick's position, she could hear her mother sigh, before taking the hint and marching down the hall towards them. As she grabbed her coat off the hook, Flick could see the fury in her mother's eyes. Understandably so in her opinion.

Brenda stopped, fixing her stare on Matthew. "You've got some bloody nerve." After a moment, she turned her attention to Flick, her voice at once softening. "I need some fresh air now anyway."

Flick nodded. Suddenly feeling a tad nauseous, she could have done with some too.

"Will you be all right?" her mother asked.

Flick took a deep breath to steady herself and nodded again.

"I've got my phone if you need me."

Brenda barged passed Matthew, and slamming the door shut as she left, the resulting boom sent an echo down the hall as it bounced off the walls. Her action seemed to surprise Matthew, but Flick more than appreciated her mother's strength of feeling and she certainly wasn't going to make excuses or apologise for it, especially when her mum had been the one left to pick up the pieces after *his* disappearance.

Flick indicated to the kitchen. Following Matthew down the hall, her pulse refused to slow. Her mother was right, he did have some nerve.

"May I?" Matthew pointed to a chair.

"I suppose." Flick took the seat opposite.

"You look well."

As she continued to watch him, she couldn't believe that after everything he'd done he'd choose a statement so banal as his opening gambit. She might not have accepted it, but he could have at least begun with an apology. Then again, wherever he'd been the last months he clearly hadn't been losing sleep, because although she wished he didn't, Flick had to admit he looked well too. She knew it was intentional, that he'd purposefully made the effort, as if looking good might increase his chances of getting whatever it was he wanted. Saying that, she scoffed, his image had always been important to him. In all the years Flick had known him, he'd spent more time in the bathroom getting ready for a night out than she'd ever done.

Flick felt a mix of confusion, frustration and, just like her mum, anger, as he easily glanced around the room. This was not how she'd envisaged their next meeting. She'd wanted to see him on her terms and in her own time. She felt hijacked into a discussion she wasn't mentally prepared for. He'd caught her off guard. Flick realised this was something else he'd always done – put his own needs first. He probably hadn't bothered to consider how turning up like this would affect her.

She knew she only had herself to blame. She should never have told her colleagues back at the café in the UK exactly where she was. All Matthew had to do was turn on his boyish charm and they'd have readily given up her location; although to be fair, she hadn't exactly asked them to keep her whereabouts a secret. She hadn't expected Matthew to try to find her.

"You didn't have to track me down in person," she said. "You could have said all you need to say via a solicitor."

"A solicitor?"

"You know, the person you hire to get you through a divorce."

Met with silence, Flick glared at him, struggling to keep a lid on her emotions. "Why else would you be here? Married life obviously isn't for you. The fact that you did a runner on your wedding day proved that. And while we're on the subject, just answer me one question – *Why?* Why not just tell me you didn't want to go through with it? Hell, why not just leave me standing at the alter if you had to?"

She continued to look him square on, holding her head high, as she waited for him to answer, but he refused to meet her gaze. Instead, he stared at his hands resting on the table. *Coward!* she thought.

"It's hard to explain."

Flick refused to budge on the issue. She didn't just want answers, after everything he'd done to her, she deserved them. "Try me."

He swallowed hard before speaking. "I was scared, I suppose. I felt under too much pressure."

Flick's eyes widened. "Pressure? About what, getting married?" She'd heard it all. "Because it was you who asked me, remember?"

"I know. And I shouldn't have."

"No. You shouldn't." Despite this being an understatement, at least they agreed on something. "How is Sarah, by the way?"

At last, Matthew looked up. "That was a mistake."

"I think you'll find it was more than that." As far as Flick was concerned, a mistake was putting sugar in her coffee, or a pink bra in the laundry amongst the whites. As for his dalliance with Sarah, Flick couldn't think of a remotely adequate word. She felt her blood begin to boil, feeling her embarrassment over the whole thing as if it were only yesterday. "Do you know how humiliating it all was? It wasn't enough for you to disappear like you did, oh no, you had to take one of the bridesmaids with you?" She closed her eyes for a second, trying to calm herself down. "So, where is she?" Flick scoffed. "How is she?"

Matthew shrugged. "I don't know and I don't care. Anyway, this isn't about her."

"Isn't it?"

"I told you, she was a mistake."

"Just like our marriage?"

"That's not what I said."

Flick bit down on her lips, not sure if she could listen to any more.

"Nothing happened between us, you know."

Flick raised her eyebrows. Did he really think she was that stupid?

"I knew as soon as we were out the door that she wasn't the answer."

"So, what? You dumped her as well?"

He shifted in his seat, enough to tell Flick that, yes, he had.

"Unbelievable."

"I'm not proud of any of it."

Flick sneered.

"And I really did want to marry you. Just not then. It wasn't the right time."

She folded her arms tight across her chest. "Again, you asked me."

"You were so upset with what was happening to your dad, it was like watching you fall apart. I just wanted you to be happy, to have a reason to smile."

Flick thought back to that awful time. Her dad was her hero, a man capable of anything. He was always so emotionally and physically strong. Then one day, all his strength went, just like that. Seeing him so vulnerable had been devastating and she couldn't count the number of times she prayed for him to get well. As for Matthew's proposal, it *had* shone a light into all of the darkness. Of course, back then she'd thought he really did want to spend the rest of his life with her. She'd thought that her father's condition had reminded Matthew about what was important, hence his need to show Flick how much he loved her. How could she have been so foolish?

"So, you felt sorry for me? You asked me to marry you out of pity?"

"Come on, Flick, stop twisting my words."

She sighed. How else was she supposed to interpret it all?

"I just hated seeing you like that. I wanted to do something to help. And then your dad died and things got worse."

Flick's back straightened and her hackles rose. "What's Dad got to do with any of this? Please tell me you're not about to blame him for your actions?"

"Of course not. The problem was you."

"Me?" Flick had heard everything.

"You became so needy," Matthew said.

"Excuse me?"

"I don't know how else to describe it. You weren't eating properly, you cried all the time, like you hadn't done enough of that already. Then after the funeral, instead of trying to get on with things you just gave up."

"I was grieving."

"I know that. But I felt like your carer, not your future husband."

Flick knew her dad's death had hit her hard and that she'd struggled to get back to normality. And, yes, she appreciated she'd probably leant on Matthew for support. But wasn't that what partners did in times of need?

"And then when you did sort yourself out, our wedding became more about your parents than us. You kept going on about their perfect marriage, insisting ours would be the same."

Flick stared at him, incredulous. "That's because I thought it would be."

"Nobody's perfect, Flick. No relationship is perfect."

"Just because your mum and dad couldn't make things work."

"And just because yours could."

Flick fell momentarily silent. Despite all the crap pouring out of his mouth, she could see he had a point there at least.

"It all got too much. Our life together was never going to live up to your expectations. We're us. Me and you, not them."

"None of this explains why you went through with the wedding though, does it? Or why you did a runner after the fact."

"No, it doesn't. And I'm sorry. I should have talked to you, expressed how I was feeling."

Flick waited for him to continue, but he chose to do nothing of the sort. Instead, he sat there playing the innocent, as if he were the victim. She waited some more, before her patience ran out. "It seems you've said what you came to say." She rose to her feet. "So now you can leave."

Her suggestion appeared to be met with surprise.

"And as I stated earlier," she continued. "You really didn't have to come all this way to speak to me. Please ensure any future contact is made through the proper channels."

Matthew remained seated. "Why would I do that?"

"Because that's what usually happens when two people divorce."

"I'm not here to talk about a divorce, Flick."

"Divorce, annulment, call it what you want, Matthew. It makes no difference to me as long as we get it sorted."

"But I don't want any of those things."

Flick had had enough. She'd given him more of her time than he deserved already. "Then what do you want?" she asked, wishing he'd just leave once and for all.

"For us to get back together."

Flick fell silent. She sat back down, unable to believe what she'd just heard. "For us to what?"

"Look, I know how stupid I've been. How selfish I've been. Like I said, I panicked, I buckled under the pressure of having to try to be perfect, when Lord knows none of us are. But I never stopped loving you and I've missed you these last few months like you wouldn't believe. Please, just give me another chance. Give us another chance."

Flick listened to his heartfelt plea, saw the desperation in his eyes. Usually so cocksure of himself, this was a side to Matthew that she'd never experienced.

"At least think about it."

Stunned into silence, Flick couldn't get her head around any of it. What on earth did Matthew think he was playing at?

"You're right, I should go," he said, finally getting up from his chair.

Flick awkwardly followed suit, tracing his footsteps as he headed down the hall to the front door.

"I'm staying at *Le Grand Hotel*. I'll be there until Saturday." He stopped and turned to face her. "I want you to come back to the UK with me, Flick." He opened the door, before pausing again. "I'll be in the reception at 7pm waiting for you."

"But–"

"Please. Don't make a decision now, think about it first." He leaned in and kissed her cheek. "And know that I love you," he said, before finally letting himself out.

Flick stood there, no longer able to think straight. Did Matthew mean what he was saying? Or was this some sort of game? She felt rooted to the spot, watching him as he walked down the long sweeping drive.

CHAPTER THIRTY-FOUR

With a hot cup of coffee in one hand, Flick pulled her coat snug across her chest with the other. Grey clouds overhead threatened rain and a cold wind blew around her as she stared out at Nate's cottage on the other side of the lake. Smoke rose from its crooked chimney and a light shone out from one of the windows. It was like looking at some wintry scene on a postcard – picture perfect.

The sound of her phone ringing filtered out from the kitchen, but she ignored it. It was probably the café again, they'd been ringing non-stop for the last twenty-four hours. It had been a while since she'd spoken to them and they probably wanted to know when she was going to be back at work. Either that, or to apologise for Matthew's sudden arrival.

In no mood to answer, she chose instead to listen to the sound of Nate's chainsaw, just a faint whirring by the time it reached her. She sighed. To think only twenty-four hours earlier she'd been looking forward to their date. Thanks to her growing feelings for the man, getting to know him more had felt like the right thing to do. Matthew turning up, however, had changed that. Matthew's arrival had left her confused and she found herself questioning her feelings.

Was her attraction for Nate genuine, or was she experiencing a rebound? After all, he was the only man she'd allowed herself to get close to since Matthew's disappearance. As for her husband, beneath the anger towards what he'd done, was there a chance that she still loved him? Of course, it didn't help when every time she thought of Matthew the words *for better, for worse* sprang to mind; a reminder that did nothing to help untangle her current emotions.

She shivered and insisting it was too cold to be standing outside, she took herself back indoors.

Placing her cup on the table, Flick moved to the front of the fire to warm herself. Orange flames danced in the hearth, crackling and spitting as they wrapped themselves around the burning logs.

Brenda entered the room and joined her at the fireside. "Just what we need on a day like this," she said.

Flick couldn't agree more. It was by far the warmest room in the house. Winter was creeping up on them and everywhere else in the chateau was freezing. "I can understand why this feels like the heart of the home. I bet we're not the only ones to ever stand here like this." She took in her mum's attire and laughed. Jeans, shirt, jumper, cardigan, shawl, and none of them matching. "You have looked in a mirror today, haven't you?"

"You mean the layered look is out this year?"

"A case of needs must, more like."

"It won't always be like this," Brenda said. "Especially now we've put a rehaul of the heating system to the top of our list." She raised her eyebrows. "We are still doing a to-do list, aren't we?"

Flick left the fire and grabbed her cup to pour another drink. She knew this conversation was coming, she just didn't know what to say, she hadn't worked out how she felt yet. "When I made my wedding vows, unlike Matthew, I meant them."

"And now?"

"Honestly? I don't know. He really did sound genuine about wanting to try again, but how can I trust him?" Flick poured her mum a drink too and took both cups to the table before sitting down. "So much has changed since I last saw him. I've changed. What if I agree to give things another go and it turns out I've changed too much?"

"Only you can decide whether that's worth the risk."

"And what happens to this place?" She glanced around the room, knowing how much she'd miss it.

"Did he mention the chateau?"

Flick shook her head. "No."

"Don't you think that's a bit strange?"

"I'm not sure. If he really wants me back, he might've thought asking about it would make him look bad. As if it's the building that he's really after."

"Maybe it is. Maybe he's playing a sly game. Lulling you into a false sense of security just to get his hands on what he thinks is his half."

Flick tightened her lips as she considered the possibility. "I didn't get that impression. But then again, I didn't think he'd leave me on our wedding day." She took a sip of her drink. "So, if that is his intention, he's got a fight on his hands." She let out a woeful sigh. "Why couldn't he just stay away? I was moving on, starting a new life."

Brenda sniffed. "Because he's like a bad penny, that's why."

"I can understand some of the things he said though. Not the stuff about him being a carer, obviously. He's always known how close we are as a family. Losing you or Dad was bound to pull the rug out from under me. And even if I acknowledge that not all families are like ours, you still do what you can for the person you claim to love. You don't see them as too demanding, you're there for them no matter what."

"Of course you are."

"As for everything else he said, I have to admit he has a point. I did go into our marriage thinking we'd be just like you and Dad, that everything would be perfect."

"Ha! I wish."

Flick smiled. "You know what I mean."

Brenda smiled too, forced to concede. "We did okay, I'll give you that."

"You did more than okay. But when it came to me and Matthew, I should have known it was wrong to keep comparing our relationship to yours. We had to find our own way, start our own traditions. Live our own kind of life, I suppose. No wonder he got scared and felt pressurised into being someone he wasn't."

"But it's not just about you and Matthew now, is it?"

"What do you mean?"

Her mother appeared pensive, as though trying to put her thoughts in order. "I'm not saying you owe anyone anything. At the end of the day you have to do what's right for you, because you're the one who has to live with the consequences."

"Good or bad."

"Exactly. But people have gone to a great deal of effort and the chateau is attracting a lot of attention as a result. And because of everyone's help, you've been able to think about a different future. You've been able to start thinking about turning your dreams into a reality. This place was going to be the art school you've always wanted, remember."

Just the thought of having something like that made Flick smile.

"You'd started to think about you. I mean does Matthew know any of this?"

Flick shook her head. "How would he?"

"But if he did, would he still want you to pack up and go back to the UK? Or would he stay here and help you build that dream?"

Flick couldn't ever imagine Matthew being happy in the wilds of Brittany. He'd love all the video and film shoot opportunities but he'd hate all the stuff in between, including the need to mingle with her fellow artists. Moreover, this part of France would be far too quiet for him. She could already hear his complaints about the lack of nightlife or nearby shopping centres. He'd never get to grips with Sunday being a day of rest, it would be the five and a half day shopping week that Matthew found sacrilegious. *But that was the old Matthew*, thought Flick. Surely the new Matthew would do everything in his power to make her happy?

"Then there's Nate to think about," Brenda said.

Just hearing his name made Flick feel all warm and fuzzy again. But she couldn't have met a man so contrary to her husband if she'd tried. She wondered if that's why she liked him as much as she did. Had Matthew hurt her so much that her subconscious thought his opposite number would be a safer bet? Whatever the reason, she couldn't deny she had feelings for Nate. The physical attraction alone was driving her crazy.

But it was more than that. Despite his early aloofness, Nate had shown himself to be a good man. Not only did they have lots in common, he accepted her for being her, he'd never trivialised her ambitions to paint and run an art school the way Matthew had done. To the point that on the rare occasion she'd allowed her mind to run away with itself, she hadn't just hoped she and Nate would develop an intimate relationship, she'd envisaged the possibility of a professional connection too.

But she was married.

She sighed at her predicament. Maybe she should just bag them both off? That would certainly make life simpler.

"Do you think word's got out yet?" Brenda asked.

"About what?"

"Matthew being here. I mean he only has tell one of the locals who he is and they'll all know. This is a small town and in small towns there's always gossip."

Being the subject of tittle-tattle was something Flick knew all about. She took another intake of breath and loudly exhaled. "I hope not."

CHAPTER THIRTY-FIVE

Nate switched off his chainsaw and taking off his ear defenders stood back to admire his latest creation. Even without features, he knew the tall faceless angel smiled back at him. With long flowing hair, she wore a floor length gown and her wings were the shape of a giant heart. Nate had never had a muse before and as he examined the simplicity of the piece her influence was obvious. This work had a modern feel that wilfully contrasted with the more ornate, traditional style he usually fashioned and liking what he saw, his smile turned to a grin as an image of Flick sprang to mind.

Just the thought of her made his insides giddy and he couldn't wait for the weekend to come around so he could see her again. *The weekend*, he thought, his need to do things right continuing to feel strange.

His mind drifted back to the party. After their kiss it would have been so easy to invite her back to his for the night. God knows he'd wanted to. But instead, he'd stayed just long enough to show his support for the event and to ask her out on their all-important date. Nate laughed at himself. "A bloody date, for goodness sake. When did you become such a gentleman?"

He didn't know where this need to be all proper had stemmed from. Maybe it was because they'd both been hurt in the past. Maybe it was because he felt what they'd started was special. He just knew he wanted to get to know Flick, both inside and outside of the bedroom. He tingled with excitement, it was a prospect he relished. All he had to do was figure out where to take her, which wasn't exactly easy in a sleepy little town like theirs.

Nate's stomach grumbled, reminding him that he hadn't yet eaten lunch. Checking his watch, it was clear he'd been so engrossed in his work that the hours had flown by and as he put his chainsaw to one side, he supposed Rufus would also be ready for a walk. He brushed himself down and a huge cloud of sawdust began swirling around him. The downside of his art, he considered, as he wafted the millions of tiny orange specks away. However, as he continued to look at his angel and smiled again, on this occasion having dust in every orifice seemed worth it.

Nate had a spring in his step as he made his way round to the front of the house, something he hadn't experienced in what seemed a very long time. Finally, life seemed to be looking up and it was all thanks to Flick. He never thought he'd say it, but thinking about recent events he even felt grateful towards Brenda for having blackmailed him. Were it not for the video shoot, Flick would probably be back in the UK and he'd be sat here, not just pining, but surrounded by architects, builders, and whatever noisy machinery these people needed when turning a beautiful building into a block of flats. And then there was Matthew, a man who without even knowing it, had done him the biggest favour of all. Although after all Flick's heartache, Nate would never openly admit that.

As Nate let himself inside, Rufus jumped up and down, his tail wagging, as he raced to greet his master.

"What do you think, boy?" Nate reached down to give the dog a fuss. "Is it going to be a happy ever after?" He watched Rufus's tail speed up, wagging faster and faster. "Me too," he replied, taking this to mean a big fat yes.

Ready for something to eat, Nate straightened himself back up and headed for the cupboards. "So, what do you fancy?" The 'Old Mother Hubbard' nursery rhyme suddenly played out in his head once he saw how bare the shelves within were. And opening the fridge door, that fared no better. "Looks like we're dining out," Nate informed his dog. "Come on, boy," he said before grabbing his van keys.

The drive into town was both pleasant and quick and the lack of tourists around meant he easily found a parking space once he got there. Climbing out of the van, he smiled. The place was dead; a bad situation for local businesses, he realised, but an excellent one for him. On quiet days like this he could walk with his head held a little higher and he could lower his guard slightly. Oh yes, Nate loved the current time of year.

He was still smiling when he and Rufus entered Café Ange. "*Bonjour*," Nate said, spotting Pete in his rightful place behind the bar.

Pete, elbows on the counter and resting his chin in his hands, looked up. "Is it?" he asked, signalling to the empty room before him. "Because me and my till don't think so."

"Nate," Jess said, breezing in from out back. "Lovely to see you."

"At least one of you seems happy," Nate said.

"Oh, don't mind him." Jess kissed both his cheeks. "He's always this miserable." She clasped her hands in anticipation. "Now, what can we do for you?"

"You can start by feeding me. And Rufus. We're starving."

"Quick," Pete said to his wife, "rustle him something up then *he* can tell you how much you're wasting your talent. You might listen to him and we can start earning some money again." He turned to Nate. "The feedback she got the other night and she still doesn't think she's good enough to turn this place into a restaurant."

Nate looked at Jess, opening his mouth ready to tell her that he agreed with her husband, that he thought she should do more with her culinary skills. Not that he got the chance, Jess made sure of that.

"Not you too," she said, and sighing at the mere suggestion she turned, continuing to shake her head as she retreated back into the kitchen.

Nate sat on a stool at the bar while Pete opened them each a bottle of beer.

"I don't get it," Pete said. "She must know what a great cook she is? In fact, she's more than that. When it comes to food, Jess is like you, she's an artist."

"She doesn't seem to think so."

"I'm wondering if I'm the one who's putting her off. Let's face it, I'm not what you'd call a natural entrepreneur."

As much as he wanted to, Nate couldn't deny this.

"She probably thinks I'll muck it up for her, like I do with everything else."

"Or it's a confidence thing?" Nate suggested. Trying to make his friend feel better, he could see Pete didn't quite agree.

"Either way, I haven't a clue what to do about it. The last thing I want is for her to be held back, for *any* reason. I don't suppose you've got any ideas?"

Nate thought for a moment. If a successful catering event like the video shoot didn't instil a sense of confidence in Jess, he felt at a loss as to what would. "Maybe a restaurant is too big a venture for her? It's too all or nothing?"

"Maybe."

An idea formed in Nate's mind. "What if you suggested she started small? Private catering for dinner parties, say? Or you could hold the odd food night here, once a month, just to start off with?"

A smile formed on Pete's lips. "That way she's not risking the security of the bar side of things." He looked around the empty room. "For what that's worth."

"And starting small would certainly enable her to build a reputation for when she is ready to take the leap."

"Friend." Pete raised his beer bottle and clinked it against Nate's. "Cheers. I think you might have just hit on something."

As Nate joined him in taking a swig, he remembered his dilemma over where to take Flick on their date night. "I might even be able to help with the first booking. If Jess is up for it."

"If Jess is up for what?" she asked. Re-entering the room, Jess carried a tray that she placed down on the bar. Taking the solitary piece of meat on offer, she gave it to the little Jack Russell who immediately snatched it in his jaws. Passing Nate his lunch, she waited for an answer. "Well?"

"Never mind that…" He stared down at a bowl of the tastiest-looking French lentil soup. "This looks wonderful. How do you do it?"

"Don't get too excited, it's nothing special. I was making it anyway."

"Nothing special. You've got to be kidding me." Nate picked up his spoon and stirred the perfect mix of lentils, onion, celery, carrots and stock, enabling an aromatic hint of garlic and thyme to rise up and meet his nostrils. Scooping up a spoonful, he blew on its contents to cool them a little before putting it in his mouth. He closed his eyes as he savoured the flavours, groaning a little as each and every one danced on his taste buds.

"Enough already," Jess said. "Sod the food, I want to hear all about you and Flick."

Nate opened his eyes. "What about us?"

"It's no good acting the innocent with me. It was pretty obvious to everyone at the shoot that there's something going on between you two. Of course, we all also know what that something is, I want all the gory details." She jumped up onto the stool next to him, fixing him with an expectant gaze.

Nate looked to Pete, hoping for a bit of male support, however, none was forthcoming. Instead, his friend offered a raised eyebrow, making it clear he wanted the low down on events so far too. "Cheers, mate." Nate returned his attention to Jess. "If you must know, there's nothing to tell."

Jess gave him the hard stare, refusing to blink even once.

"Okay, okay." Nate relented. "We're seeing how things go."

Jess let out a loud squeal and clapped her hands together. "I just knew you were perfect for each other. The first time I met Flick, I thought of you and what a great couple you'd make."

"Really. And what made you think that?"

"Because she's real and smart and pretty. She's authentic, nothing at all like the women in your past and everyone and their dog knows how those relationships turned out. Flick will tell you how it is, she won't massage that ego of yours."

Jess's observation made Nate a tad uncomfortable. "What do you mean? Massage my ego?"

"We all know you can be a bit precious sometimes."

"Precious? Really?" Nate didn't know whether to laugh at hearing this or feel affronted. But while he might not have agreed with Jess on that particular observation, he knew she was right when it came to his previous relationships. The women in his past weren't ever interested in him, they were interested in what he had. Or, more to the point, what they thought he had. Flick was the complete opposite.

Again, his insides came over all funny as he pictured her. She looked beautiful the other night, on the terrace by the lake under the moonlight. His lips formed a little smile, a smile that didn't go unnoticed.

"Could it be that our Nate's in love?" Pete asked, both his and his wife's knowing eyes suddenly upon Nate.

"I can neither confirm nor deny that," Nate said.

"Spoilsport," Jess said.

Nate's phone suddenly rang, to his relief, preventing any further discussion on the matter.

"Saved by the bell," Pete said, much to Nate's amusement and Jess's disappointment.

He checked the number. "It's Aunt Julia. Wonder what she wants." Clicking to answer, she launched into a tirade of ramblings and he was forced to pull the mobile away from his ear for a second. Listening once more, Nate's jovial expression vanished as he struggled to get his head around what she was saying.

No way would Flick do that. Would she?

CHAPTER THIRTY-SIX

Foot down on his accelerator, Nate didn't care about speed limits. Red mist had descended and all reason had abandoned him as he raced out of town. Heading straight for the chateau, he gripped the steering wheel so tightly his knuckles turned white. His temples bulged as fury coursed through his veins. How could she do this to him? How could he be so stupid as to fall for it?

Staring ahead, he drove on automatic pilot, only hitting his brakes when he needed to come off the main drag. He swung the van into a right turn, struggling to control the vehicle as he forced it back into a straight. Bounding over numerous potholes, he found himself thrown in all directions, however, keeping hold of the wheel he still refused to slow down. He drove through the chateau's open large iron gates, all at once skidding as the van's tyres hit the gravel drive. They had to have planned this. Why hadn't he seen it coming?

He depressed the accelerator further and, picking up more speed, waited until the chateau entrance was upon him before slamming on his brakes. The van's wheels locked, bringing him to an abrupt halt. Unclipping his seatbelt, Nate fought with the strap in a desperate attempt to free himself before managing to climb out. He marched towards the entrance door and despite its weight, flung it open as he let himself in. Voices sounded from the kitchen and he charged down the hall.

Flick and Brenda were already out of their seats as he pushed the kitchen door open and with such force it hit the wall. Their faces showed a mixture of fright and confusion. Not that he cared. They had done this. Not him.

"Jesus Christ," Flick's mother said. "What do you think you're doing?"

"What do *I* think I'm doing?"

"Nate," Flick said. "What's wrong?"

She took a step towards him, but he put a hand up warning her to stay put. He hadn't felt so angry in a long time and he was in danger of saying something he'd regret.

She froze. "Nate?" she said again, her voice meek.

He looked from her to Brenda, the fear in their eyes enough to shock him back to his senses. He had a rule when it came to women, there was a line he refused to cross. Besides, showing any temper would only play into their hands, no doubt, giving them more ammunition when it came to their scam. He forced himself to calm down, letting some of the red mist dissipate before speaking again. "Why?" he finally asked. "Why would you do this?"

"Do what?" Flick replied.

Nate might recognise the need to keep his rage in check, but that didn't mean he'd let the two women continue to treat him like an idiot. Flick could portray the vulnerable, little innocent all she wanted but her act didn't work any more. The game was up. "I have to hand it to you both. I actually fell for your sob story. Poor deserted bride looking for a new start."

"Excuse me," Brenda said. "How dare you…"

"How dare I what?"

The woman fell silent.

"If this is about Matthew," Flick said. "I'm as shocked as you are about him turning up. I…"

"Matthew? What's he got to do with anything?" Nate scoffed. "At this moment, I seriously doubt the man even exists."

"Of course he exists," Brenda snapped.

"And he's in on it too, is he?"

"In on what?" Flick asked.

"I'm sorry, Nate," Brenda said, coming to her daughter's side. "But whatever's going on here, I think you're talking to the wrong people."

Determined to keep it together, Nate let out a short sharp laugh. "Really?"

"Yes, really."

"The blackmail was a nice touch by the way. You're one hell of an actress. I genuinely thought you were desperate to help your daughter."

He took in Brenda's glare as she willed him to shut up. Talk about trying to keep up the pretence.

"I should have just taken my chances with the developers," Nate continued, regardless.

"What do you mean *blackmail?*" Flick asked. "Why would anyone want to blackmail you?"

Nate didn't deign to answer, he just sneered. As far as he was concerned, the women were in it together.

"Mum, do you know why anyone would want to do that?"

Refusing to speak, Brenda flushed red. Not because she felt any shame, Nate knew that. She was just pissed because they'd been caught out.

"Mum?" Flick asked again.

Nate shook his head at the pair of them. "Of course, that was just the beginning of your little plan, wasn't it? The set up."

"I'm sorry, but you really have lost me, Nate." Flick's confusion seemingly fast turning to frustration, her eyes went from him to her mum and back again. "Can one of you please tell me what's going on here?"

Again, Nate scoffed. He pulled out his phone and clicked on the screen before shoving it towards Flick's face. "Ring any bells?"

"What is it?" She took the mobile from him and scrutinised the photograph on display. "But this is a newspaper's website. How did they get this? Why would they even want it?"

"Keep swiping. There's more, although I'm guessing you already know that." Nate watched her follow his instruction, her brow furrowing deeper and deeper as each image appeared.

"I don't understand."

"Of course you don't," Nate said, mocking her claims of virtue. "So how much did they pay you?" he asked, ignoring her wounded expression as she passed the phone to her mother.

"Pay me?"

"Any other year and I doubt they'd have been interested, something else you probably already know."

Flick just looked at him.

"Oh come on." Nate's accusations appeared to hit a brick wall. Snatching his phone back, he addressed both women. "You really expect me to think you're not responsible for this?"

He watched Flick take a seat at the table, then looked at Brenda who seemed frozen to the spot. Their sudden silence on the matter told him all he needed to know. "I just hope that whatever money you did get was worth all the effort." He waited for an answer.

Met with nothing but continued quiet, his shoulders dropped before he turned to leave the room.

Making his way down the hall and back out through the front door, he shook his head. He no longer felt angry, or frustrated, or stupid. A sadness enveloped him. Were there no good people left in the world?

He got into his van and, after staring at the chateau for a moment, started up the engine and drove away.

CHAPTER THIRTY-SEVEN

Flick sat in silence trying to make sense of what had just happened. "Why?" she finally asked. "Why would a newspaper be so interested in me and Nate? I don't get it, we're nobodies." She crinkled her nose, screwing her face up in confusion. "And how did they even get the pictures? As far as I know there weren't any journalists at the video shoot or the wrap party. But even if there were, why us? Why not take photos of the band?" She looked to her mum who leant against the kitchen counter. "They must have confused us with someone else. There's no other explanation."

She fell quiet once more, convinced she'd crossed over into some twilight zone. None of what had just happened seemed to make sense. "And what about Nate's reaction? Instead of coming around here blaming us for whatever's going on, he could have just as easily asked the paper's editor. That's the first thing I'd have done." She tried to recall each of the pictures, hoping for a clue as to which paper had featured them. She'd been so engrossed in the actual images that she hadn't thought to look. If she had, she could have contacted the editor herself. She turned to her mum again. "And all that rubbish about being blackmailed. Who does he think he is? I've never heard anything so preposterous." Her voice quietened as she envisaged his downright fury. "I've never seen anyone so angry."

She stopped speaking, her eyes narrowing as she waited for her mother to join in the conversation. She'd been unusually quiet throughout the whole episode, quite out of character when she normally had something to say on every subject going.

Brenda remained tight-lipped. However, moving to straighten up the already aligned tea and sugar caddies, her sudden shiftiness made it clear that she knew more than she was letting on.

"Mum?" Flick said.

Her silence continued.

"Fine. If you won't give up the reason for all of this, I'm sure Google will." Flick picked up her mobile ready to do an internet search of the week's news. "French chateau, Brittany, France, Argon Fire," she read, as she keyed each word into the search bar. "This should give me what I'm looking for." She paused before hitting the search symbol, turning her attention back to her mother. "I mean, what newspaper editor doesn't want a quote from one of their headlining stars?"

Brenda finally relented. "Okay, okay."

Flick's thumb continued to hover over the screen. "So, you do have something to do with this?"

Brenda turned mute again.

"Mum, whatever it is you've done you need to tell me."

Like a wronged teenager, Brenda sighed. Dragging her feet as she approached the table, she took Flick's phone and she seated herself opposite. She pressed a few keys and then scrolled before handing it back.

"Great," Flick said. "More pictures."

Flick looked at the screen and took in the photo before her, her eyes immediately drawn to the young boy featured. It seemed to be a holiday snap, and going off the clothing alone, it was obviously taken a few years earlier. There was no denying the boy's identity; aside of ageing he'd hardly changed a bit. "That's Nate," she said.

Her gaze moved to the woman at his side. She knew she was staring at Nate's mother, they were the image of each other. "She's beautiful and I can't believe how alike they are." Flick continuing to scrutinize the picture. There was a sadness in the woman's eyes, something her beaming smile couldn't disguise no matter how hard it tried. "I still don't understand. Why are you showing me this?"

Brenda reached over and retrieved the phone, her expression serious as she once again began searching. She handed it back.

Flick smiled as she looked at Nate's mother once more. She was younger in this one and appeared to ooze glamour, her hair and make-up were perfect. And the dress she wore, it was stunning. "She looks familiar, although I can't think why."

"Growing up, you preferred to be stood in front of an easel rather than sat in front of the telly. I'm surprised you recognise her at all."

"What do you mean?" Flick looked down at the photo again, focusing on the statue the woman held in her hands. "Is that what I think it is?"

"An Oscar? Yes."

"She was an actress?"

"Yep. And a very good one, at that. There was a time when all the big producers and directors wanted her in their films, all of which I've seen, by the way. She had such a talent and talk about screen presence."

Flick struggled to take this information in. Nate had never once mentioned his mother, no one had. But why all the secrecy? "Where is she now?" Flick asked.

Brenda gestured for the phone again and conducted another quick search. She gave it back to Flick, before rising from her seat to go and pour them a coffee from the machine.

Flick stared down at the next image – this one a newspaper article. However, it was the grainy, black and white photo accompanying it that caught her attention. Her eyes widened in horror as she looked down at the ambulance men wheeling a body bag to the back of their van.

Her mum placed a coffee cup in front of her.

"Nate's mum?" Looking up, Flick wasn't sure she really wanted an answer.

Brenda nodded. "I'm afraid so."

Flick's heart automatically went out to him. She knew first-hand the pain of losing a parent and that was hard enough. But to have to cope with this kind of attention as well. She glanced at the news article again, unable to imagine how Nate got through it. "What happened to her?"

"An overdose."

Flick put a hand up to her chest. "How awful," she said, looking down at the image again. "Poor Nate."

"He's the one who found her."

"No!"

"She'd had an issue with prescription drugs for some time, apparently. There was an accident on one of the sets years before that had left her with chronic back pain. When the pills stopped properly working she began self-medicating with alcohol and as you'd expect, it was all downhill from there." Brenda sighed as if recalling the waste of life. "I blame that manager of hers, Bruce somebody or other. He pushed her too hard, like she was his own personal cash cow." Brenda took a drink of her coffee. "And the press. Once it became obvious that she needed help, that what she was doing affected her work, they seemed to turn on her. She couldn't leave the house without someone shoving a camera in her face. It was as if they wanted her to snap."

Flick indicated to the photo on the phone. "Looks like they finally got what they wanted."

"The overdose was accidental, by all accounts, but I get what you mean. Bloody vultures. Even now there are those intent on putting her death down to something more sinister. I often wonder if the poor woman will ever be able to rest in peace."

"When did all this happen?"

"Coming up ten years ago. That's probably why that paper published those pictures of the two of you. A bit of anniversary melodrama."

Flick fell silent, as she tried to digest what she'd just heard. If she struggled to get her head around it all, how must Nate feel? She felt sad for him. This was his mum, no wonder he was angry.

"It looked like Nate was following in her footsteps for a while."

"Nate was an actor too?"

Brenda half laughed. "Sadly, no. But like his mum he became a bit of a drinker. Her death sent him off the rails, I suppose. He was always out partying and getting himself into trouble for one thing or another. And for quite a few years. Of course, the paparazzi loved his antics, reporting every sordid detail. They did to him what they did to his mother, I suppose. And the 'kiss and tells' that came out about him. In my view, some women should be ashamed of themselves."

"Really." Flick couldn't imagine the Nate she knew falling out of nightclubs after getting up to goodness knew what.

"Then one day he just vanished. He grew up I suppose. Came out to France and got his act together."

"I still don't understand why he came around here shouting the odds though. Anyone of those people at the shoot could have taken those pictures. And because of the industry they're in, they'd have known exactly where to flog them."

"More coffee?" Her mum grabbed both mugs as she jumped out of her seat.

Determined to get to the bottom of it, Flick thought about everything Nate had said. He'd talked about them scamming him, selling photos, and... *Oh Lordy*. Closing her eyes, she dropped her arms and head down on the table as realisation dawned. "You blackmailed him, didn't you?"

"Yes. No."

The woman clearly couldn't make her mind up.

"Maybe."

Flick forced herself to sit up straight. "Which is it?"

Brenda plonked two freshly poured drinks down on the table. "I asked him for some assistance," she said, sitting back down.

Flick cringed. "What kind of assistance?"

As if recognising the game was up, her mum seemed to crumple in front of her eyes.

"I knew you were torn about being here, that a part of you wanted to stay but didn't have a clue what to do with this place. I mean, what do you do with a blooming, great big chateau that needs loads of work? And somewhere along the line you said that if you had a proper choice you'd at least try to start a new life here, which is all I ever wanted you to do. There was nothing left for you back in the UK thanks to that husband of yours. Then the idea of an art school came up, and suddenly you had something wonderful to focus on. But like you said, neither of us had the cash for something like that..."

Flick put up her hand to interrupt. "Please tell me you didn't ask Nate for money," she said, her insides filling with both dread and humiliation at the mere prospect.

"Of course not."

Flick supposed that was something. "Then what did you ask for?"

"I simply asked Nate if he could help."

As far as Flick was concerned, there was nothing *simple* about any of this. "You asked him for help? That's it? Nothing else."

"Yes. One neighbour to another."

Flick almost laughed. "Then why did he just accuse us of blackmail?"

Her mother came over all sheepish, twisting her wedding ring around her finger like she always did when she was uncomfortable, first one way and then the other.

"Well?" Flick nudged.

"I may have dropped into the conversation the fact that I knew who he was."

Flick stared at her mum. "So, let me get this straight. You're telling me you just let him *think* that you were blackmailing him."

Brenda nodded.

"Because that makes a whole heap of difference, doesn't it?"

"There's no need to be snarky. I can't help how the man's mind works now, can I?"

Flick couldn't believe what she was hearing. No wonder Nate thought they were responsible for this whole mess. Although thanks to her mother they probably were. If her mum hadn't approached him for help, as she put it, the video shoot wouldn't have ever taken place. Which meant there'd have been no photo opportunity for whoever did take the damn pictures and, therefore, no resulting newspaper article.

"Oh, Mum. How could you?"

CHAPTER THIRTY-EIGHT

"Here you are, ladies."

As Pete placed two large glasses of wine on the table, Flick tried to decipher his accompanying smile. Was it meant to be reassuring? Or was it given out of embarrassment? Watching him head off, she decided it was probably a mix of the two.

Her stomach churning, she turned her attention to Jess who sat with her. "I wasn't sure if either of you would talk to me," Flick said, picking up her drink.

"What made you think that?" Jess replied.

Flick tilted her head, one eyebrow raised. Did the woman really need to ask? "Nate's a friend of yours. And as far as he's concerned, me and Mum are public enemy number one."

Jess proffered a dismissive hand, clearly wondering what all the fuss was about. "He's also a big boy who'll get over it. In my view, the whole thing's hilarious. Who'd have thought it, eh? Your mum a blackmailer."

While Jess giggled, Flick cringed, wishing she could see the funny side too.

"You shouldn't laugh. Not really." She put her glass back down. "I know Mum was only trying to do the right thing by me, but to resort to extortion. How could she? Especially when she knew everything Nate's been through. I'm so frustrated with her right now. It's no wonder he hates us. As for everyone else, I can only imagine."

"I, for one, think you're being too hard on her," Jess said.

"You do?"

"Yes, I do. Taking a step like that can't have been easy, particularly for someone like Brenda who obviously doesn't have a malicious bone in her body. She risked her own reputation for her one and only daughter. Fair play to her. I'd like to think I'd do the same thing for mine if I had one."

Flick wondered what else Jess thought Flick's mother had been up to. It was one thing taking responsibility for what she had done, but as for anything else. Flick felt a thickness in her throat as she considered the shame of it all. "You do know she didn't take those pictures though, don't you? I wouldn't want anyone adding that to her criminal record."

Jess laughed. "I was there that night, remember. And I never saw Brenda with a camera or her phone out all evening. Believe me, the way I was milling around with those canapés, I'd have noticed."

Relieved, Flick drank a mouthful of wine. "Nate thinks she did."

"Nate's wrong."

"Not that I blame him. Mum would be the first on my list of suspects too if I were in his shoes."

"Nate needs to climb out of his own backside," Jess said, causing Flick to almost choke.

"You can't say that!"

"Why not? Don't get me wrong, Nate's one of my best friends. I love the man to bits but he does take himself too seriously sometimes."

Flick jerked her head back in surprise. Considering the man's history, she expected more sympathy. "He has had it rough, by all accounts."

"Of course he has. His mum was in the spotlight for most of her life and for all sorts of reasons, good and bad. Nate too for that matter. And the way she died… I wouldn't wish that kind of grief on my worst enemy. When I think about what he went through, it's no wonder he went off the rails for a while. And boy, did he go off the rails. It's no wonder he went from grieving son to spoilt trust fund brat in all the papers. His behaviour was enough to make your eyes water." She picked up her glass. "Anyway, there comes a time when we have to deal with our baggage. And thanks to your mum, that time might well have come for our Nate. The way I see it, she's done him a favour really."

Flick didn't know what to say. Recalling his anger over the whole thing, she doubted he would agree.

"Don't worry," Jess said. "This isn't anything I wouldn't say to his face."

Glad to hear it, the last thing Flick wanted to do was to cause trouble between friends.

"He just needs to stop skulking about and face his demons. Stop hiding from the past and accept it."

"You can understand why he might be loath to do that though, can't you?"

"Most definitely. At least, here he has a *bit* of anonymity. But getting back out there is the only way to stop all the curiosity surrounding him. If he really wants to step away from the limelight, he's got to move on, take a few risks, show the world who he is today. The press will soon lose interest when they realise how boring his life is compared to before."

The woman next to her may have sounded harsh to Flick, but admittedly she also made sense.

"Don't get me wrong, Nate's a wonderful bloke, he can just be his own worst enemy sometimes. You looked great in the photos by the way."

"You saw them?" Flick wanted the ground to swallow her whole.

"Of course I did. Two friends appearing in the national press, I wasn't going to let that slide without taking a peek. And it was a lovely article, all very romantic. It's a shame Nate didn't bother to read it."

Flick felt herself blush. Unlike Nate she'd never experienced being in the news. All those breakfast tables, daily commutes, lunch break reads, how many people had seen that kiss?

"But anyway, enough about him. How are you?" Jess asked.

Flick ran her index finger around the rim of her glass. "Embarrassed. Feeling sorry for myself. Wishing none of this sorry affair had ever happened. And my phone hasn't stopped ringing thanks to my work colleagues wanting all the juicy gossip. I've had to turn it off." She considered the ridiculousness of her situation. It was like she'd gone from one soap opera straight into another. "After what went on with Matthew, I thought I'd finally found a way forward, some direction. Thanks to Mum, things are worse than ever."

"I can't think why."

Flick laughed; that was easy for her to say. Flick thought for a moment. "Coming here made me step out of my comfort zone, see life through a different lens. Yes, doing something with the chateau would be hard work, but exciting at the same time. A challenge."

"And that's changed?"

"Definitely." She couldn't understand how Jess could even ask that. "You know what small towns are like. Even if people accept I didn't know what Mum was up to, I'll still be guilty by association. At least back in the UK I was only the jilted bride."

"Only?"

Flick smiled an empty smile. "It's funny how things turn out, isn't it? Compared to being labelled an extortionist, *jilted bride* doesn't seem quite so bad."

Jess took a sip of her wine, swishing it around her mouth before swallowing.

Flick could see that she wanted to say something but wasn't sure if she should. "What is it?"

"About Matthew…"

Flick closed her eyes for a second. Her heart sank; she could guess what was coming. "What about him?"

"Tell me to butt out if you want to…"

"You know he's here, don't you?"

"It's been mentioned."

"Of course it has." She let out a laugh. "See what I mean about small towns? I was wondering how long it would take before word got out."

"Rumour has it that he wants a reconciliation."

Flick sighed. Was there anything about her love life that wasn't common knowledge? "Then rumour would be right."

"Do you still love him?"

"To be honest, I think a part of me must care about him on some level. Despite being angry with him, he is my husband. But I can't help questioning why he's really here? For me, or for what he thinks is his half of the chateau?"

"No, surely not."

"Is it really a coincidence that he turned up the day after that piece in the paper?"

Jess shrugged. "Who knows? Only he can answer that, I suppose. And Nate? Where does he feature?"

Flick recalled his fury over the newspaper debacle, the anger in his eyes was so intense, it was frightening. And the pain that surrounded him when he finally left...

After the things he said, never mind the scorn in his voice, he was never going to see this situation for what it was – a single act by a mother trying to help her daughter. She and her mum were always going to be guilty of so much more. Flick sighed, saddened by the thought of what could have been. "I think that ship has sailed. Don't you?"

CHAPTER THIRTY-NINE

Nate willed himself not to wake up, but thanks to the banging about downstairs, his brain had other ideas. Ignoring it, he didn't even question who was responsible. There could be a burglary in progress for all he cared, he just wished they'd be quick and take what they wanted so he could go back to sleep.

With the noise continuing, he knew he should go and investigate, but as he tried to open his eyes, thanks to a combination of light streaming in through the window and a blinding headache, the best he could muster was a squint. He repeatedly smacked his tongue against the roof of his mouth, however, it was no good, it remained as dry as a desert flip-flop. Having obviously murdered his saliva glands, he needed water and he needed it now.

Throwing the cover back, Nate groaned as pain ricocheted from one side of his skull to the other. How could such a simple movement cause so much agony? Still wearing the previous day's clothing, he noted, he eased himself into an upright position before manoeuvring his legs over the edge of the mattress. He paused as a wave of nausea swept over him. *Great*, he thought. *That's all I need.*

Nate rose to his feet. As he headed for the bathroom, the sound of a sizzling frying pan filtered up to him, the smell of its contents making him feel even more sick. He checked his watch and scoffed. *Lunchtime.* Whoever the house invaders were, they were certainly making themselves at home. Entering the room, he turned on the cold tap and stuck his mouth under the flowing water, guzzling as much of it as he could. Turning the tap off again, he wiped his mouth with the back of his hand, making a conscious decision to avoid the mirror as he left the room to make his way downstairs.

"You're still alive then," Aunt Julia said, busy at the stove.

Nate took a seat at the table, clocking the large collection of beer bottles gathered together at one side of the kitchen counter. Had he really drunk that much? He supposed he must have done, looking at the evidence.

His aunt plonked a large glass of water and a cup of strong black coffee in front of him. "Drink."

Nate grimaced. Opting for the coffee first, he had neither the physical nor the emotional strength to argue. He leant an elbow on the table and rested his chin in his hand, feeling sorry for himself throughout. The tapping of his aunt's heels, as she utilised the length and breadth of the cooking area, hurt his already-painful head and he was convinced she didn't need to clatter those pots and pans quite so much.

"I hope it was worth it," she said, approaching the table again, this time with a plate of food. "Eat," she added, handing him an unwelcome knife and fork.

He looked down at the runny egg, juicy sausages and greasy bacon slices. Eating was the last thing he wanted to do. He'd have given some of it to Rufus were the dog not too busy sucking up to his aunt, trotting dutifully in line with every step she made. *Traitor*.

Julia returned with a rack of toast, causing Nate to sigh at her lack of empathy and realising he had no choice but to follow her orders, he readied himself to do as he was told.

She took the seat opposite, watching him struggle with every mouthful.

Sadist, Nate thought, feeling the weight of her stare. He'd have been in safer hands with the burglars.

"I hope you're proud of your behaviour."

He forced himself to swallow. "I fancied a drink, that's all."

"I can see that," his aunt replied, indicating to the bank of bottles. "But that's not what I'm talking about."

Nate continued to eat, unable to stomach a lecture as much as he couldn't the food hitting his belly.

"Brenda is distraught after your little visit. I've just left the poor woman in tears."

As far as Nate was concerned, his aunt's pity was misplaced.

"To go in there all guns blazing. How could you?"

Nate couldn't believe what he was hearing. He didn't give a toss about Brenda, she wasn't the one plastered all over the British press. He was. As for her daughter, just like the others, she was, no doubt, revelling in her fifteen minutes of fame.

Nausea swept over him again. He didn't think he'd ever felt so betrayed.

"I tried to tell you not to jump to conclusions," Julia continued.

"Conclusions?"

"But would you listen? No, you wouldn't. What did you do instead? You put the phone down on me, while I was still speaking I might add, to go shouting your mouth off at two defenceless women." She sighed. "I've seen you when you're not happy, the pair of them must have wondered what the hell was going on."

Thanks to his hangover, Nate didn't have the energy to stick up for himself. He simply let her words wash over him as he pushed away his plate. He couldn't eat any more.

His aunt pushed it back. "You still need to finish your coffee too."

"I've had enough."

"Haven't we all."

Nate pulled a face. "What's that supposed to mean?"

"It means it's high time you grew up, young man. It's time you stopped living in that bubble of yours and realised you're not the only one who's hurting here."

"What are you talking about now?" he asked, wondering where all this was coming from, let alone where it was going.

"You know exactly what I'm talking about. You weren't the only one to suffer because of your mum. Watching her go from one bad relationship to another, popping pills every second of the day, and washing most of them down with any drop of alcohol she could get her hands on, throwing her career away, neglecting her responsibilities. And, yes, by that I do mean you. Then to do what she did, to kill herself."

Nate flinched at the memory, doing his best not to picture her lifeless body strewn across the bed. He could still hear the frantic 999 call, how he struggled to breathe as he begged the operator to send help. He could feel his desperation as he tried to force air back into her lungs and the tiredness in his arms as he pushed on her chest. But it was no good, he was too late. She was gone. As for the note, if you could call it that, it simply contained two words. *I'm sorry*. As if that's all he and his aunt deserved.

Thinking back, he should never have hidden it. But in his young, naïve mind, she'd been crucified enough. No way could he let the papers drag her through the mud for taking her own life as well and to this day, the only two people that knew what she'd done were him and Julia. It was their secret, one he often wished they hadn't kept. Telling the world might have stopped all the conspiracy theorists out there insisting his mother was Britain's answer to Marilyn Monroe.

"Of course that left the rest of us feeling guilty for not doing more," Julia carried on. "When deep down we all know we did everything that we could." She finally paused, as if recognising the need to calm down. "She was my sister, Nate. Everything that happened pains me as much as it does you."

He didn't know what to say. He'd never heard his aunt talk like that before.

"There comes a point," she said. "When we just have to get on with things. Stop blaming ourselves for the choices your mother made. And we certainly can't blame everyone else for the choices *we* make."

Nate considered the last couple of days. "I didn't *choose* for any of this to happen."

"No. But you did choose to be judge and jury."

Now what was the woman going on about? "Meaning?"

"Meaning if you'd bothered to find out the facts before flying off the handle, you'd have saved yourself a whole lot of heartache these last twenty-four hours."

Nate scoffed at his aunt's gullibility. "Please don't tell me they've fooled you too."

"All those two are guilty of is trying to start a new life here in France. Brenda asked you for help for the sake of her daughter, nothing more, nothing less. She was never going to blab about your whereabouts. Five minutes in her company and any fool could see that."

Nate shook his head. Yep, they'd got to her.

"As for Flick, she's the best thing to happen to you in years. And what do you go and do? You blow it. All because you're too arrogant to see that you're not the only victim in this world. She didn't want her picture plastered all over that paper any more than you did."

"That's what they told you, is it?"

"Yes."

"Then I'm sorry, Aunt Julia, but you're the fool here, not me."

His aunt sighed, her eyes showing a mix of frustration and disappointment. "I got a call from Bruce this morning."

"And what did he have to say? I bet he's loving all this crap. Jumping on the bandwagon to promote his documentary."

"He was in a bit of a panic actually, worrying that you might think he's responsible for those photos."

"In case I pull out and ruin his viewing figures?" Nate knew he sounded sarcastic, but he couldn't help himself. "He's another leech trying to make money out of Mum's demise. Then again, what's new there?"

"I also got a call from Lenny."

"Well, well, well. They're all coming out of the woodwork."

"He wanted to apologise."

"For what?"

"The pictures."

"Why would he do that?"

"Because it was the kid from Argon Fire's fan club who actually took them."

Nate froze. It couldn't have been. He felt any semblance of colour drain from his face.

"I thought that might get your attention. But it gets better, because even he's innocent of this so-called crime."

Nate looked at her confused. Either he did take the photos, or he didn't.

"The poor lad had never even heard of you or your mum," she carried on. "He was simply taking photos of his fun few days away for posterity. It was his father who recognised you. His father's the one who sent them to the newspaper." Nate's aunt was clearly on a roll. "And for your information, there was no malice intended on his part either. He was simply a big fan of your mother's and after everything that had happened to the both of you, he just wanted to let other fans know how happy you are now."

Even Nate could see the irony in that. Happy was not how he'd describe his current feelings.

"I'm guessing that's why he handed them over without asking for a single penny. You see, not everyone in this world is out to get you, Nate. It's about time you realised that."

A sense of nausea swept over him again. "I feel sick."

Julia shook her head as she got up from her seat to go and fetch the coffee jug. "I bet you do," she said, refilling his cup.

Not that Nate could blame her for the lack of sympathy. Even he knew he didn't deserve it. "Why didn't you just tell me all this at the beginning?"

"Because I thought you needed to hear a few home truths first."

She was right, of course. He closed his eyes, realising what a spoilt brat he'd been and what an absolute fool he'd made of himself. The things he'd said and the way he'd said them. Flick and Brenda were never going to forgive him.

"Now drink up and finish your breakfast," Julia continued.

Nate knew he was in no position to argue.

"Just make sure you leave some room."

Nate looked from his plate to her. "What for?"

His aunt smiled. "For all the humble pie you're about to eat."

CHAPTER FORTY

Nate opened the door to his workshop. Stepping inside, he glanced around at his sculptures. He took in the painstaking detail in each and every piece, thinking about all the hours upon hours he'd spent learning his craft. His personal life might still be in tatters, but he'd come a long way as an artist.

He picked up a chisel, running his fingers over the cold metal. From day one, he'd always valued his time in there, he loved being surrounded by the tools of his trade, even when he hadn't known how to use them. It was funny how one little room could give his life its sense of purpose. He laughed. Had it really done that? Or had it simply given him a place to hide away from everyone and everything.

He breathed in the woody aroma. It smelt like over-baked biscuit, it was comforting. It reminded him of his mother.

His mother. How could a man both love and hate someone in such equal measure?

Standing there in the quiet, it would have been so easy to open his mouth wide and spew out his frustrations in one loud roar. Despite the temptation, however, he stopped himself. In his view, it would take a lot more than a bit of shouting to sort out his head.

He thought about what his aunt had said – about his arrogance, his need to grow up, how not everyone in the world was out to get him. Her straight-talking about his mum had been especially difficult listening, she'd really gotten her point across. His shoulders drooped. It saddened him to think he'd been so wrapped up in his own anguish over the years that he hadn't seen hers. He might not have wanted to hear it, but she was right to talk to him the way she had.

He'd been selfish and, looking back, had no doubt been a source of worry in much the same way as his mum had been. Not only had Julia had to watch her sister drive herself into an early grave, she'd been forced to cope with her nephew going down the same path for a while too. The stupid choices he'd made, the excuses he'd had every step of the way and all of them wrapped up in self-pity. He was definitely his mother's son. His aunt must have dreaded the phone ringing. To have *that* call once was more than enough.

Nate never thought he'd ever understand his mum's final act, but he had to admit that a part of him was starting to. He might not have stopped his heart from beating, but just like her, he'd certainly given up on life. He looked around the room again, realising just how much he'd locked himself away these last years, as if the outside world had hardly existed.

His eyes settled on the tall faceless angel. Grabbing a stool, he perched himself down in front of her. "And then you came along. And enticed me back."

He couldn't believe that in a few short weeks, Flick had managed to do what his aunt had spent years trying to achieve. In her own sweet, albeit unintentional way, Flick had shown him that his mother didn't dictate his identity.

His smile faded as he recalled their last encounter. The confusion in Flick's eyes, how could he not see that that was real? He could still hear the venom in his voice, feel the hardness in his face as he spat his words out. As for Brenda, of course she wasn't the criminal mastermind he'd made her out to be. He scoffed. Having spent years telling himself he knew exactly what people were about, it turned out he knew nothing of the sort.

They were never going to forgive him. And why should they?

The pit of his stomach felt heavy with shame, which would have been enough to make the old Nate drown his sorrows in drink. He'd be staring at the bottom of an empty beer glass by now, because just like the other night that's what he always did. Not this time though, this time there were no excuses. He had to face up to his behaviour, it was just a case of how?

He thought for a moment, before reaching into his pocket for his phone. Scrolling down his list of contacts he finally clicked 'call' and waited. "It's me. I need a favour."

CHAPTER FORTY-ONE

Flick's boots rubbed as she made her way towards the chateau. Shoving one foot in front of the other, she groaned, the sweeping drive seemed never-ending. She hadn't intended to be out that long. After Julia's visit and subsequent explanation as to the mystery photographer's identity, Flick had thought a stroll in the fresh air might help clear her head. She stopped for a moment to give her feet a rest. There must have been more going on in her mind than she'd realised, her quick walk having somehow turned into a long constitutional. She sighed, supposing the blisters were worth it. She might not have all the answers yet, but she'd had plenty of time to think.

Setting off again, she wondered how Nate was feeling now the truth was out. She sighed again. He probably still hated her and her mum. Flick might not have appreciated his outburst, but she could certainly understand why he'd put two and two together and got six.

Finally, Flick reached the chateau entrance and she let herself in. *Home at last*, she thought, at the same time shrugging away her coat and kicking off her boots.

Heading for the kitchen, she wasn't surprised to find her dad's casket of ashes had reappeared on the fire's mantelpiece. The atmosphere in the chateau had been tense over the last day or two and her mother seemed to gain comfort in having him close by. Flick had to admit she felt the same and approaching the wooden box, she let her fingers trace the carved inscription – *Forever Loved*. Flick knew he'd hate the current strain between her and her mum. She hated it too. "Don't worry, Dad. We'll get it sorted."

As if on cue, Brenda entered the room. "I thought I'd make some lunch. Would you like some?"

Watching her head to the fridge, Flick could see the situation was taking its toll. Usually so positive, the glint in her mum's eyes had waned and she seemed smaller somehow, older. "Let me help." Flick stepped forward to get a knife and cut the bread while her mum grabbed the butter and cheeses, before preparing a simple salad. The silence as they worked was deafening, the quietness continuing even as they sat down for their meal.

Brenda suddenly stopped eating. "This is awful," she said, putting down her knife and fork.

Flick popped a forkful of tomato into her mouth. "Tastes all right to me."

For the first time in days, Brenda smiled. "You know I'm not talking about the food."

Flick also placed her cutlery on the table. "Everything's going to be fine. You've no need to keep punishing yourself."

"But I want to show you how sorry I am for all of this. Lord knows I can't just keep saying it. I want to put things right. If I'd known what the fallout was going to be I'd have kept my big fat mouth shut. Nothing's worth coming between me and my daughter, not Nate, not this chateau…"

"And nothing has come between us, Mum. Not really. I admit I'm not happy about you threatening to out Nate, but what's done is done. And I know you had nothing but good intentions, you had my best interests at heart like always. We just have to figure out how to move forward."

"So, what's the answer? Because I'm happy to go along with whatever you decide."

Flick got up from her seat and headed for the cupboard. "I know this is going to sound daft." She pulled out a couple of glasses and a jug, heading to the sink to fill the latter with water. "It's just that when I look back on everything, it almost feels like

I've forced people in to keep saving me. And because of that, be them good or bad, I haven't been able to make my own choices. Not proper ones, anyway."

"How so?" Brenda asked as Flick set the glasses and jug down on the table.

Retaking her seat, Flick tried to order her thoughts. "Put it this way, if Dad hadn't suffered his stroke, Matthew wouldn't have asked me to marry him. This isn't about blame, being ill wasn't Dad's fault, I just handled it so badly."

"Go on."

"If I'd been stronger, there'd have been no reason for Matthew to step in. He wouldn't have felt the need to rescue me. Yes, his proposal was commendable, it came from a good place, however, it was also just plain stupid. I mean, of course I was going to say yes. He offered me a lifeline when I felt like I was drowning. But let's face it, I was in no position to make that kind of commitment. And as it turned out, neither was he."

"You can say that again."

Flick smiled. As far as she was concerned, none of that mattered any more.

"Coming to France was the same. Would I have chosen to own a place like *Chateau D'Enchantement*? Probably not..."

"But..."

"Look, I'm not saying the pair of you were wrong for buying it. I think this place is wonderful. To be honest it's given me a new zest for life. But it wasn't your job to keep my ambitions alive, was it? To turn my dream of running an art school into a reality. I should have done that for myself." She paused to pour them a drink. "If I had, you and Dad could have spent your money on enjoying yourselves."

"Maybe."

"Even the video shoot was thanks to you and Nate. And it was a great solution to a big dilemma. But you shouldn't have had to resort to blackmail on my behalf."

"I am sorry for that."

"Don't be, Mum, I'm the one who's at fault. I should have taken charge of events, come up with my own plan to make this place work for us. I've been such a bloody wimp, all I seem to have done, especially in the last year, is feel sorry for myself. I've turned everyone I know into some knight in shining armour on a *rescue me* mission."

"We only wanted to help."

"And I understand that. But it's high time I helped myself, don't you think?"

"And how do you plan on doing that?" her mother asked.

Thanks to her walk, Flick had already done a lot of soul-searching and, admittedly, most of it thanks to something Jess had said about Nate. It was pretty obvious that he wasn't the only one carrying emotional baggage, she seemed to have collected quite a few suitcases of her own. Suitcases that, like his, needed offloading.

The beginnings of a smile appeared on her face and her chair legs suddenly scraped against the hard floor, as she jumped up from her seat. "You'll see," she said, all at once grabbing her bag and exiting the room.

"You're going out?" her mum asked, following her. "Why? Where to?"

Flick donned her boots and coat before opening the door to leave, her smile replaced with a wide grin as she raced out to the car. "I'm going to take charge. Starting with my love life."

Brenda put a hand up to her chest, her concern continuing.

"Don't worry," Flick said. "I know what I'm doing."

Climbing into the vehicle, Flick rooted in her bag for her keys. Finally locating them, she started up the engine and set off down the drive. Leaving the chateau behind, it got smaller and smaller with every check in her rear-view mirror. Her pulse quickened the further away she drove.

As she approached the large iron gates, Flick eased off the accelerator, forced to bounce up and down in her seat as she negotiated the potholes. Bringing the car to a standstill, she checked the road was clear before pulling out onto the main drag. "There's no turning back now."

Continuing on her way, it wasn't long before she reached her journey's end.

Parking up, she didn't have a clue what she was going to say, she didn't even know if he'd be there. Her chest felt light thanks to the anticipation. "You're doing the right thing," she told herself, and taking a deep breath got out of the vehicle.

She stared up at the building. With its four floors and numerous large green shuttered windows, *Le Grand Hotel* certainly lived up to its name. Not that she should be surprised, Flick realised, Matthew had always liked the finer things in life and she dreaded to think what its room rates must be. Climbing the steps up to the ornately porched entrance, she was keen to see inside and glancing around, it didn't disappoint. From the antique furniture, to the designer wallpaper, to the massive reception desk, it was all very posh, and she'd have put money on the artwork adorning the walls being original.

The receptionist, a very smart suited chap, looked up from his work. "*Puis-je vous aider, madame?*"

Flick stared at him blankly. She didn't have a clue what that meant.

He smiled. "Can I help you?" he said, clearly recognising the rabbit in headlights expression coming back at him.

She quickly took another glance around, spotting Matthew through an open door that led to what seemed to be the bar area. "*Non, merci.* May I?"

The receptionist nodded, indicating that, indeed, she may, and thanking him once more, she approached the doorway. She suddenly paused before entering, it appeared that her husband had company and while she watched him easily chat to his female companion, she used the time to gather her thoughts. She let out a laugh, when her husband finally noticed her presence. The poor man looked mortified.

He seemed to garble some excuse as he jumped out of his seat to join her. "Flick," he said, rushing over. "I didn't think I'd see you until tomorrow."

"I noticed," She nodded to the mystery blonde.

"What?" Matthew said, his voice panic-stricken. "No. Please don't think I'm–"

"It's okay," Flick interrupted. "I don't think anything."

At last, he began to relax. "Good. Because after you know what…" He paused, clearly expecting Flick to silently fill in the gap. No longer willing to vocalise his past behaviour, Matthew was obviously ready to brush it away as if it hadn't happened. He looked at her directly, his gaze suddenly eager. "So, does this mean you've decided?"

Flick took a deep breath. This taking charge business was scary. "I have."

"And you're coming back to the UK with me?"

Flick scrutinised his expression. It wasn't hopeful, or anxious, or desperate even. It was self-assured. He was so used to getting his own way, he'd assumed her return would be a done deal. She gave him a gentle smile. "No, Matthew, I'm not."

"Oh." He put one hand on his hip, the other up to his chin, as he shifted from one foot to the other. "I wasn't expecting that."

Flick took in his confusion and having never seen him so lost for words before, she actually felt a bit sorry for him. Not enough to give their marriage another go however. As far as she was concerned, that part of their relationship had ended before it began. Realising she'd said what she came to say, she didn't see the point in dragging things out. "I'll let you get back," she said and gesturing once more to the blonde she turned to leave.

"Flick," Matthew said, stopping her.

"Yes."

"You didn't ask me to stay."

She smiled. "No. I didn't."

CHAPTER FORTY-TWO

As she headed downstairs, Flick smiled. There'd been a definite loss of tension since the previous day's visit to see Matthew. Her future at the chateau might not be certain, but she felt positive and looked forward to giving it her best shot. As did her mum, who cried when Flick explained why she'd run out on her. They just had to come up with a concrete plan to turn her dream of running an art school into reality.

Flick made her way to the kitchen, but she paused as she entered, wondering where her mother had got to. Flick's eyes scanned the room until she finally spotted her, forced to ask why her mum would be out on the patio instead of in front of the fire? No matter how many layers they dressed in, it felt below freezing inside, let alone out there.

Joining her, Flick shivered as she took in her mum's contemplation. Her demeanour seemed a far cry from the happiness she'd demonstrated the day before. "You okay?"

"Just thinking," Brenda replied.

"About?" Flick asked, although it didn't take a genius to figure it out.

Keeping her eyes on the lake, Brenda let out a heart-felt sigh. "You and Nate."

Flick knew why, of course. It was Saturday, that evening was meant to be their big date.

"You were so looking forward to getting to know him more," Brenda continued. "And when I think about how happy he made you. Why did I have to go and ruin everything?"

As much as she wanted to, Flick couldn't deny her previous excitement. In fact, Nate had stirred up all sorts of emotions in her and most of them good. He hadn't just made her feel human again, he made her feel wanted, attractive, sexy even. As daft as it seemed, she'd thought that night was going to be the start of some great romance. Sad really. Whatever connection they'd shared, it clearly wasn't meant to be. "Maybe it's for the best? Seeing my face in a newspaper once was too much. Now I know who he is, who his mother is, I'm not sure I'd have coped with all that scrutiny. Life's complicated enough."

"I must admit that did cross my mind. But that was before everything came out. You're stronger than you think."

Flick smiled. "Let's just say I'm getting there."

Brenda turned to face her. "Call it a silly question, but after everything that's happened, do you think there's still a chance?"

Flick had to admit that half of her hoped so. In all honesty, she'd started to fall for Nate and those kinds of feelings didn't just switch off. The other half knew better though. And as she stared over at his house, it felt cruel to know he was so near, yet so far. She recalled the previous day's walk.

Wandering through the chateau grounds, she'd felt more than a tad tempted to just turn up at his door. Of course, it didn't help that she kept hearing her father's voice, insisting that she seized the day and embraced life for once. Not that Flick listened. It was one thing knowing that she had to end things with Matthew, but thanks to their farce of a wedding day, she didn't think she could face another rejection. "Probably not."

Suddenly suspicious, Flick's eyes narrowed as she looked at her mum. "If you've got any ideas about hatching some sort of plan, then please don't. I mean it. No more meddling."

Brenda laughed. "Don't worry. I've well and truly learnt my lesson. There'll be no more interfering from me."

"Good." Flick gave her mum a well-received hug. "Now, let's talk about something else."

Footsteps on the gravel piqued their attention, causing Flick's stomach to immediately lurch. She put a hand to her belly and although in that moment a part of her hoped it was Nate, after the week she'd had, she'd gotten to the point where she dreaded unexpected guests.

"There you are," their visitor said as he rounded the corner. "What are you doing out here? No wonder you didn't hear me knocking."

"Pete," Flick said, happy to see him. "What a surprise."

"No Jess today?" Brenda asked.

He commenced a round of *faire la bise*. "I'm afraid not," he said, cheek kissing finally over with. "But I do come bearing gifts."

"Really?" Flick said.

Pete smiled. "Come on. Follow me."

Flick and her mum did as they were told and shadowed him back round to the front of the chateau.

"You've still got the hearse, I see," Brenda said.

Pete smiled. "Of course. And she's coming in very handy, I have to say."

Intrigued, both women watched him head for the front passenger seat and pull out some sort of wheel-based contraption. It reminded Flick of a folded-down pram frame, but she couldn't think why anyone would want one of those. She leaned towards her mum. "What is it?" Flick asked, as he set it on the ground.

Brenda shrugged. "I'm sure we're about to find out."

Continuing to observe him, Pete produced what looked like a remote key fob from his pocket. He seemed very proud as he placed it flat on his palm. "Are you ready?" he asked, reminiscent of some magician about to do a magic trick. The two women nodded and he made a show of using his index finger to press the button, enabling the contraption to both rise and unfold at the same time.

"Oh, Lordy," Flick said, realisation dawning.

"You managed to get your coffin trolley then?" Brenda called out, chuckling as she stated what was obvious.

"Isn't it fantastic. It's surprising what you can buy over the internet these days."

Like a child with a new toy, Pete used the button to manoeuvre it towards the back of the hearse, but he clearly hadn't got the knack. And forced to stifle her giggles, Flick watched it swing first to the left and then to the right. As if refusing to maintain the necessary straight line, the thing seemed to have a life of its own.

"Sod it." Finally giving up, Pete simply pushed the trolley instead.

"That's not a body, is it?" Brenda asked.

Curious, Flick's eyes widened as he began hauling what looked like a shrouded figure out of the vehicle and onto his trolley, her intrigue continuing as he began wheeling it towards them. And careful to keep it hidden under its sheet as he tipped it into an upright position, she watched Pete compose himself. He obviously saw this as some big reveal.

"Ready?" he asked his audience once more.

Flick and her mother nodded again and in one swift movement, he pulled the shroud away.

Flick stared in amazement. Taking in the wooden sculpture, with its long flowing hair and giant heart-shaped wings, it was the most beautiful angel she'd ever seen. "It's stunning," she said, reaching up to touch the perfectly smooth surface where her face should be.

"Wow!" Brenda said. "She's beautiful."

"I don't have to tell you who it's from," Pete said. "But just in case." He pulled an envelope from his pocket and handed it to Flick before stepping back.

"Thank you," she said, not quite sure what to make of it all.

Her hands shook as she looked down at her name neatly written on the front. Opening it, she didn't have a clue what to expect. Not that she needed to worry; as soon as she saw Nate's words she felt her eyes light up. Her heart skipped as she digested his simple message – *I'm sorry. Please forgive me.* Maybe she'd been right to live in hope.

"We've all told him what an idiot he's been," Pete said. "Just so you know."

Flick let out a laugh, appreciating the body of support. "That's very kind of everyone." She suddenly heard her father's voice, as he again insisted she follow his lead.

Embrace life. Take a risk, he seemed to say. *What have you got to lose?*

She looked from the note to her mum, who appeared to understand.

"Go!"

Flick smiled as she shoved the envelope into her mother's hand. "Are you sure?" she asked. After all, the trouble with Nate had affected both of them.

Brenda nodded.

"Thank you," Flick said, and giving both her mum and Pete a kiss and a hug, she ran up to the chateau to grab her coat.

"Cup of tea?" Brenda asked Pete.

"Don't mind if I do."

Flick reappeared from the entrance hall and happy to leave them to it, headed off round the back.

CHAPTER FORTY-THREE

Flick made sure to keep the lake in sight as she continued on her way. After all, having never been to Nate's house before, the last thing she wanted was to get lost in the woods.

With her dad encouraging her each and every step, she tried to practice what she was going to say when she got there and listening to herself, she quite liked this taking charge malarkey. It gave her a sense of power. She stopped occasionally though to look back at the chateau. Not only did she find it reassuring, thanks to its close proximity to the water, she'd never before been able to appreciate its rear façade in quite the same way.

Similarly, Flick had only ever viewed Nate's property from a distance and as she neared, she was pleased to see it was as pretty as she'd imagined. Taking in the plume of smoke rising from its crooked chimney, it reminded her of the cottages often featured in children's fairy tales. She smiled. It was perfect.

She slowed her step as she approached, at the same time feeling her nerves start to kick in. What if he didn't want to see her? Even worse, what if he didn't feel the same way and she was about to make a complete fool of herself? Thanks to her mother's extortion attempt, she'd suffered enough embarrassment already.

Suddenly the front door opened and Rufus raced out to greet her. And realising she'd missed her chance to back out, Flick reached down to gather him up. "Hello, boy," she said, dodging his tongue as the little dog tried to lick her face and nibble her ears. "At least someone's pleased to see me."

She spotted Nate standing in the doorway and setting Rufus down, returned Nate's gaze. His hair looked wet as if he'd just showered and he wore faded jeans and an unfitted, white T-shirt that hung loosely over his hips. He looked good and her heart raced as she stepped forward. "I came to say thank you." Studying his face, she tried and failed to read his expression. "For the angel. She's beautiful."

"I'm glad you like her," he replied, but just like his expression, his voice gave nothing away.

Flick stuffed her hands in her pockets and looked down at her feet. Now that she'd got there, any sense of confidence she'd experienced seemed to desert her. Of course it didn't help that he wasn't making this easy and she began to feel a bit stupid.

"Would you like to come in?"

Flick immediately looked up. "I'd like that very much."

As she approached the doorway, Rufus at her heels, he stood aside to let them both in. Flick felt herself blush as she squeezed past and attempting to focus on something other than him, she forced her attention towards the room. Glancing around, the only sense of home came from the roaring wood burner that the little dog plonked himself in front of. The house definitely needed a woman's touch, she considered, her cheeks reddening even more as she realised she was there for the job.

"Is tea okay?" Nate asked, setting the kettle to boil.

"Yes, please." Feeling hot and bothered, she took off her coat and hung it over her arm.

"Here, let me," he said, racing over to take it from her.

As she handed it to him, their eyes locked. Flick knew she should say something, but as usual when he held her gaze she felt too captivated to speak.

The kettle boiled, its whistle breaking the spell.

"Excuse me." Nate headed back to the kitchen to see to their drinks.

Watching him, Flick sensed he was on his best behaviour, something that made her uncomfortable. She'd come here to see the Nate she knew, the one full of banter and who made her laugh. The man before her felt more like a stranger. Then again, she considered, maybe that's what he was? "Leave them."

He appeared to freeze for a second, before turning to face her again. "Okay." He leaned back against the counter.

She took a deep breath, gearing herself up. About to declare her feelings, it was her big moment. Determined to be as direct with him as she had been with Matthew, her pulse quickened as she opened her mouth to speak. "I just want to say that I'm sorry," she said, instead. "Mum should never have blackmailed you." As soon as the words were out, Flick felt like a complete chicken. "Even she knows that now and can't apologise enough."

"No." Nate shook his head as he moved towards Flick. "It's me who needs to say sorry. To both of you. I should have known you weren't responsible for those photos."

"Yes, well, Mum didn't exactly make herself look innocent, did she?"

"But I should have gotten my facts straight before shouting my mouth off."

Flick recalled his behaviour and the downright fury he demonstrated. "Yes," she said, her expression stern. "You should."

Nate seemed surprised by her bluntness, then his face suddenly broke into a smile.

"What?" Flick asked. "What's so funny?"

"You. You're so straightforward when you want to be. Even now."

"You mean you expected me to be different?"

"Maybe."

While Flick appreciated why he might think that, his assumption annoyed her. She wasn't there to see the son of an Oscar winner and she certainly wasn't there for an autograph. If he expected special treatment he was in for a shock. Had he not learnt anything about her in the last few weeks. "Look, mate, you might have a famous mother, and just because you've pulled a few stunts in your time…"

"You know about all that stuff?"

"Of course I do. I might not be up to date on the latest celebrities, but that doesn't mean I'm not nosey." Seeing his embarrassment, it was Flick's turn to feel amused. "You were quite the lad back in the day."

Nate flashed her a look. "It's all exaggerated."

Enjoying the tease too much, Flick didn't answer.

"I'm telling you, it is." He seemed desperate for her to believe that.

Finally Flick relented. "Of course it is. Although you must know I don't care either way. That was the old Nate. It's *my* Nate that I'm interested in."

He looked at her directly again. "Your Nate?"

Flick put a hand up to her neck, suddenly self-conscious. "Yes." There, she'd said it. Not quite in the way that she'd planned, but still.

"I like the sound of that."

Flick's heart felt giddy. So, he did feel the same.

"But when you say interested?" he asked, coming over all coy. "How interested would that be?"

Flick smiled. This was more like it. She took a step closer, happy to play along. "Very, if you must know."

"And how much is very?"

Flick closed the gap altogether and placing both hands on Nate's hips, she used them to steady herself as she stretched up to his level. Keeping her eyes on his, she paused before giving him a gentle, yet short-lived, kiss. "That much," she said, lowering herself back down.

"You call that a kiss?"

Flick giggled as he pushed her hair behind her ears, at the same time stretching and puckering his lips.

"Now this is a kiss." Suddenly serious, Nate's gaze intensified. Continuing to stroke her hair with one hand, he used the other to tilt her chin and tenderly draw her lips towards his.

Butterflies seemed to play havoc in Flick's tummy as their mouths drew closer and closer, his lips, feeling soft and inviting as he planted one gentle kiss after another, each one lasting that little bit longer. She felt his tongue searching for hers as their embrace became more passionate, her body stirring as Nate took control and slowed things right down again.

Without warning, he pulled away, suddenly serious.

"What?" Flick asked.

"Before we take things any further, you do know this isn't a game to me, don't you? I'm not looking for anything casual."

Waiting for an answer, he looked so vulnerable and Flick knew that couldn't have been easy for him to say. "I should hope not," she replied, deciding it was time for her to be honest too. "Because I think I'm falling in love with you."

"Only think? Because I know I've fallen in love with you." He drew her close again and kissed her forehead, before looking into her eyes for a moment. He smiled. "Fancy that cup of tea now?"

Flick nodded and coming over all warm and fuzzy, she watched him return to the kitchen. She hugged herself, grinning widely as she looked to the heavens. "Thanks, Dad."

THE END

Acknowledgements

Thank you to everyone at Bombshell Books, especially Betsy, Sarah, Sumaira, Heather and my editor Morgen. You're all brilliant.

Special thanks also go to Marie Laval, Esme Buckley and Nathalie Barret, my go to people when it came to the nuances of the French language. Without you three my characters would be like Flick's father, speaking more Franglais than Français. Thank you to Katherine Bolton, too. You described your local mayor's office perfectly and before you ask, no, I still haven't visited mine.

I'd also like to say a big thanks to Bronwen Hockerday. It's funny to think that by the time you read this we'll have already met!

And finally, my heartfelt thanks go out to you the reader.

Lightning Source UK Ltd.
Milton Keynes UK
UKHW040819021118
331645UK00001B/68/P